Dorsey frowned and lowered herself onto one of the chairs, a bad feeling snaking its way around her insides. "What's up?"

"I just caught a report that was coming in from HQ. Case in Georgia I thought you should know about."

"Go on," she said cautiously. It wasn't like Decker to hedge.

"The body of a woman was found a couple of weeks ago. The ME's best guess is she'd been dead less than eight hours."

"Cause of death?"

"From the preliminary report, looks like multiple stab wounds to the torso, exsanguination."

"Sexual assault?"

"Not sure."

"O-kay . . ." She dragged out the word. *And I need to know this because . . . ?*

It wasn't as if she had no corpses of her own to deal with. And Georgia wasn't her territory, so what was Decker's point?

Decker sighed. "There's no easy way to do this. The woman had no identification on her, so the locals faxed her description to other agencies in the surrounding area hoping someone would be able to match her to a missing persons report."

"And . . ." Dorsey felt impatience rise within her chest.

"I'll cut to the chase. The victim has been positively identified as Shannon Randall."

"Not possible." Dorsey felt herself relax. This had nothing to do with her after all. "Shannon Randall died in 1983. The state of South Carolina executed her killer, remember? This has to be a different Shannon Randall, Decker."

mariah STEWART

LAST

A novel of suspense

look

BALLANTINE BOOKS • NEW YORK

2007 Ballantine Books Mass Market Original

Copyright © 2007 by Marti Robb
Excerpt from *Last Words* copyright © 2007 by Marti Robb
Excerpt from *Last Breath* copyright © 2007 by Marti Robb

Published in the United States by Ballantine Books, an imprint of The Random House Publishing Group, a division of Random House, Inc., New York.

BALLANTINE and colophon are registered trademarks of Random House, Inc.

This book contains excerpts from the forthcoming mass market edition of *Last Words* and the hardcover edition of *Last Breath* by Mariah Stewart. These excerpts have been set for this edition only and may not reflect the final content of the forthcoming editions.

ISBN 978-0-7394-8354-1

Cover design: Tony Greco
Cover image: woman: Jupiter Images

Printed in the United States of America

For Dennis

Acknowledgments

In the wake of Hurricane Katrina's devastation, those wild, wacky, and totally wonderful readers who hang out at Adwoff.com opened their generous and loving hearts with a drive to raise money to be donated to the Habitat for Humanity (donation matched by Nora Roberts). When they asked if I'd donate autographed books for their raffle, I threw in an offer to name a character after the drawing winner, who could chose to be a villain, a victim, or a vixen.

The winner—the always delightful Ms. Edith Chiong—decided to throw caution to the wind and chose for her namesake a character who was the absolute polar opposite of the real Edith. And so Edith the hooker was born.

However, the softhearted real-life Edith was concerned about the future of fictional Edith, and wondered if by the end of the book the character might be redeemed. I think she'll be pleased with the path her character chooses to follow. Just as I think she'll be pleased to know that the entire story grew from fictional Edith's refusal to allow her friend's disappearance to be ignored by the authorities—that she was the catalyst that began the search for the truth—and that, in the end, her desire to do the right thing indirectly led to the unraveling of a very tangled web of lies and deceit.

Prologue

February 25, 1983

"Tell me what you did with her body."

The broad shadow of the FBI agent loomed large over the teenager seated at the pockmarked table. His head down, eyes closed.

He leaned in from behind, his breath going down the neck of the boy's shirt, his mouth close to the boy's ear.

"Where is Shannon Randall?" he asked.

"I don't know."

"Sure you do." The agent leaned in a little closer.

"No." The boy stared straight ahead. "I don't know where she is."

"We know she was with you on Wednesday night. Tell me what happened to her." He inched even closer, his voice a flat whisper. "Tell me what you did to her."

Eric Louis Beale, eighteen years old and scared to death, shook his head side to side in an uneven motion. "I didn't do anything to her, I swear."

"You picked her up in your car. You took her out to the lake . . ."

"What?" Beale frowned. "I didn't drive to the lake."

"Oh, come off it, Eric. We both know you're lying."

"I'm not lying. I didn't take her to the lake."

"We have a witness who saw you driving out of town in the direction of the lake with Shannon in the front seat next to you."

"No, that's not true."

"Why would someone make that up, Eric? Why would anyone lie about that?"

"I don't know, but I know I didn't drive to the lake. I never left town."

"Next thing you know, you'll be telling me you didn't see her on Wednesday."

A long silence followed. Eric Beale's gaze darted around the room.

"Look, Eric, we know you had a thing for her. Her girlfriends already told us how you followed her around. Always offering to drive her places. To school in the morning, home again in the afternoon. To the library. Any place she wanted to go." Special Agent Matt Ranieri stood with his hands on his hips, his jacket unbuttoned. He walked casually from behind the chair in which the suspect sat to the front of the table, so the kid could see the harness that held the gun just out of view under the jacket.

Ranieri stopped and turned toward Beale. "Where did you take her on Wednesday, Eric?"

"Nowhere," Beale whispered.

"Are you going to try to tell me she wasn't in your

car on Wednesday?" Ranieri stared at the kid, his eyes boring into him. "Because we both know that would be another lie, don't we?"

Beale went still as a stone, his eyes no longer flitting around the room but focused now in a rigid stare.

Ranieri sat on the edge of the table, his eyes still on Beale's face, returning the stare.

"Want to know what we found under the passenger seat of your car, Eric?"

When no response came, Ranieri said, "A shirt—I'm thinking it's yours—with blood on it. Quite a bit of blood, in fact—I'm thinking that's Shannon's—front and back. The tests we're running right now will tell if I'm right. I'm betting I am. What do you think?"

Beale continued to stare.

"Now, you're probably thinking how you're going to explain that. You're thinking, hey, they can't prove that the shirt wasn't there a week ago. Even if it is Shannon's blood, they can't prove it wasn't there before Wednesday. They can't even prove she was in my car on Wednesday. That what you're thinking, Eric?"

Ranieri crossed his arms over his chest.

"Well, guess what, loser. We sure enough can prove it. We can because Shannon left us a little something to let us know she was there. On Wednesday."

From his left jacket pocket, Ranieri took out a small notebook. He slapped it on the edge of the table to make the kid jump, to put him even more on edge than he already was.

"Shannon's homework assignment book, Eric."

He flipped through almost to the last page, then read, "Wednesday, February 23." He paused and looked at Beale.

"You know what Wednesday's date was, Eric?"

Beale nodded slowly.

Ranieri continued to read. *"History. Read pages three hundred and two through three hundred fifty-two and be ready to discuss economic reasons for westward movement. English. Read act one,* As You Like It, *and write a short—"*

"I didn't hurt her, I swear to God I didn't. She was already messed up when I saw her."

"Saw her where, Beale?"

"On Edgemont. She was running . . ." He swallowed hard.

"Tell me right from the beginning."

"I was driving home from work, I was—"

"What time?"

"It was just after five. I got off work at the gas station at five o'clock."

"And you left right at five?"

"I . . . I got a drink, a can of Pepsi, from the case there in the office. I talked to one of the mechanics, Billy, for a few minutes."

"What did you talk about?" Special Agent Matt Ranieri already knew what they'd talked about. He'd interviewed Billy Tomlinson earlier that afternoon. He wanted to hear it from Beale. There was no reason for the boy to lie about this part of his story. The agent merely wanted to see how the boy's eyes read when he was telling the truth, so that maybe, if the kid kept lying, Ranieri would be able to tell the difference.

"Conan the Barbarian." The kid looked slightly embarrassed by the admission.

"Conan the Barbarian," Ranieri repeated flatly. Then once more for good measure. "Conan the Barbarian."

"Billy got this poster—from the movie?—and he'd hung it up in the garage just for laughs. Big poster of that guy, Schwarzenegger, whatever his name is."

"And you talked for how long?"

"I don't know—ten minutes, maybe. Then we talked about the Rocky movie that came out last year. Billy's into those action flicks, you know?"

This jibed with what the mechanic had related, so the agent let it go.

"So you leave the gas station at ten after five or so, then what?"

"Then, like I said, I started home. Up Edgemont Avenue toward the pond."

"But you live on Taylor, right?"

Beale nodded. "Yes."

"Isn't the pond on the other side of town from Taylor?"

"I had things on my mind. I wanted to just be alone for a few minutes."

"Things like what?"

"Just . . . stuff." He shook his head wearily. "There was a dance that was coming up, I was waiting to hear from a college, I was—"

"You wanted to be alone, but you picked up Shannon Randall?"

"She came running down the road, where it dead-ends by the library. She's my friend. I stopped to see if she wanted a ride."

Ranieri leaned in again. The movement was intimidating, as it was intended to be.

"She wasn't just your friend. You had a crush on her. You followed her around, didn't you? Followed her after school? Kept tabs on her . . ."

"No, I—"

"You were thinking about the dance because you were thinking about asking her to go with you, isn't that right?"

"Shannon's only a freshman, I'm a senior. No way would her folks let her go to the dance with me. Besides, some other girl had asked me but I'd pretty much decided not to go because I need the money for the deposit for college. To save my spot for next year."

"You're not going to have to worry about where you're going to be living next year, pal." Ranieri stood up again and walked around to the front of the table, where he could look the kid in the eye. "That money you saved for tuition? I don't think you're going to be needing it."

Beale broke then, and started to cry.

"Did Shannon cry, Eric? Did she cry when you hurt her?"

"I swear to you . . . I swear to you, I did not hurt her."

"Where'd the blood come from, Eric?" Ranieri stood across the room, his arms folded over his chest. "Why was her blood on your shirt?"

"I told you, she was messed up when I picked her up. Her mouth was bleeding. Her eye was swollen. She asked me to take her to the park so she could go into the ladies' room and wash off her face. And I did. I gave her the extra shirt I had in my gym bag so she could clean her face."

"What did she say happened to her?"

"She didn't say."

"Wait a minute. You see this girl, your 'friend,' running down the road, her face bleeding and swollen, and you don't ask her what happened?"

"I did ask. She wouldn't tell me."

"What time was that?"

"I don't know. Five thirty or so, I guess."

"Tell me about taking Shannon to the park."

"I just drove in, the gate was still open. I parked in the lot near those log buildings where the bathrooms are. She jumped out of the car and ran in. She was in there for maybe ten minutes or so. She came out, her face was cleaned up, but I could see she was going to have a black eye and her mouth was going to be all swollen the next day."

"Did you beat her up there in the park?"

"I didn't beat her up." Eric Beale looked pale and defeated.

"Right. So then what happened?"

"She got back in the car and gave me back the shirt and said she was sorry she got blood on it. I told her it was okay, to just toss it in the back and I'd take care of it. I asked her again what happened, asked her who hurt her, but she just shook her head and looked out the window."

"And she didn't say anything? You're telling me that someone beat her up, you helped her, but she wouldn't tell you who?"

"All she said was, it didn't matter. She just kept saying that over and over. 'It doesn't matter.' I started to drive her home, but when we got to Montgomery, she asked me to stop the car, so I pulled over. She picked up her book bag and thanked me for the ride and for helping her, but she said she had to get out there."

"In the dark? Three blocks from home?"

Beale nodded.

"And you let her?"

"I couldn't stop her."

"You know what I think, Eric? I think you picked her up there on Edgemont, and I think you drove her to the lake, not to the park. And I think she was just fine when she got into your car, Eric. I think you took her out to the lake and you—"

"No!"

". . . tried to get it on with her, that's what I think. And then I think you—"

"I never would have done anything like that! Shannon was my friend!"

". . . slapped her around a little when she wouldn't put out."

"Don't even talk about her like that!" Beale's hand slammed the table defiantly. "Shannon's a good kid. I would never treat her like that!"

"Where is she, Beale?" The FBI agent's eyes narrowed. "Where is Shannon Randall? What did you do with her? Is she at the bottom of the lake? In one of the caves, maybe, or dumped into one of the ravines out in those hills outside of town? Why don't you just tell us, save everyone a whole lot of time?"

"I swear, I didn't do anything to her. I swear it." Beale was sobbing now. " It's all like I said. I took her to the park like she asked, so she could clean herself up. I asked her and asked her, but she wouldn't tell me who hurt her. She got out of my car at Montgomery Avenue and that was the last I saw of her. I swear to God I haven't seen her since."

"How do you explain that someone saw you— *you*—driving on Lakeview, headed out of town with Shannon after seven o'clock?"

"I don't know." The boy was shaking now. "I don't know why someone would say something that isn't true. There has to be a mistake."

"The mistake, Eric, is lying to me."

Matthew Ranieri remained standing, his arms still folded across his chest, thinking of the pain the Randall family was going through at that very minute, certain in his heart that this eighteen-year-old punk not only knew where the girl was, but had been responsible for whatever happened to her.

A cold fist closed around his heart. His own daughter was just two years younger than Shannon Randall. What would he do if someone took off with her and she never came back?

He'd do exactly what he was doing now. And he'd make certain the son of a bitch paid.

1

June, 2007

Hot summer closed around the Florida panhandle like a tightly clenched fist. Soaring afternoon temperatures and suffocating humidity had thickened the night air, sending those poor souls who lacked air conditioning to seek respite in the nearest source of water, which for the prudent was a swimming pool or the shower. Only a fool would have taken to the lakes or ponds, especially in the dark, gators being what they are.

Dorsey Collins abandoned the air-conditioned comfort of her apartment for the balcony off her living room. The unrelenting sun had faded the orange-and-white-striped cushions on the two patio chairs she'd bought at the end of last year's season. She'd known when she purchased the chairs with the matching table that the fabric wouldn't stand up to direct sunlight, but she'd bought them anyway. When you're on the job, and dealing with life and death on a daily basis, it's life's small pleasures that keep you going.

Dorsey leaned over the railing and tried to ignore

the mosquitoes buzzing around her face. In the past, mosquitoes rarely bothered her, but lately, everything in her life had been totally screwed up. She was thinking her body chemistry must be reflecting this somehow, drawing a cloud of the little bastards to her whenever she stepped outside.

It really did figure, didn't it?

She twisted the cap off her beer, took a long, serious swallow, and stared out into the parking lot beyond her apartment building. She'd met very few of her fellow residents in the complex, so she didn't expect to recognize any of the tenants who were parking in their assigned spaces. By the time the last of the arrivals had disappeared into their respective buildings, she'd finished the beer. She debated whether or not to have another for all of three seconds.

Maybe, she told herself as she pushed aside the sliding door to her living room, just maybe she'd get lucky and pass out while leaning over the side of the balcony, fall three stories to the pavement below, and break her neck, thereby putting herself out of her misery.

It could happen, she reasoned as she opened the refrigerator door just far enough to grab another bottle. She was twisting the cap as she walked back toward the balcony when the phone began to ring. She stopped midstride to listen to the message.

"Dorsey, it's Scott Murphy."

She groaned at the sound of his voice, then walked to the patio door even as the message was being left on her machine.

"I was hoping to catch you at home . . . I mean, I know you're busy, but I was hoping . . ." Breathy asthmatic pause. Big sigh. "Anyway, I was hoping to catch up with you before the weekend, see if you were free for Saturday night. Or Friday."

He paused again, just as she slid the door closed.

"Or Sunday. . . ." was the last she heard of the message.

Damn, she wished he'd stop calling. That was the third message he'd left for her since last weekend. She knew she should return his calls. He was a nice guy, just trying to be nice to her, even though she'd been a total shit to him.

Dorsey sat on the chair closest to the balcony and rested her feet on the railing. She looked up just as a frothy bank of clouds shifted from the face of the moon. A minute later, stars could be seen winking here and there overhead.

If I could have one wish, she thought, I'd wish for . . .

What?

She closed her eyes, knowing damned well what she'd wish for. She'd wish she could go back in time to 4 P.M. last Friday afternoon, and then instead of letting her friends talk her into going to a barbecue for a retiring agent, she'd go home to that book she'd been planning to read.

But no. When her fellow agents gathered around the door to her cubicle and harassed her, she gave in.

"Honestly, Dorsey, you live like a hermit. You need to get out once in a while."

"Come on, Dorse. Just for an hour or two. It'll do you good to have a little fun. You deserve a night out. You've been working nonstop for the past three weeks."

"Yeah, well, there was that little matter of Hector Rodriguez and his buddy, Jon Mattson, and that young girl they kidnapped," she'd reminded them dryly.

"Hey, just for a while, okay?"

"Yeah, come with us now, or we'll follow you home and make rude noises outside your apartment until you cave in. Come along quietly, Agent Collins, and no one will get hurt."

And no one did, but me. . . .

Things had been just swell until sometime after ten when *He* walked in.

With Maddy Chambers, an agent just transferred from San Francisco, and Wilbur, the dog he'd shared with Dorsey.

He was Davison Everett Kane Haldeman.

Jesus, Dorsey chastised herself, with a name like that, she should have known.

It was bad enough he'd brought along the woman he'd left Dorsey for, knowing there was a good chance she'd be there, but the bastard had the nerve to bring Wilbur.

Up until then, she'd been mourning the loss of the dog almost as much as she'd been mourning the loss of the guy. But damn that Wilbur, fickle mutt that he was. His heart always did belong to whoever held the treat box. And these days, all the treats were in

Maddy's hands, along with the brown leather leash Dorsey had picked up on the way home, the day Davis had called to tell her he was bringing home a dog he'd seen sleeping in a vacant lot three days in a row.

It had been hard enough, watching the flirtation in the office once word had gotten out that Davis had moved out on Dorsey—taking Wilbur. ("Hey, I was the one who found him. He goes with me.") Harder still to maintain a professional demeanor when she had to work with either Davis or Maddy. But she'd drawn the line at socializing with them.

Dorsey tossed back another long swig of beer and questioned her ability to make sound decisions in her personal life. What in the name of God had she been thinking when she'd let Davis move in with her? And more recently, whatever had possessed her to throw caution to the wind on Friday night and hit on Scott Murphy, the new prosecutor from the state's attorney's office?

God, she cringed whenever she thought about it.

Not that he'd been a bad guy, or anything. He was nice enough—too nice, actually—when she found herself the next morning hung over and embarrassed in his apartment.

Scott had compounded her humiliation by sending her flowers and repeatedly assuring her—and anyone else who'd listen—that absolutely nothing had happened; she'd merely passed out on his sofa and he'd let her sleep it off right where she'd slumped.

God, what ever possessed me. . . ?

She leaned forward, her arms resting on her knees, and watched dark clouds roll in and lightning move across the sky. *Maybe if I sit here long enough, it'll strike me.*

If nothing else, she knew, she should go back inside and return his call. Thank him for the flowers, at the very least. She owed him that much. The roses had set him back a pretty penny. She could at least thank him for his thoughtfulness.

She took a swig and wondered if she'd ever make the call.

The humidity continued to rise by the minute, the sultry air thick in her nostrils. The closeness made her slightly claustrophobic. She'd be infinitely more comfortable in the apartment, but she just couldn't bring herself to go back inside. It was too quiet. Too empty. Too lonely.

She watched a jagged spear of lightning stab at a grove of trees and thought, *God, I am pathetic.*

When she finally did go back in, she stayed only as long as it took her to grab another beer. She twisted off the lid and it lifted with a soft pop. She dropped the lid on the counter and went back to the balcony. The rain was just beginning to fall with a few fat drops here and there.

Maybe she should look for another place. One that had no memories, good or bad. Sort of like starting over.

Damn it, she didn't want to start over. She'd been here for six years. She loved this apartment. It had taken her days to find it when she first moved to Florida, freshly divorced and living alone for the first time in her life, focused solely on her career. The apartment was perfect: a big airy bedroom and bathroom, large living room with a small dining area at one end, and a nice eat-in kitchen. A balcony with a view of the lake, and some gorgeous sunsets. Good parking, convenient location, decent rent. Pool, gym, and spa, though she never used those amenities.

No, damn it, she wasn't giving up her perfect apartment just because the man she'd recently shared it with had turned out to be a perfect asshole.

Sooner or later, the last trace of him would fade and she'd be comfortable here again.

She wondered wryly if the psychic in that little stucco house down on Lakeview had any experience with exorcisms.

She was only half kidding.

She drained the bottle and set it next to the two others on the table and leaned over the rail, debating whether or not to go in for another. She'd needed a good buzz the night before—and the one before that—to get to sleep. Every time she closed her eyes, she saw that moment when he walked in with her dog, Maddy, clinging to his arm, and everything had gone white before her eyes.

The rest of the night was a blur, which was probably just as well.

The front pocket of her jeans began to ring. She pulled out her phone and checked the caller ID. She was more than a little surprised to see a Virginia number displayed.

This was a call she should probably take.

"Collins."

"Dorsey, Steven Decker."

The SAC she'd worked for after graduating from the academy.

"Hey." She brightened, happy in spite of herself to hear his voice. He'd been a great boss, fair and smart and always accessible. She'd missed him. It had been what, two years since they'd last been in touch? "It's good to hear your voice."

"Yours, too. Listen, Dorsey, I wish this call was strictly social, I'd love to catch up, but there's something that's come to my attention that I think you need to know."

"Make it good news, please."

"Wish I could, but I'm afraid there's no way to clean this up." His voice was sober, serious.

Not a good sign.

"What?" She frowned and lowered herself onto one of the chairs, a bad feeling snaking its way around her insides.

"I just caught a report that was coming in from HQ. Case in Georgia I thought you should know about."

"Go on," she said cautiously. It wasn't like him to hedge.

"The body of a woman was found a couple of weeks ago. The ME's best guess is she'd been dead less than eight hours."

"Cause of death?"

"From the preliminary report, looks like multiple stab wounds to the torso, exsanguination."

"Sexual assault?"

"Not sure."

"O-kay . . ." She dragged out the word. *And I need to know this because . . . ?*

It wasn't as if she had no corpses of her own to deal with. Georgia wasn't her territory, so what was Decker's point?

Decker sighed. "The woman had no identification on her, so the locals faxed her description to other agencies in the surrounding area hoping someone would be able to match her to a missing persons report."

"No TV, no newspaper reports?"

"Nothing. The body was found on Shelter Island, which is about as big as your thumb, and is just an inch south of the line separating South Carolina and Georgia. No local paper. Nearest city is Savannah." He cleared his throat. "The police in Deptford— Georgia, right over the border—had been sitting on a report that appeared to be a match. Seems a woman had come in to the station a few weeks back, said her roommate had been missing since the night before. Said they always kept in touch with each other throughout the night—both of them are working girls—so when the girl didn't return by morning, the roommate knew something was wrong. I got the feeling the Deptford cops didn't invest a lot of time looking for her—

hookers come and hookers go. The roommate apparently had gone in to talk to the cops several times, but not much was done. No APBs, no mention in the news, nothing."

"And . . . ?" Dorsey felt impatience rise within her chest.

"And . . . I'll cut to the chase. The victim has been positively identified as Shannon Randall."

"Not possible." Dorsey felt herself relax. This had nothing to do with her after all. "Shannon Randall died in 1983. The state of South Carolina executed her killer, remember? This has to be a mistake, Decker."

"Shannon Randall's family was notified, Dorsey. Her sister went to the morgue and identified her. It's Shannon."

"Someone's playing a nasty hoax on them. Not funny."

"The dental records match. Fingerprints from the body matched fingerprints on items from Shannon's room that her mother had kept all these years. They're running DNA from the hairbrush the mother sent down. The results won't be back from the lab for at least a week, you know how that goes. But the sister was positive once she saw the birthmarks. The body is definitely that of Shannon Randall."

"It has to be a mistake," she insisted, a buzzing starting inside her head.

"If a mistake was made, it was made in 1983," he said softly.

"If this is true . . ." She shook her head, swallowed

hard. "If this is true . . . if this is really Shannon Randall . . . *the* Shannon Randall . . ."

She took a deep breath, blew it out again, still trying to gather her thoughts.

"If this is true, who's going to tell my father?"

"Well, we were hoping you could give us a hand with that. . . ."

The ringing phone sounded so far away, farther still if one pulled a pillow over one's head.

Which is what Special Agent Andrew Shields had done in an effort to muffle the incessant noise. Finally, recognizing the futility of his efforts, he rolled out from under the pillow and felt along the bedside table for his cell phone.

He blinked several times to clear his vision. He picked up his watch and blinked again. It was barely five in the morning. There was only one person who'd be calling him this early. And odds were, it wasn't going to be a social call.

"Shields."

A cheery voice greeted him. "Good morning, Andrew."

He knew it. John Mancini. His boss. Andrew sat up and ran a hand over his face.

"Morning, John."

"How's it going?"

"Not bad, for the middle of the night."

"Oh, did I wake you?"

"Very funny." Andrew covered a yawn.

"So I was looking over the assignments last night, and I noticed you're working on the Gilchrist case."

"Right."

"I need you somewhere else."

Andrew waited. He'd been half-expecting this. The Gilchrist case wasn't exactly low profile, and he knew several of the other agents working the case were less than happy when he'd been assigned to join them. Less than happy? Who was he kidding? A couple of them looked downright pissed to see him show up on the job that first day.

Andrew wasn't sure he could blame them.

"Andy?"

"Yeah—I'm listening."

"I need you to pack for maybe a week."

"Where am I going?"

"Shelter Island, Georgia, to start . . ."

"What's there?" Andy asked.

"A public-relations nightmare, if what I'm hearing is true." John sighed.

"What's this all about?"

"It's about a twenty-four-year-old case that just came back to life."

"Want to fill me in?"

"In 1983, the Bureau got a call to lend a hand with an investigation in Hatton, South Carolina. One of the daughters of the local preacher had gone missing two days earlier, and all indications were that she'd been murdered by a young guy she knew from town. The Bureau sent a team with one of its up-and-comers— Matt Ranieri—to lead the investigation."

"Ranieri. He's the guy on TV every time there's a big case ongoing. He's like Mr. Crime on the talk show circuit."

"Right. After the Randall case—that was her name, Shannon Randall—Ranieri landed a lot of TV gigs." John cleared his throat. "Anyway, the young kid was arrested, the case went to trial even though the body had never been found—revolutionary down there in that day—and the kid was convicted on circumstantial evidence."

"What evidence?"

"A shirt covered with her blood was found under the seat of his car, along with her school assignment book, and an eyewitness saw him driving her out of town. She was never seen again."

"And the boy's explanation?"

"The kid admitted he picked her up that afternoon, but said she was bloody when she got into his car, that someone had worked her over, and he'd given her the shirt to wipe her face on."

"He say who beat her up?"

"He maintained he asked, but she refused to tell him. Says he drove her to a park, she went into the ladies' room and cleaned up, and then he drove her home. Says she asked to get out a few blocks from home, so he let her."

"And the cops didn't believe him."

"They had a witness who said otherwise."

"Who was the witness?" Andrew asked.

"A friend of the girl's. Said the guy had a big crush on Shannon, was hanging around her all the time but

Shannon wouldn't give him the time of day. You know the rest."

"So where's the problem? You had an arrest and a conviction . . ." Andrew stopped and thought for a moment, then said, "Let me guess. There's DNA evidence to prove his innocence and he's getting out."

"No, and there will be no getting out for him," John told him. "He was executed back in '91."

"So what's the deal?"

"The deal is, we just got word that a body found in Georgia has been positively identified as Shannon Randall's."

"The vic whose body was never found?"

"Right."

"So great, case closed."

"Not quite," John said. "The body had only been dead for maybe eight hours."

"What?" Andrew frowned. "How can that be?"

"That's what we're sending you down there to find out."

Andrew hesitated, then said, "John, if this is true, if this is Shannon Randall, this could become a high-profile case."

"Not could," John corrected him calmly. "Will."

"So, don't you think you'd rather assign someone else?"

"If I wanted to assign someone else, I'd have called someone else," John said coolly.

"This could be national news."

"Say it, Andy. Say it once, and get it over with."

"Look, I'm just back from leave." He wanted to keep going, but the words stuck in throat.

"I know that. Go on."

"You're going to make me say it?"

"Damn right I am." John sounded angry.

"I'm just saying, a Shields may not be the best man for the job. After everything that happened last year—"

"I will tell you this one more time, and if I ever have to say it again, I'll fire your ass on the spot. I never want to have this conversation with you again, understand?" Without waiting for a response, John said, "You are not your brother. Many families have a black sheep. Brendan was yours. He betrayed everyone who loved him. His family. His friends. The Bureau. But—and this is the important part, so listen good—you are not Brendan. You are not responsible for what he did, and you are not expected to pay for his sins. If anyone in the Bureau thinks otherwise. want to know who, because I will personally straigh out his or her ass. Are we clear on that?"

"Yes, sir," Andrew said quietly.

"You're a damn fine agent, Andy. I have dence in you. This case is going to blov faces unless we get to the bottom of it most likely going to blow up anyway shot agent pushing for the death p that was happy to give it to him. was well-known and highly re the family of Eric Beale was portedly were drunks, dad had

ing up the wife and kids on more than one occasion. Older brother served time for assault. The kid who went to jail had apparently had a run-in with the nephew of the police chief's wife the week before."

"So back then, it almost didn't matter if he was guilty or not."

"Well, that was then, this is now. It matters. I want to know the truth. I want to know what happened to this girl, and how." John paused, then added, "Did I mention that Shannon had apparently been making her living as a prostitute all these years?"

"Ah, no. I think you left that part out." Andrew swung his legs over the side of the bed. "They're sure it's her? They're positive?"

"Positive."

"Shit."

"My thoughts exactly."

"So when do I leave?"

"This morning. I want you there before noon. I don't know how long before the press gets wind of this, so you're going to have to move fast. Go over the original file with a fine-tooth comb and find out what went wrong. Figure out where this girl's been all these years, and why no one knew she was still alive. And then, after you've done all that—"

"I'm going to have to solve the case," Andrew fin-ished the sentence. "Who killed Shannon Randall, and why."

"You're pretty good at this, you know."

"Hey, I'm a special agent with the FBI. You can't

put much over on me." Andrew smiled. "By the way, who's working with me on this?"

"No one. You're on your own. It's a sensitive case, and I expect you to treat it as such."

"I will."

"Stop in and pick up the file on your way to the airport. I'll have everything copied and ready for you."

"I'll be there within the hour." Andrew stood, ready to hang up.

"Oh. There's one more thing," John said.

"What's that?"

"You're going to have company."

"You just said you weren't assigning anyone else," Andrew reminded him.

"I'm not." John paused. "I mentioned Matt Ranieri . . ."

"You have to be kidding." Andrew laughed out loud. "You couldn't possibly let him in on this."

"Of course not. You will, however, be joined by his daughter."

"His . . . John, that's almost as bad."

"His daughter. Dorsey Collins, you hear of her?"

"The name sounds familiar. She's with the Bureau?"

"She's been working out of the Florida office for the past six years or so. She's good, she's smart, she's tough, and she's honest. She can't be officially connected with the case, I don't want her name showing up on so much as one damned scrap of paper, but she can shadow you."

"If anyone figures out who she is . . ."

"Then she's out of there in the blink of an eye. But I don't know how anyone would know. She has a different last name and she's never exploited the relationship with her father. I heard from Decker that even after her divorce, she kept her married name so as to not ride Matt's coattails. I don't think more than a handful of people at the Bureau know she's his kid."

Andrew sat silent.

"Look, from what I hear, she's going to want in on the investigation. I figure she can work with us, or she can go off on her own and end up working against us. I'd rather have her right there where we can see her."

"May I say something?" Andrew asked.

"Of course."

"I don't think this is a good idea, John. I know you're the boss and it's your decision, but I have to go on record and say I don't think this is good."

"Objection noted. Just trust me on this. Decker says she's good, Andy. I wouldn't saddle you with anyone who isn't. And she's going to have to play by my rules if she wants to be allowed to play at all. I don't think she'll be a problem. If she is, she's gone."

"So when can I expect her to show up?"

"I don't know. I haven't spoken with her yet."

"Not at all?"

"No."

"Then how do you know she's going to want in?"

"Because I know her reputation. And I know Matt. I spoke with Steven Decker last night. He's already told her about the situation. I don't expect it will be much longer before I hear from her. I'll have her call you."

"You think you have everyone figured out, don't you?" Andrew said, only half kidding.

"That's why I'm the boss of the best of the best." Andrew could hear the humor in John's voice.

"John, the boy who was executed . . . if this is really Randall, and it sounds like it is, someone's going to have to talk to his parents before word gets out to the press."

"That's my problem. I have someone trying to locate them as we speak," John told him. "Now, if there's nothing else, I'll be expecting you by 6:30."

The line went dead, and Andrew folded his phone shut.

He was well aware of the gift he was being offered, but didn't know quite how to express his thanks. His family had a proud history in the service of the FBI almost since its formation. His father and uncle had served, three cousins, both his brothers, his only sister. Theirs had been a respected name for decades, their collective record impressive. And in one moment, as long as it had taken for a high-powered rifle to be fired, their name, their reputation, had been destroyed.

Andrew's brother Brendan was the black sheep John had referred to. He'd marked their cousin, Connor, for murder, and mistaking Connor's brother Dylan for Connor, pulled the trigger on the wrong man and blew away a one-in-a-million guy. In Dylan,

both the family and the Bureau had both lost an irre-
placeable member.

But even that had not been the worst of Brendan's
sins.

Somehow, Brendan had gotten mixed up with another rogue agent and became a willing participant in
a sex-slave ring kidnapping children out of Central
America. When Brendan suspected their brother
Grady's wife might be catching on, he facilitated her
murder as well.

Andrew still couldn't quite believe it himself. Nor
could he understand how someone you know and
love—someone you have known and loved your entire life—how that person could turn into a monster
right before your eyes without you seeing, without
you knowing. How is it possible that none of them
had recognized the evil in him? Had any of them even
known him at all?

More than a year later, Andrew was still asking
himself the same question. How could we have not
known?

Andrew thought back to the Christmas before it all
fell apart, to their cousin Aidan's wedding, to family
dinners where they'd all gathered. If there had been
anything in Brendan's behavior that might have
tipped them off to the demon that dwelled within
him, why hadn't they recognized it? Try as he might,
Andrew could not recall one incident that might have
given it away. Brendan had always been . . . Brendan.
Fun loving, happy-go-lucky. When had his jovial
façade become a mask for something sinister?

Andrew would never know. None of them would. Brendan now lay as dead as Dylan. Because of him, the family had lost two of their beloved. Grady had been the big loser. He'd lost not only his brother and his cousin, but he'd lost the love of his life as well. After it was all over, Grady had retreated to the house in the Montana hills he'd shared with his Melissa. Other than an occasional call to their father, no one had heard from Grady in months. Andrew knew his brother would never be the same—how could he be?—nor would his father. Frank Shields had given thirty years to the Bureau, and it was mostly because of him that Andrew had decided to return to the job after his leave was over. Not to have done so would have been, in Frank's eyes as well as in Andrew's, cowardly. The name Shields had stood for something. Andrew knew it was up to him, and his sister, Mia, to make certain it still did.

He went into the bathroom and turned on the shower. He'd have to hustle if he was going to make it into the office before rush hour traffic clogged the highways. He wished John had given him a choice about whether or not Dorsey Collins should be permitted to tag along through his investigation—silent partner or no—but as John had pointed out, he was the boss. In general, John was a damn good judge of character, which is how he'd managed to put together the best and most specialized unit within the Bureau. Well, except for Brendan, but if his own family hadn't seen his flaws, John couldn't be expected to.

Then again, John admitted he hadn't even met this

woman yet. So why, Andrew asked himself, would John go out on a limb to let her become part of an investigation when all the facts seemed to indicate she shouldn't be permitted within miles of Shelter Island?

Good question. Andrew turned on the water and set it for hot. Just one more to be answered before the investigation was over.

Just one more to be added to a long list of questions: What really happened that night twenty-four years ago? Where had Shannon Randall been all that time? How did she get there? And why? Had anyone known she was still alive? If so, why didn't that person speak up? And who killed her now, and why?

And why was John Mancini so insistent that Dorsey Collins—the daughter of the man who pushed the case to a faulty conclusion all those years ago—be permitted to work with Andrew behind the scenes in search of the answers?

2

Dorsey parked her rental car on the shady side of the street across from her father's house. Matt Ranieri lived in a tidy half-brick split-level in a sprawling 1960s-era Philadelphia suburb. Back then, the neighborhood had been mostly upwardly mobile middle-class and totally Catholic. St. Patrick's Church was two blocks to the right on this same street, and St. Francis of Assisi three blocks to the left, cleanly dividing the neighborhood into the Irish parish and the Italian parish. Over the years, members of other faiths had moved in, and the parishes had shrunk. Several years ago, the doors of the elementary school serving St. Francis had closed and the students were directed to St. Patrick's, which had the larger building. These days, as many kids from the neighborhood attended public school as they did St. Pat's. When the diocese consolidated the two parishes, enrollment at St. Francis had declined further. Dorsey had been in her old parish church exactly three times since she graduated from college. One wedding—hers—and two funerals, her former mother-in-law's and her grandfather's.

She crossed the street, toying with the house key on the chain inside her right pocket as she glanced down the empty driveway. Walking around to the back porch, she paused at the bottom of the steps to note the condition of the yard. The grass was neatly cut, the roses had been pruned, some of the shrubs cut back, and the flower gardens weeded and freshly mulched. Her dad must have been here for at least a week, she reasoned; it would have taken him that long to prune and weed and mow. She climbed the steps and unlocked the door, stepped into the stillness.

"Dad?" Even knowing he wasn't at home, habit found her calling as she walked through the kitchen into the hall that led to the front door. "Dad?"

The downstairs windows were all tightly shut and the shades pulled down. She scooped up what appeared to be several days' mail from the floor and skimmed through it while she carried it into the kitchen and placed it on the table. She opened the refrigerator and took out a diet soda, popped the tab, and took a few sips before closing the door. She exhaled loudly, looked around, and headed into the living room. The message light was blinking red and silent on the answering machine. Without hesitating, she hit the play button. If someone had already called her father to tell him about Shannon Randall, Dorsey wanted to know.

"Hi, Matt?" The woman's voice, soft and tentative, played in the quiet room like music. "This is Diane." Nervous laughter. "I guess you know that." More laughter. "I . . . um . . . just wanted to thank you for last weekend. I had a really good time, and . . . um . . .

well, I just wanted to thank you again." Another pause. "I'd like to do it again sometime. You have my number. . . ." The fumbling sound of the phone being returned to its cradle.

Diane?

Dorsey didn't remember having heard about a Diane. Not that her father had to keep her up to date on his social life, but the last Dorsey had heard, he'd been dating a woman named Anna.

She sat in the overstuffed green chair near the fireplace and sipped the soda. The air was close and warm to the point of being stuffy, and would get warmer as the June sun continued to beat down on the roof. On the mantel a series of photographs paraded left to right, achingly familiar pictures of her mother, Bernadette—Bernie to all—some with Dorsey, some with Matt, the occasional shot of a smiling Bernie alone. The last photo was from their last Christmas, right before Bernie had stepped off the curb in front of the real estate office where she worked and had been struck by a car driven by an eighteen-year-old college freshman home on winter break.

Dorsey had been nine, old enough to recall every minute that followed a neighbor banging frantically on their front door. She'd heard his breathless speech, watched her father run barefoot out into the snow and down the six blocks to the site of the accident. Dorsey had run, too, but had been stopped by one of her mother's coworkers far short of the white sheet that lay on the ice-covered street.

The boy who'd been driving the car stood on the

sidewalk ten feet away from Dorsey, sobbing loudly and inconsolably, his face blotched red from the cold and tears. Whenever Dorsey recalled that scene, what she thought of was bone-numbing cold and the tears of a stranger who had changed their lives, and her father yelling at the paramedics to do something, *do* something. The empty feeling of being abandoned would wash through her every time, choking her with the memory of her father scrambling into the ambulance with her mother's body. He'd never looked back, never given a second thought to Dorsey, who'd stood forgotten and alone in the cold.

Years later, Dorsey had tried to rationalize, reminding herself that her father had been in deep shock. That maybe he hadn't known she'd followed him from the house. That he hadn't been thinking of anything at that moment but hoping to save the life of his wife, even though everyone there knew it was already too late.

That had been twenty-seven years ago, and her father had never remarried. So, Dorsey reminded herself as she returned to the kitchen, if her dad was dating more than one woman, he's certainly entitled, and it was certainly none of her business.

She poured the rest of the soda into the sink and tossed the can into the recycling bin, then called her father's cell phone again. Still no answer. She left the house the same way she'd entered it and locked the back door.

"Hey, Dorsey, is that you?" a voice from the next yard called.

"Hi, Mr. Genzano, how're you doing?" Dorsey stepped across the stretch of grass that marked the property line to give her father's elderly next-door neighbor a quick hug.

"Can't complain." Thin, weak arms encircled her and gnarled hands patted her back. Mr. Genzano was eighty-eight that year. Or was it eighty-nine? "No one cares if you do, so what's the point?"

"You're looking well."

"I'm looking older than dirt, but nice try, Dorsey." He beamed. "So, you thought you'd pay a surprise visit to your old man, did you?"

"And you know it's a surprise because . . . ?"

"Because if you'd called ahead of time, you'd have known he was at the beach house." A bony elbow nudged her ribs. "You're not the only one in the neighborhood who can put two and two together and get four, eh?"

"Anytime you want a job with the FBI, Mr. Genzano, you give me a call. I'll put in a good word for you with my boss."

"If I thought they'd give me one of those glockenspiel guns, I might consider it. I used to be quite the shot, you know, back in Double-u Double-u Two."

Dorsey laughed. "You just say the word, Mr. Genzano. The Bureau can always use a good man."

Mr. Genzano chuckled, then coughed. "Asthma. Gonna be the death of me. Gotta get back inside and outta the yard. Pollen everywhere."

He shook his head and turned toward his house. "You tell your father to give me a call when he gets home, hear? We're going to need to do something about that old maple out back. Split in half and ready to fall . . ."

He continued to talk as he returned to his own yard and up his back steps. Dorsey waited until he opened the back door, then waved. The old man waved back, and she sighed with relief that he hadn't gone into respiratory failure right there in the driveway.

Dorsey crossed the street and opened the driver's side door, leaning against the car momentarily, looking back at her father's house. The last place they'd all lived together as a family—it held so many memories. She turned away abruptly and got into the car.

She checked her voice mail, then turned the key in the ignition. There was no point in returning to the airport. The beach house was less than three hours away. She might as well just drive down and see what her father was up to.

Had he already heard the news?

Part of her almost hoped he had, so she wouldn't have to be the one to tell him.

She dialed his number again. This time she left a message. "Pop, I'm on my way down to the beach house. We need to talk. I should be there in a few hours."

The drive to Hathaway Beach took longer than Dorsey had expected, due to road construction on Route 1 just south of Dover, then again on Route 36 going toward Slaughter Beach on the Delaware Bay. Hathaway sat midway between Slaughter and the

Old Mispillion Lighthouse, at the end of a road that was newly paved. Dorsey could remember a time when the road was mostly sand and dirt going down to the beach, back before the old Delaware fishing towns had been discovered. Twenty years ago, when Dorsey's grandmother had considered putting the house on the market, she could barely have given it away. Now, local realtors stuffed the mailbox with solicitations, dying to market the old place to the people driving by who'd love to call it theirs.

Well, it was a pretty fine house, Dorsey reflected as she parked at the end of the drive behind her Dad's dark blue Explorer. Built in the late 1890s by her maternal great-grandfather, James Mills, the old clapboard Victorian stood tall and stately and tightly laced as a spinster, all by itself on a large lot smack in the center of Hathaway. Behind the house stood the remnants of the old carriage house, which her father insisted he would someday renovate, and the remains of her grandmother's gardens, in which neither she nor her father had any interest.

The grass in the front yard grew in tufts through the yellow sand, and three old pines along the side of the house leaned westward, as if exhausted from having stood against the wind off the bay for so many years. Across the street, two more houses from the same era sat on either side of a large square building of block construction that dated from the 1960s. The newer structure housed not only the small two-room post office, but the general store, a luncheonette—the town's only dining spot—and a newsstand as well.

Dorsey climbed the five steps up to the freshly painted front porch and pulled the screen door open. The inner door stood ajar and she called to her father as she walked through the downstairs and out the back door, which was unlocked as well.

She checked inside the garage and around the back of the carriage house, but her father was nowhere to be seen. There was only one other place he'd be.

Dorsey walked two hundred yards to the path leading over the dune. She slipped out of her shoes and tucked them under her arm, and walked toward the bay. The sun was dazzlingly bright off the water, the tiny waves of low tide rolling gently onto the sand with barely a sound. She shielded her eyes from the sun with her right hand and saw her father far down the beach, almost to the cove that led to the lighthouse.

She dropped her shoes and walked over the coarse sand, avoiding the jagged edges of crab shells and the driftwood that had washed up during the last storm. By the time she was near enough for him to hear if she called out, the dread that had begun as a tiny flutter swelled to fill every pore. The speech she'd practiced all the way down in the car began to fall apart, leaving her with facts but no coherent way of delivering them.

"Know who's driving that boat?" He spoke without turning to her, but pointed out toward the bay and the ferry that ran between Lewes, Delaware, and Cape May, New Jersey.

"You mean the bow rider at two o'clock?"

"Right. Mike Patton's boy, Tom. Remember him? He used to tease the hell out of you because you were so short."

"I remember." She nodded, recalling that Tommy Patton had been a bully who'd made the life of every kid in Hathaway Beach miserable at one time or another.

He looked over his shoulder and smiled. "He's about five seven now. And you're . . . ?"

"Five nine." She smiled too, thinking it might be a good sign to know that mean Tommy Patton had gotten his, so to speak.

"Tommy's grown up okay." Matt Ranieri turned and reached for his daughter with both arms and hugged her. "He's settled down and from what I hear, he hasn't set rotten eggs under anyone's tires in a long time."

"Good to know." She forced the smile to hold for a few moments more while she returned the hug.

"So. What brings you here?"

They stood side by side, his arm draped over her shoulder casually, but the tension between father and daughter was as tangible as a third entity there on the beach with them.

"What's up?" He stared out at the horizon, as if he knew whatever news she was about to break would be devastating.

She cleared her throat, but before she could speak, he asked, "Are you all right, Dorse? Something happen to you? Something going on . . . ?"

"Oh." Her eyes widened slightly in surprise. It had

never occurred to her that her message might have given her father the impression that this had to do with her. "Oh, no, Pop, no. I'm fine."

"Good, honey." He exhaled a breath as if he'd been holding it since he'd heard the message she'd left. "Then tell me what's so important that you had to drive all the way here from . . ." He paused. "Have you been transferred?"

"No, I'm still in Florida. I flew to Philly, then rented a car and drove to the house. Mr. Genzano said you'd be here."

"Must be important, then, for you to do all that traveling. You get promoted?"

"No, but—"

"Fired? You weren't fired, were you?" He turned fully toward her, his face creased with concern for his only child. "Because I still have friends in the Bureau, the director and I—"

"No, Pop, this has nothing to do with me."

"Then what?"

"It's . . ." Her stomach clenched. She did not want to do this. "Maybe we should go back to the house."

"Spill it, kiddo."

"I got a call from Steve Decker last night." She swallowed hard.

"And?" He made an impatient gesture with his right hand, urging her to continue.

"Pop, three weeks ago, they found the body of a woman in Georgia who has been positively identified as Shannon Randall. She'd been dead for less than half a day. She's been alive all these years."

He stared at her as if she'd spoken a foreign language.

Finally, he laughed awkwardly. "That's impossible. We both know that Shannon Randall died twenty-four years ago. There's been a mistake."

"No mistake, Pop. They've matched the dental records and the fingerprints. DNA is being tested as we speak. Decker says it's definitely Shannon."

"I don't believe it. Someone screwed up someplace. No way." He shook his head slowly side to side. "No goddamned way."

He broke away from her and paced several steps down the beach, then turned back to her.

"That was a good arrest. Eric Beale was guilty as sin, and everyone knew it. The jury knew it. He was convicted—"

"Pop, they never found her body."

"And they still haven't." His voice grew louder and his dark eyes flashed. He looked at his daughter as if seeing her for the first time. "You believe this bullshit, don't you?"

"Pop, Decker says a positive identification has been made by one of her sisters—"

"What positive identification? No one's seen that girl since she was fourteen, that's been, what . . . twenty-four years?" His voice continued to rise. "You wouldn't recognize yourself after twenty-four years. And they expect me to believe . . . ?"

Matt shook his head adamantly. "No goddamn way, Dorsey. No *goddamn* way is anyone ever going to convince me that Shannon Randall was alive all those years. Eric Beale killed her back in 1983. He was tried, convicted, and executed for her murder. No goddamn way was that a mistake."

"Pop . . ."

She reached for him, but he pushed past her, heading back up the lonely stretch of beach that dead-ended across the cove from the lighthouse. She watched him go, watched his stride increase with each step. She knew better than to follow him.

Dorsey walked back to where she'd dumped her shoes and gathered them up, then returned to the house. She walked around back and sat on the top step of the wooden porch, then reached into her pocket and pulled out her phone. She debated for several minutes who to call.

She'd start with Decker.

"Tell me again why the body in Georgia is Shannon Randall. You can't possibly have any DNA results back yet," she said when he picked up his private line.

"Fingerprints. Dental records. Identification of her birthmarks." Her old boss sighed. "You're at your dad's."

"Right."

"And he's pissed off and thinks this is all bullshit."

"Wouldn't you?"

"If I were in his shoes, yeah, I probably would want to see every scrap of evidence. However, in this case, under the circumstances, your father can't be anywhere near this, Dorse. For the obvious reasons."

"Like, he was in charge of the Bureau's investigation?"

"It isn't just that he was lead on our investigation, he made the case. It was a noteworthy case, one of the first trials in South Carolina where a defendant was convicted on circumstantial evidence alone, where no body had ever been found." On the other end of the line, Steven Decker took a deep breath before adding, "And I probably don't need to remind you that your father's made quite a career out of this case."

There was no denying that Matt Ranieri had become the poster boy for the FBI following the swift arrest and conviction of Eric Beale for the murder of young Shannon Randall, daughter and granddaughter of the ministers of a popular church in Hatton, South Carolina. Tall, handsome Matt had been a public-relations dream, and over the years had gone on to become the face of the FBI on every television news and talk show. He'd retired from the Bureau ten years ago and was still everyone's favorite talking head. After every horrific crime, you were sure to see former FBI superstar Matt Ranieri on your favorite news talk show later that night, and for several nights thereafter. At one time, one of the cable networks had even talked about giving him his own show, where he'd interview law enforcement agents who'd been instrumental in the investigations of high-profile crimes.

"So, where does the case stand?" Dorsey asked tersely. "Who's in charge of the investigation? Locals? Sheriff? State investigators?"

Decker laughed. "You're kidding, right? The sheriff's department in Georgia caught the case when it first came in. But once the ID came in from Deptford, and they realized who they had in the morgue, they called the Bureau and pitched that hot potato off to us like it was on fire. They want no part of it."

"Odd. You'd think they'd like the opportunity to show up the Bureau."

"I think they thought it would be more fun to watch us fall all over ourselves trying to spin it. Which sooner or later, someone is going to have to do. We've been trying our damnedest to keep a lid on it, but sooner or later, word will start to spread. I don't know how much longer before something leaks out."

"Shit." She grimaced, knowing it would only be a matter of time before her father's media contacts would catch up with him. "Who's on it for the Bureau?"

"Andrew Shields."

"I thought he quit after his brother went wacko last year and killed one of his cousins."

"He didn't quit. He took some time off, that's all. But God, what a mess. The Shields family have been serving the Bureau for years. Damn shame, for everyone involved."

"So is Andrew Shields still in that special unit of John Mancini's?"

"Yes. He still is."

"So, Mancini's effectively calling the shots."

"Stay out of it."

"I can't."

"Don't go near the case."

"Look, I just want—"

"Doesn't matter what you want. Just keep your fingers off it."

"This is going to destroy my father. I have to know for certain, because if it's her—"

"It's her, Dorse. Accept it."

". . . if it's her, where's she been all these years? What the hell happened to her? Was she a runaway? And if so, why? The Randall family was very respectable. Father was a minister, mother a schoolteacher. This kid came from a good background, Decker. Why would she have run?"

"Let someone else find that out. Kids from good homes run away every day, you know that. Just leave it in Andy's hands and stay out of it."

I can't, was again on the tip of her tongue. Instead, she said, "Okay. Thanks a lot. For giving us the heads up. I—and my dad—appreciate it."

Decker sighed, as if he knew his advice would be ignored the second he hung up the phone.

"Give your dad my best. And if there's anything I can do . . ."

"Appreciated. Thanks again."

She disconnected the call and walked to the end of the driveway, but her father was nowhere in sight. He'd be a while working this one out, she knew. She went inside and found a cold bottle of water in the refrigerator. She took several long deep swigs and returned to her perch on the back porch. She sat with her knees apart, swinging the bottle around by the neck in a mindless circle.

She tapped the phone against the palm of her left hand, then opened it again and dialed.

Grateful for once to be connected to voice mail, she left a brief, to-the-point message for her boss.

"Sorry I missed you, but I need to take some time off. I'm sure you can figure out why. I'll take whatever personal days I have coming and however many vacation days I have left. Talk to you soon."

She forced from her mind the open cases she'd left on her desk. They could be reassigned, she rationalized, but there's no one else to do this for Pop. She reached for her phone one more time. She dialed the number she'd memorized weeks ago while she'd been trying to get her nerve up to call to ask if there was an opening. When the call was answered, she cleared her throat before speaking.

"This is Special Agent Dorsey Collins. I'd like to speak with John Mancini. . . ."

3

It was well past dusk when Dorsey heard her father's footsteps on the front porch. The squeal of the screen door followed, then its slap against the door jamb.

She waited silently in the living room, seated in her grandmother's rocking chair, which had sat for sixty-some years in that same spot near the bow window overlooking what had once been gardens. If Dorsey closed her eyes, she could almost imagine herself curled on her grandmother's lap, secure and sheltered, the gentle to and fro of the rocker lulling her to sleep.

But there'd be no comfort tonight. Anger, frustration, denial, indignation—her father's emotions would run the gamut. She wondered if Matt—whose arrogance was a given to all who knew him well—was capable of considering the possibility that Decker had been telling the truth.

"I just saw Mike Summers out on the beach." Matt made an attempt at normal conversation in spite of the fact that his face was flushed and his voice shaky. He sat in the old wing chair near the fireplace, the same chair he'd been sitting in for over forty years.

Like the rocker, it had never been moved. She couldn't recall that anything in this house had been moved out of place, ever.

"How's he doing?" Dorsey responded, because she had to.

"He just sold his place up on Bay Road. You won't believe how much."

"How much?"

"Seven hundred grand. For that shack." Matt shook his head. "Just think what you could get for this place. You could sell it, you know. Your grandmother left it to you, not me," he reminded her without rancor. "You don't need my permission."

"It's not for sale."

"You're never here. Why hold on to it?"

Because it is the only place I ever lived that when I left, I had only good memories.

"Sentimental value," she told her father.

"Nice that you can afford to kiss off that much money for sentiment."

She shrugged and rocked the chair slowly, knowing he was working up to what he really had to say.

His cell began to ring and he took it from his pocket and checked the number.

"Owen Berger," he told her. *"And Justice For All."*

"Don't, Dad." She shook her head.

"Owen's a good guy. I've been on that show a dozen times."

"That was then, this is now."

"I'm not afraid of the media, Dorse. I've always gotten along well with those folks."

"Yeah, when you had a good story to tell. Now, you *are* the story. Whole 'nother ball game."

"Look, I've been thinking about this. There has to be a mistake." He shut off the ringer, set the phone to vibrate, and stuck it in his shirt pocket.

She sighed and opened her mouth to speak, but he cut her off.

"I'm not worried. It's only a matter of time before they realize. . . ." He cleared his throat. "Dorse, it has to be a mistake. I figure I'll call the director, tell him I'm going to come back on active and work this thing out."

She stared at him in disbelief.

"Do you really think for one second they'd let you anywhere near this case?"

"I worked it the first time."

"Which is precisely why you can't work it now. Come on, Pop, you know better than that." She stopped rocking. "And I've already spoken with John Mancini. I asked him to take me on, give me a place in his unit. I'd heard there was an opening, and I thought maybe . . . well, I thought maybe he'd hire me."

"And?"

"And, he said he'd consider me for the unit but he couldn't put me on this case. It would look really bad all around. If the press got wind I'd been assigned, well, it would not look good for the Bureau. Or for you, for that matter. Bottom line, if they're not willing to put me on board, they sure as hell aren't going to let you anywhere near it."

Matt sat forward in his chair, his arms resting on his thighs, and stared at the floor. Finally, he said, "What are they doing to prove that it isn't Shannon Randall?"

"Pop, there are fingerprints, dental records—they're checking DNA right now. It's her."

"You think they couldn't have made a mistake? Happens all the time, you should know that," he said angrily. "Could we just consider they made a mistake? I'd think at the very least, you of all people, *my daughter,* would want to take a look at the evidence before accepting this as true just because *they* said so. Could you at least do that?"

She nodded but did not speak. Instead, she raised herself from the chair and patted the pockets of her jeans, looking for her car keys.

"Damn it, I'll call Mancini myself. Son of a bitch, after all I did for him, he can't help me out here?" Matt stood, his hands on his hips, his anger exploding.

"Let me tell you something about John Mancini." Her father's jaw tightened. "Seven, eight years back, John caught a case, Sheldon Woods. Homicidal pedophile. Murdered—tortured, mutilated—fourteen young kids before he was caught. Bastard used to call John, every day, taunt him. Would never talk to anyone but John. Finally got to the point where Woods called him while he was torturing a kid. John had to sit there, helpless, listening to this little boy being murdered."

Dorsey had heard the story before. She knew where her father would be taking it this time around.

"John kept his head, tracked Woods down, brought him in. John was just as cool and calm as could be. And when it was over, he broke. Started drinking. Got so bad, they finally made him take a leave. Spent six months with a shrink the Bureau handpicked to work with him." He paused for effect, the way he always did when he got to this part of the story. "And who do you think they called to take this wounded agent under his wing, huh? To find him—Christ, he was holed up in this cabin in the middle of nowhere for a while—talk to him, bring him in, bring him the hell *back*. Me, that's who. I'd already retired, and they called me back to bring him around. And he can't help me now?"

Matt was close to shouting.

"I spent six weeks with that man. And he's going to shut me out of this? I don't think so."

"Pop, when I spoke with John, he said he couldn't assign me. I understand that. And you should too." She held up a hand to delay the protest she knew would be coming. "But he told me if I just happened to stop at Shelter Island to say hey to an old friend from the academy, he couldn't stop me."

"Shelter Island?" Matt frowned and shook his head. "What old friend of yours lives on Shelter Island?"

"Shelter Island, Georgia, is the place where the body was found. And Andrew Shields would be the old friend from the academy."

"You weren't at the academy with Andy."

She shrugged. "Guess John forgot."

"John doesn't forget anything." Matt sat back down in his chair. "So he's giving you an opening. . . ."

"Not officially, no. But he's made it clear he'd turn the other way as long as I was not publicly involved in the investigation and as long as no one knows I'm your daughter. If that gets out, I have to duck and run."

"So, in other words, Andy can tell you what he finds out, but you can't investigate on your own."

"Right, but I can shadow Andy and I'll know if there are any loose strings."

"If there are, I'll expect you to pull them."

"Of course."

Matt thought it over, then nodded slowly. "I guess that's as good as it's going to get."

"And we're damned lucky we got that much. I half expected him to tell me I'd be arrested if I set foot in the state of Georgia."

"All right. Do what you have to do without getting fired. In the meantime . . ." He took his phone out of his pocket and checked the ID of the call coming in. He looked across the room to his daughter. "I can't keep putting these guys off indefinitely. Sooner or later, I have to talk to them."

"I wish you wouldn't."

"I'm no coward, Dorse. Don't ask me to act like one. If I made a mistake . . ." His face went white, as the full implication of his having made a mistake sunk in.

"Just don't talk to anyone for a while, okay?" She

walked to him and knelt down. She understood what had just occurred to him, and knew he must be in terrible pain as a result. "We're going to find out what happened, Pop, back then, and now. We'll put it all together, I promise."

"Jesus, Dorse, I can't believe this is happening." He ran a hand through his hair, then rubbed it across his chin. "I remember it like it was yesterday. Beale all but admitted that he'd killed her."

"After how many hours of questioning, Pop?"

He shot her a look.

"Listen, the first thing I was told when I showed up in Hatton was that the cops knew who did it, that the kid had all but come right out and confessed. They told me this kid, Beale, had had the hots for Shannon Randall big time, but other than let him drive her home from school once in a while, she didn't have any use for him. We spoke to her girlfriends, they all said the same thing. And he admitted to having picked her up late that afternoon; one of her friends said she saw the girl in his car an hour or so after he claimed to have dropped her off, and that the car was heading out of town, in the direction of the lake. He finally admitted the girl had been in his car—he couldn't keep denying it because we found her things in his car. But he said he never left town, so we know he lied about that."

"Because a witness saw him."

"Right. And you know yourself, one lie leads to another. A suspect lies about one thing, chances are he's lying about something else."

"Did he ever confess, Pop?" she asked softly. "You were there when he was executed. Did he ever admit that he killed her?"

"No." Matt suddenly looked like a balloon that was leaking air. His voice dropped and he could not meet her gaze. "No, even then, at the end, he didn't admit to a damned thing. Still swore he was innocent."

"Pop, we're going to have to consider that he was telling the truth."

"Jesus, Dorse, if I made a mistake," he whispered, as if he'd not heard a word she'd spoken. "If I was wrong back then, that means . . ."

He looked at her through eyes dark with growing despair. "If Eric Beale did not kill Shannon Randall . . . dear God, I sent an innocent kid to his death. God forgive me, I watched an innocent boy die. . . ."

Matt stood at the end of the drive and watched his daughter's car grow smaller and smaller, then finally disappear around the first bend on Dune Road. He sighed and looked up at the sky as if hoping to see something other than what he saw every time he'd closed his eyes since Dorsey had given him the incredible news: Eric Beale's face moments before his execution, eyes wide with fear and confusion, skin so pale as to be almost transparent, mouth moving in prayer.

His stomach wrenching, Matt went into the house and directly to the bathroom, where he dry heaved for the fourth time that day.

When he was done, he went back outside, hoping

to find a place to sit and figure out what to do next, but he was uncomfortable everywhere he went. He set out on foot down Dune in the same direction Dorsey had driven. The cattails grew twelve feet tall along this side of the marsh, and he was just as glad for it. There'd be little traffic this time of day, but he had no desire to stop and chat with whoever might be driving through.

He was still working on getting past denial, to a phase where he could think. He'd lain awake all night trying to make sense of it all. How could something that had seemed so certain, so sure, have been so insanely wrong?

He walked along the sandy shoulder to where Dune met up with Hook Road, and took a right onto Hook, barely noticing what he was doing and giving no thought to where he was going. His pace quickened as he neared the inlet where the old lighthouse lay in ruins. The road narrowed to one wide dirt lane and a bit more, and the tall reeds on either side gave him little shelter from the sun overhead. Some slight breeze set the grasses dancing, their hushed rattle the only sound other than his breathing and his footfalls.

The lunch spot that had once been housed in the base of the light was gone now, pushed down in a hurricane several years ago. The roof had collapsed to one side, and swallows had come to build nests almost as soon as the rain had stopped falling and the wind had ceased to blow. They swooped around Matt as if they barely noticed his presence. He walked past the lighthouse to the sturdy pilings that still stood like fearless sentinels and looked across the inlet to the bay.

He exhaled deeply and blinked back the tears behind his dark glasses.

He walked to the end of the rickety pier with no thought that it could very well collapse under his weight and lowered himself so that he was sitting with his feet dangling just above the water. He remembered another time, a lifetime ago, when he'd sat in this very spot with Bernie. He'd been nervous as all get-out, the engagement ring in his pocket and his heart in his throat. He tried really hard, but he couldn't see her there anymore. He remembered how she looked, her dark auburn hair pulled back in a ponytail, sunglasses perched on the edge of her nose, her legs long and tan—but he just couldn't see her there.

All he could see in his mind's eye was Eric Beale sitting at the table between two public defenders—both fresh out of law school, the low men on the county's legal totem pole—as the trial had progressed.

Matt squeezed his eyes shut against the image, but it was still there. The boy's mother and father sat next to each other but apart, a void between them, the kind of void that sits between strangers. Matt had never seen them speak to anyone, not even each other, so detached were they from the proceedings. He remembered thinking how odd it was, the way the parents had never turned to each other for comfort throughout the entire trial, as if each had shut out everyone else. Someone had told him that they were both alcoholics, and he had wondered if that might explain the sense of disconnect he had when he looked at them. Especially the father. Matt had never gotten the feeling that the father was actually there in the courtroom with the rest of them the way the mother was.

Jeanette, her name was, Matt just remembered that. Jeanette Beale sat through every minute of every day as if watching a movie she wasn't enjoying. Her eyes rarely left her son. The father, on the other hand, showed up sporadically, and even then hadn't seemed to be affected by what was going on.

Matt was aware it was only a matter of time before his phone began to ring and he'd have to answer it. He'd told Dorsey he wasn't afraid to face the press, that he wasn't a coward, and he'd meant it. What he hadn't said was that he was afraid he'd have to face Jeanette Beale and explain to her how he'd been so wrong. That his mistakes had caused the son she'd obviously loved to die.

There was just no damned way he could make this right. The best he could hope for was to figure out where he'd gone wrong—and God knew that wouldn't be consolation to anyone.

The box with his notes on this case was in the attic back home. He needed to get his hands on the old files, find some quiet place where no one could find him, where he could go over every word of every report without being disturbed by ringing phones, so he could reconstruct the entire thing in his head, until he understood and could explain to himself how he could have been so far from the truth. Then maybe he could explain to her—to Jeanette Beale, whose eyes had never left her son. Those eyes had expressed no shock when the conviction was read, nor when the death sentence had been announced, almost as if she'd expected no less than this from her life.

Matt needed to understand, not so that he could offer excuses when the cameras caught up to him and the microphones were shoved in his face, but so that he would have the strength to face her, to tell her what had gone wrong, to explain to her how he and the system had failed her son. How he had failed her. How regardless of what else in life had let her down, she should have been able to count on him to find the truth, and on justice being done.

He reached up and grabbed one of the pilings, pulled himself to his feet, and stood for one moment more to watch the gulls dive for the small fish that swam close to shore. On the way back to the house, he took his cell phone from his pocket and dialed a number. He knew just the place where he could hide out and relive the past for a few days.

"Hey, Diane? Matt. Yeah, great, thanks. Yes, I got your message. You said something about taking your boat out on the Chesapeake for a few days? I think I changed my mind. Yeah, sure. I can be ready to leave in the morning. . . ."

4

Another airport. Another rental car. Another winding country road heading toward another marsh. Dorsey couldn't help but make the parallels between where she'd been yesterday and where she was today.

The big difference was that Hathaway Beach had not been the scene of a recent murder, a murder certain to gain national attention once it became known this was the case that had made Matt Ranieri, if not a household name, certainly a recognizable one.

Shelter Island was located off Georgia's coast, a pretty, privately owned island which had once been the exclusive domain of a family named Sheldrake. In the early-1800s, Horace Sheldrake purchased the island from its original owners and turned it into one big cotton plantation. The mansion Horace built for his family had since been renovated and was now a luxury hotel. Much of the rest of the small island had been turned into a private golf course. If you wanted to play the course, you booked a room or a suite or perhaps one of the small guest cottages, and you played for free. Otherwise, you didn't play at all.

The island lay across a two-lane bridge. At its foot, Dorsey took a right turn and followed a sandy patch of road to Calvin's Crab House. Special Agent Andrew Shields had promised he'd be waiting at two o'clock. She was fifteen minutes early, time enough, she figured, to get her bearings.

She parked next to a battered station wagon and left the air-conditioned comfort of the Taurus and stepped into the muggy world of Low Country summer. The thick air held the distinct odor of fish and the hum of insects. She walked to the wooden deck that surrounded the ramshackle structure and looked for the door.

She was halfway around the building—still looking—when she heard her name. She glanced down to the dock below and saw a tall, dark-haired man looking up.

"Dorsey Collins?"

"Yes."

"I'll be right up." He waved, then turned back to the man he'd been speaking with.

Dorsey leaned over the railing and watched a small boat pass under the bridge and head to the dock where the two men stood. Of course, the man who'd called to her was Andrew Shields. She'd have recognized him anywhere. Not because they'd met before, but because she knew several of the other members of the Shields clan and rumor had it they all bore a striking resemblance: tall, athletically built, dark hair and eyes, strong features. Dorsey had worked a case, early in her career, with Aidan Shields, Andrew's cousin. Even from this far away, the resemblance was unmistakable.

When he reached the top of the step, he put out his hand. "Andrew Shields."

"Dorsey Collins." She accepted the hand he offered and shook it. "But I would have recognized you."

"Because I look like my . . . who? Brother? Cousin? All of the above? And you worked with one of them at some point."

"Actually, I did work with Aidan a few years back. And I was in a criminal investigation class with Grady when I was at the academy." She hesitated before asking, "How is Grady?"

"About as you might expect." He brushed the query aside and gestured to the front of the building. "Let's go in and grab a bite, and we'll talk."

She followed him around the corner of the building, and stepped inside when he held the door for her. There was one large square room with a dozen or more tables for four set here and there. He gestured to one that had a view of the water below.

"Is this okay?"

"Fine. Thanks." Dorsey seated herself, placed her handbag on the edge of the table, and reached for the menu.

"Don't bother with the menu," he said as he sat across from her. "They only have a few selections, and I can tell you from experience that this place makes the absolute best Low Country boil you will ever taste."

"What's in it?"

"Sausage, shrimp, potatoes, corn, spices . . . it's really a treat."

"Sold."

"What would you like to drink?" he asked. "I can recommend the beer and the iced tea. Anything else, you're on your own."

"I'm guessing they don't have much call for light beer here."

"You'd be right." He smiled. "Draught okay?"

"Sure."

He pushed back his chair and walked to the bar on the opposite side of the room to place their order. Someone dropped coins into an ancient jukebox, and Otis Redding started singing about watching the tide roll away.

"He was from Georgia, you know." Andrew returned with two glasses of beer.

"Who?"

"Otis Redding."

"Oh." She smiled her thanks for the beer and took a sip. It was delightfully cold. "I didn't know."

Andrew tapped his fingers on the table, then said, "So, let's cut to the chase. What is it you want?"

"You're kidding, right?" She almost laughed in his face. "I thought I made myself clear on the phone."

"On the phone you said you wanted to stop down to talk with me. You're here. Now I'm asking what you want."

She stared at him hard across the table. "Please don't play games with me, Andrew. You know why I'm here."

He returned the stare for a long moment.

"Look, I don't know what John Mancini told

you. . . ." She stopped and said, "Maybe we should start there. What exactly did he tell you?"

"He told me that you'd be calling, which you did, and that you'd be interested in the Shannon Randall investigation. You mentioned that on the phone as well. He also said you'd probably want to play an active role but I was to keep your fingerprints off everything. He did say he explained to you exactly what that meant."

"He did."

"But what he didn't say was whether or not his terms were acceptable to you."

"I don't recall him saying there was a choice."

"There isn't."

"So what part don't you understand?"

"I don't know what your expectations are, Dorsey. I don't know what you're hoping to find."

The bartender waved to Andrew that their order was ready, and he excused himself. Dorsey watched him walk to the bar and retrieve the tray holding two steaming crocks of spicy stew. He set one in front of Dorsey and the other at his place, then set the tray on the table behind him.

"They've been short on help all week," he explained as he sat back down in his chair. "Go ahead. Give it a try."

She tasted a bit of shrimp. "It's spicy."

"I probably should have warned you."

"No, it's fine. Delicious, really."

They ate for a few minutes in silence.

"Look, I'm not trying to be a hard-ass." He leaned

across the table and lowered his voice. "I just need to know that you understand exactly how sensitive this is." There was something almost naively earnest in the way he was looking at her.

"Of course I understand."

"If anyone suspected that Matt Ranieri's daughter was anywhere near this investigation—"

"I said I understood."

"Convince me."

"I am not to sign any reports, I may not talk to anyone without you present, I may not speak with the media, and I may not initiate anything without your knowledge."

"I'm sure John told you it was a take-it-or-leave-it situation."

"Obviously, I took it."

"But you still didn't answer my original question. What is it you want?"

"You mean, ultimately?"

"Yes."

"I want to know the truth. If this woman is definitely Shannon Randall, I want to know where the hell she's been all these years. And how did she get there? And why?" She placed both hands flat on the table in front of her and stared down for a long time. "And I want to know what happened that night back in 1983. If she knew that Eric Beale had been arrested, tried, and convicted of murdering her. Was she aware he'd been executed?"

"The only thing I didn't hear you say is that you want to exonerate your father of Eric Beale's death.

You know, of course, that if Beale didn't kill Shannon, your father is going to be accused of rushing to judgment, of leading the team that prosecuted an innocent man. Of being responsible for his death."

"If Beale didn't kill Shannon, my father has a lot to answer for. I am aware of that. So is he." She nodded slowly. "Believe me, no one is more aware than he is."

"And you really think you could be impartial? We may find things that could make your father look really, really bad."

"I am aware of that possibility, yes." She sat stiffly now, uncomfortable under his scrutiny.

"You don't think you're going to be tempted to influence me to bury facts or to—"

"I'm going to pretend you didn't say that." Her temper flared. "You can ask anyone I've ever worked with, they'll tell you I don't give a shit about anything but the bottom line."

"Which is?"

"The truth, of course."

"Even if the truth destroys your father."

"Whatever the outcome, he'll have to deal with it." She said softly. "And so will I."

"And he knows you're doing this?"

"He encouraged it." She tried to smile. "Since they wouldn't let him back on the job to do it himself."

"He didn't really expect . . ." Andrew frowned.

"Of course not." This time the smile was genuine, if weak. "But he wants to know. Something convinced him back then that Beale killed the girl, that there was no other explanation for her disappearance. If he missed something, he needs to know."

"And Beale?"

"My father will have to find a way to make his peace with it. I can help find the truth, but I won't be able to help him deal with the consequences. We both know that."

"All right, then." Andrew drained his beer. "Finish up, and we'll go for a ride. I'll drive."

"The body was found here." Andrew pointed to a slight depression in the sea grass that grew in thin clumps on the side of the dune.

"Who found her?"

"One of the guests at Sheldrake Hall was out jogging early in the morning, and tripped over the body."

Dorsey stood on the gravel path and looked at the dump site. "Whoever left her here had to know she'd be found before too long."

"Maybe they were hoping the gators would get to her first."

"This is a salt marsh," she said as she knelt to take a closer look. "Gators live in fresh water."

"Right, but maybe whoever dumped her here didn't know that."

"Maybe whoever dumped her here just wanted to get rid of her." She swatted at a mosquito that flew directly at her face. "Cheeky bugger," she muttered.

"Or, as you said, wanted to make certain her body would be discovered quickly." Andrew looked over his shoulder in the direction of the main house, which was hidden from view by a long row of gnarled live oaks that formed an allée from the main road to the front door. "It could have been brought in by car under cover of night. The guests and employees of the inn have all been interviewed, and no one saw or heard anything that night. But the bartender back at the Crab Shack says he saw a light-colored van coming down off the bridge when he was locking up that night. Said it was around ten after three."

"No make or year on that van?"

"He said it was going fast. He just saw that it was a light van."

"Maybe the body was brought by boat," Dorsey suggested.

"A boat would have been seen or heard. Because of the way the currents run, the only safe place to moor is to the immediate left of the old house. Which is why the dock was placed there. A car would actually have been the best way on and off the island if someone was trying to avoid being seen."

"How was the body left?" Dorsey stood and slapped at the back of her neck.

"Laid on her back, her hands crossed over her stomach. Legs straight out in front of her. I have photos in the car, I'll show you later."

"So she wasn't just tossed out of the car. Someone took the time to lay her carefully on the ground."

"Right. Which means this is probably no random killing." Andrew nodded. "Her clothes were carefully arranged, even the short skirt she was wearing was pulled down as far as it would go."

"No sexual assault?" Another slap, this one on her left hand.

"No. Not that the ME could tell, anyway. Remember, she was a working girl. There were signs of recent sexual activity, but according to her roommate, she'd been working that night."

"So there's no way of knowing if she'd had sex with her killer. If he was one of her johns . . ."

"Right now, we know nothing," Andrew agreed.

Dorsey knelt again to inspect the grasses. "She wasn't killed here. There would have been blood."

"Right. There was no indication she was killed here."

"So, where do we start?" Dorsey shoved her hands into the pockets of her linen pants, which had looked so crisp when she'd put them on earlier that morning but were now full of wrinkles. She should have worn jeans. "Why aren't you swatting?"

"They're not bothering me."

"That's really annoying."

"Sorry. And it's not where do *we* start. It's where am I on the investigation, which is already underway."

"Right." She bristled but nodded her understanding.

"I've spoken with the roommate briefly, but I got very little out of her. I did take a few notes, which I'll let you read, along with the statement she gave the police, but we're going to need to meet with her in person." He paused as if something had just occurred to him. "Maybe you'll have more luck with her. She doesn't seem to have a very high regard for men."

"Most prostitutes don't. But I'd be happy to talk to her, if you think it will help."

"And I'll want to talk to the family, back in South Carolina. I haven't been in touch with them yet, though I understand the state police have been. Once the locals realized what they had, they couldn't get rid of it fast enough."

"So I've heard." She turned slightly and looked out at the sea, where dark clouds were gathering and a storm was just beginning to move toward the shore. Even from the opposite side of the island, she could hear the waves pounding on the beach. The air was still, except for the hum of the mosquitoes that seemed to grow louder with every minute. She swatted at the air near her right ear and smacked her left arm.

"That's it. I've had enough for one day. I say we head inland, away from these goddamn little flying vampires."

"Good idea," Andrew said, though the insects still appeared to ignore him. "First we'll take a look at the body, then we'll visit with Edith Chiong."

"Who's Edith Chiong?" Dorsey started toward the car.

"Shannon's roommate."

"Where's the body now? She hasn't been buried yet, right?"

He caught up with her at the car.

"No. They've only just identified her a few days

ago. The body is still at the ME's. My understanding
is that it's going to be transported to a funeral home
in Hatton, South Carolina, within the next day or so,
so I want to make that the priority. I'm hoping Shannon herself will be able to give us a clue as to what
happened to her."

"That sounds like a plan." Dorsey opened the passenger door and hopped in as quickly as she could,
hoping to leave most of the swarm on the other side
of the glass. "Would you mind stopping back at the
Crab Shack so I can pick up my car? I can follow you
from there."

"Sure."

Andrew backed out of the parking spot and headed
down the narrow road that led back to the bridge.

"A profiler I worked with told me that you can't
find the killer without knowing the victim," Dorsey
said. "That the victim will tell you what you need to
know, if you pay attention."

"Anne Marie McCall." He nodded.

"Right. I worked a case with her last year. She's
great. Have you worked with her?"

"Yes." He was suddenly intent upon studying the
road.

"Oh, my God, I forgot . . ." She covered her mouth
with her hand. "I shouldn't have . . . I forgot . . ."

"Right. She was engaged to marry my cousin,
Dylan." Andrew's gaze was fixed on the road ahead.
"Who was murdered by my brother."

"Andrew, I'm sorry," she told him softly. "I wasn't
thinking."

He made a left onto the bridge.

A moment later he said, "Good point, about knowing the victim to find the killer. That's exactly what I intend to do. I'm interested in seeing just what Shannon has to tell us. Hopefully, she'll give us something that in the end will lead us to her killer."

5

"She's been a real popular girl these last few days."
The middle-aged receptionist at the medical exami-
ner's office inspected the credentials Andrew offered,
then barely glanced at Dorsey's badge as she pushed
her chair back from her desk and stood. "Course,
rumor has it she was real popular when she was alive,
too. And busy. Very, very busy."

"Are you referring to the fact that it's been alleged
she was a prostitute?" Andrew slid his badge back
into the inner pocket of his jacket, his face unread-
able.

"Honey," she drawled, "there is no alleging about
it. She was what she was. This wasn't the first time
the cops found that girl out late at night, if you know
what I mean."

She took five steps and opened the door leading to
the hall. Andrew opened his mouth as if to speak, but
the receptionist didn't seem to notice.

"Course, that don't make it right, what happened
to her. Don't make it right at all." She waved the
agents on with her right hand. "Just saying, you keep
putting yourself in harm's way, sooner or later harm's
gonna catch up with you, that's all."

It was hard to argue with that logic. Hookers were high risk, there was no way around it.

"Doc Fuller's in the back room. He told me to bring y'all on back when you got here." She continued to chat as she led them down the hall, and stopped in front of a solid gray door. "Most activity we've seen around here in a while. Can't remember the last time the FBI was here. Maybe not since that bus crash out on the old Hollow Tree Road back four years or so now. Illegal alien driving a car that hit a bus, you may have heard about that. . . ."

She swung the door back and stepped aside so they could enter.

"Doc, the FBI agents you were waitin' on are here. This here's Agent Shields," she pointed to Andrew, then turned to Dorsey. "And this is Agent Collins."

Dorsey extended her hand to the dapper white-haired gentleman in the crisp lab coat. It was so clean that she suspected he'd just slipped it on. No way could he have performed autopsies in that spotless garment.

"Agent Collins, good to meet you." He shook her hand firmly, then turned to Andrew. "Agent Shields. We spoke on the phone, I believe."

"Yes, sir. We appreciate you making time to see us. We know your time is valuable, and—"

"Not at all." The ME waved his hand dismissively. "I don't have a damned thing better to do. No autopsies scheduled today, and if the good folks of our fine county are lucky, I'll have none again tomorrow. Come on over here. Have a seat and we'll talk."

He beckoned the agents to follow him to the far side of the room, where several chairs stood around a wooden table. In the center of the table, a Mason jar held a handful of blue flowers.

"Maise's idea of decor." He nodded in the direction of the door the receptionist had left open. He walked to it and gave it a shove, to close it. "That oughta keep her guessing for a while."

He turned back to his guests.

"Now. You wanted to talk about Shannon Randall." Fuller took the chair nearest the window and rested his hands on the table. "How can I help you?"

"Actually, we were hoping to see the body," Dorsey said before Andrew could respond. She caught the look he sent her: *Back off. I take the lead.* With a slight nod of her head, she acknowledged she'd jumped the gun, and gestured to him to pick up at that point in the conversation.

"We're still not clear on cause of death," Andrew explained. "We've heard she was shot, we heard she'd been stabbed."

Dorsey's head snapped up. She stared at Andrew.

"Yes." Fuller nodded. "Yes, she was."

"Which?"

"Both."

"She was shot *and* she was stabbed?" Dorsey heard herself ask.

"Yes. And here's the odd thing: either could have killed her. The gunshot was at close range, right to the heart. Whoever pulled that trigger wanted to make sure she was good and dead, good and fast." Fuller leaned back in his chair, his hands behind his head. "And the stab wounds? Any one of three or four of them could have been fatal."

"How many were there?" Andrew asked.

"Nine." Fuller nodded grimly. "That girl'd been stabbed nine times."

"Which actually killed her?" Andrew wanted to know.

"That would have been the gunshot. Like I said, straight to the heart. But the stabbing must have been almost immediately thereafter." He shook his head. "I pride myself on being meticulous, being up on all the latest forensic techniques. I believe she was technically dead when she was stabbed. Judging by the amount of blood she lost, her heart was still pumping for a time after she was shot."

He stared at the table for a moment, then said, "I do believe it was the gunshot that killed her."

"Why stab her if you've already shot her?" Dorsey thought aloud.

"Why, indeed?" Fuller asked. "My first thought was the killer was trying to cover up the fact that she'd been shot, three of the stab wounds being precisely over the entry point."

"She was stabbed over the gunshot wound?" Andrew asked.

"Repeatedly."

"Was the gun used to kill her something out of the ordinary, something that could be easily traced?" Andrew suggested.

"Looked like your basic .38 caliber to me," Fuller told them. "Nothing we haven't seen before."

"Anything else you can tell us about the stab wounds?" Andrew asked.

"Made with a really sharp knife. Kitchen knife most likely. The kind my wife uses to cut up chickens, goes through bone?" Fuller told them. "Blade was an inch and a quarter wide, non-serrated, pushed in pretty far in most places. Two, almost three inches, in some spots." Fuller let that sink in, then added, "But here's the funny thing about that. Usually you see someone with that many stab wounds, they're jagged in places because the killer's been in a sort of frenzy, but not here. It was all very deliberate. Edges of each cut nice and clean. Took his time, whoever did this. Sliced her up nice and neat, emphasis on the neat."

Fuller stood abruptly.

"But come on, you'll see for yourself. She's right over here."

In the time it took for Dorsey and Andrew to stand, Fuller had made it across the room and was standing in front of a drawer in the wall. He pulled the door open, and the body of Shannon Randall slid out on its slab. He waved the agents closer.

Dorsey stood over the body and found it alarmingly difficult to look down, as if seeing Shannon Randall in the flesh would make this nightmare undisputedly true. If this was indeed Shannon, her father was in the deepest shit of his life.

She looked down, and thoughts of her father's predicament faded completely. She saw, not the child whose murder her father had sought to avenge, but a woman whose life had been taken from her in a violent manner. The corpse was not unlike others she had seen before. The skin dry and a particular shade of gray. The hair lifeless and matted where the skin from the skull had been peeled back. Eyes open and glassy, sightlessly staring into Dorsey's.

Traces of black mascara had flaked onto the skin under the eyes. For some reason, Dorsey's eyes kept returning to those flecks. To her, those tiny flecks were the only signs of life, the only indication that this had been a living, breathing woman before something terrible had happened to her. It was all she could do not to reach out and brush them from Shannon's face. In her mind's eye, Dorsey could see Shannon preparing to go out that night—that night she could not have known would be her last—putting on her makeup, applying mascara as she must have done thousands of times before. As Dorsey had done many times herself. As so many women do. It made the victim unexpectedly familiar, and Dorsey forced herself back to the task at hand.

Shannon Randall had been five feet, three inches tall, slim, with muscular legs and arms, and hair dyed red. Dorsey's fingers curled unconsciously into her own long, naturally red curls. She recalled from the photos of Shannon at fourteen that her hair had been light brown, and wondered whether she'd changed the color to make her stand out more on the street, or if it was part of a disguise she'd adopted long ago.

Which brought Dorsey back to the first question

that had gone through her mind when she'd heard Shannon Randall had been alive for the past twenty-four years: What had happened to this girl on that long ago night? Had she run away, and if so, from what? From whom?

"You can see where the knife went in around the gunshot wound—right here, here, and here." Fuller pointed with the scalpel he'd picked up from a nearby tray. His voice brought Dorsey back, reminded her why she was here.

"Doctor Fuller, do you have some gloves we could use?" Andrew asked.

Ever the gentleman, Fuller offered a box of latex gloves first to Dorsey, then to Andrew. They each took a pair and pulled them on.

Andrew leaned close to the chest and studied the wounds.

"May I?" he asked, and reached for the scalpel. Fuller handed it over, and watched from the opposite side of the table while the agent probed gently at the dry gray flesh to the left of the Y incision from the autopsy.

"Yes, there it is," he murmured. "You can see where the bullet entered, right here, but you really have to look for it. As you said, it's almost as if the killer tried to cover up the bullet hole." He looked up at Doctor Fuller. "Why would the killer try to disguise the cause of death?"

"Knowing the answer to that could be a clue to who the killer is." Fuller nodded, then paused and added, "Then again, maybe not. Sometimes, you just don't know what's significant and what's mere coincidence. Could be the killer was covering up, could be he just wasn't watching what he was doing."

"Even though he was doing it slowly enough to make very clean, very even wounds."

Fuller nodded. "Right. Still, as you know yourself, things aren't always what they seem."

Dorsey studied the still figure for a long moment, her eyes trailing the length of the left arm, then moving down to the thigh, then to the opposite side of the body where her gaze lingered on the right thigh and arm. Andrew watched her without comment. When she raised her eyes to his, she said softly, "She was a cutter."

"You saw that, too?"

"Probably used a razor blade—see how very thin the scars are?" She pointed with a gloved index finger to the lines that went up and down the woman's arms and the tops of her thighs like the pale, uneven rungs of a ladder.

"Judging by the scars, I'd say she'd been doing it for a very long time," Andrew noted. "Some scars have long healed, some have been reopened more than once. Some recently, I'd say."

"Interesting that it appears she might have stopped for a while, then started again." She pointed to several long marks on Shannon Randall's upper thigh.

"Right. These are fresh. And here, on her upper arm, close to her shoulder?" Andrew studied the scars intently. "Almost all of the others are old."

"I noticed those," Fuller nodded, "but I don't recall

having had this type of thing before. Read about cutting, but haven't ever seen it firsthand. We don't get a whole lot of kids in here, not like this. Most young people have left town, moved on before they reached this age."

"She cut for a long time, then stopped long enough for all those old scars to heal over and stay healed. Then something happened to make her start cutting again." Dorsey seemed to mull it over. "So maybe whatever caused her to start cutting in the first place, whatever it was she'd gotten over sufficiently that she didn't feel she had to hurt herself anymore—somehow, that *whatever* was back in her life."

Both men stared at her. She stood up straight and pulled off the gloves.

Andrew did the same, turned to Doctor Fuller. "We really appreciate your time, Doctor Fuller."

"Anytime, Agent Shields. I'm going to have to release the body to the family soon—thought they'd be wanting it sooner than this, frankly. I suspect there's some kind of to-do going on right about now, what with the young lady having been a hooker and one of her sisters being a preacher—"

"Her sister?" Dorsey frowned. "I thought her father was the minister."

"He had been, up until just a couple of years ago. Car accident left him paralyzed. Heard all about it from the director of the funeral home up there in Hatton, where the Randalls are from." Fuller covered the body with the sheet and slid the shelf back into the refrigerated drawer. "Hit and run. Car ran him off the road, then disappeared. Never even stopped. They figured it must have been a drunk driver. The man never saw it coming, apparently. Hasn't walked since. It was the youngest daughter who took over the church."

"I think I remember more than two children in the family," Dorsey said, trying to think back to her early teens when the story was fresh in her mind.

"There are three sisters. Four daughters altogether. Oldest's a state senator up in South Carolina now—she's the one who identified the body. Another sister does something on television. And of course, the minister. Can't recall the funeral director saying much more than that."

"Quite an accomplished family," Andrew remarked as he and Dorsey headed toward the door.

"Yes, so it would seem." Fuller peeled off his gloves and dropped them into the wastebasket next to his desk. "It's had me wondering how a girl from a family like that ends up like this girl did."

"Girls from all kinds of backgrounds end up like Shannon Randall, Doctor Fuller. There's no easy answer why," Andrew replied.

"True enough." Fuller nodded.

"What was the sister's demeanor when she came to make the identification?"

"Solemn, I'd say," the doctor replied after pondering the question for a moment. "Sober. Respectful."

"Emotional?"

"No, wouldn't have called her emotional." Fuller shook his head from side to side. "She didn't cry, just sort of looked at the body for a while. Asked me to raise it on the left side at the shoulder, and I did. She leaned down to take a look, and said something under her breath like, 'Yes, that's it.' "

"She was looking for a birthmark," Andrew said.

"That's right. On the back of the left shoulder, she has a little mark, sort of looks like a cigar. I'd noted it in my report, but she wanted to see for herself."

"What did she do, after she saw the mark?" Andrew asked.

"She just sort of nodded and said thanks."

"And she just left, just like that?"

"Pretty much," Doctor Fuller told him. "Oh, one thing she did do. After she'd looked and I let the body back down on the gurney, she tucked some hair behind the girl's ear. Sort of gentle, like. I remember thinking that was nice, her being the older sister and all."

"Thanks again, Doc." Andrew waved from the door, and after he and Dorsey passed through, allowed it to close quietly behind them.

The receptionist had left for the day while they'd been with Doctor Fuller, and she'd closed up the office on her way out, but there was sufficient light from the windows for them to find the front door. They walked to the parking lot in silence.

Andrew stopped at the front of Dorsey's car and looked at his watch.

"How do you read the older sister?" she asked.

"I don't know. She came alone to make the identification. Why didn't the mother or two younger ones come with her? And odd, don't you think, that she was so unemotional about it? You think your sister has been dead for more than twenty years, then you find out she's been alive all that time, but now she really is dead. Wouldn't you show more feeling when you see her for the first time after all those years and she's laying dead on a gurney in the morgue, all carved up? Wouldn't you cry for her, just a little?"

"At the very least." Dorsey nodded. "It certainly makes you wonder about the relationships among the sisters. I wonder if the other two stayed away from the morgue because they're more emotional than the oldest one."

"Maybe. But maybe there's more to it than that." Andrew checked his watch. "Look, it's almost seven. How about we find you a place to stay tonight, then grab some dinner. There's no point in trying to see the roommate tonight. Chances are she's already out on the street."

Dorsey nodded somewhat absently.

"Where are you staying?" she asked.

"The Deptford Inn, it's right as you come into town. Want to try there?"

She nodded again. "I'll follow you."

He started around the front of his car, then turned back to her.

"You're thinking that a family like the Randalls—a minister, a state senator, and someone involved in television—wouldn't be happy to have this story break right about now."

"Three siblings, all in well-respected professions.

And then all of a sudden, Shannon, who was supposed to have been dead all those years, turns up a hooker? You see something wrong with this picture?"

"Oh, yeah. But I think the real question is, when did the long lost sister turn up? Before or after she was killed?"

6

A knocking sound from someplace far away drew Dorsey from a deep sleep. She opened her eyes and blinked several times until she remembered where she was: in a small third-floor room in the Deptford Inn, and the knocking sound was coming from the door.

"Who's there?" she asked cautiously.

"Shields."

She got up slowly and went to the door.

"Sorry." She covered her yawn with both hands. "I must have conked out."

"You've been doing a lot of traveling these past few days. Travel always makes me tired, too." He leaned against the door frame.

"Come on in." She waved him inside and closed the door behind him. "Have a seat."

"No thanks. I didn't intend to stay. I just wanted you to have a chance to look over Edith Chiong's statement along with my notes before we sit down with her tomorrow."

"Are you sure you don't want to try to find her tonight?"

"Waste of time. We stand a better chance of catching her at her apartment in the morning. We'll have a better shot at getting her to sit down and talk with us during the day, too. Tonight, she's going to have her eye on the clock, time being money in her business."

"Good point." Dorsey nodded.

He handed her the file he'd had tucked under his arm.

"This can't be everything." She frowned.

"Not by a long shot, but this is the file on Edith Chiong. Her statement, notes from the Deptford police regarding the visits she'd made to the station trying to report Shannon's disappearance. It's all in there."

He moved to the door. "I guess I'm going to turn in."

She walked to the door and held it open for him. "Thanks for everything today. Especially for letting me go with you to see the body and speak with Doctor Fuller. Up until today, Shannon Randall was just a name out of my past. Now . . ."

He studied her face for a moment, and she had the feeling there was something right on the tip of his tongue. What he said instead was, "I'm in room 317 if you need me for anything. How about we meet in the lobby around eight in the morning, and we drive into the city together?"

"Great. Thanks. I'll see you then. And thanks for the reading material. I appreciate it. You didn't have to do that."

"You're welcome. I figured you ought to be up-to-date. Besides, like I said, she might open up to you more than to me."

Andrew walked through the open door and she closed it behind him, wondering what it was he'd wanted to say.

Dorsey sat on the edge of the bed and read over the room service menu, then called and placed an order for a light supper. She piled the pillows behind her and sat back against them, the manila file on her lap. She opened it and thumbed through the contents.

Edith Chiong's statement was on the bottom, and there were reports from a number of police officers relating their conversations with her. Notes written on scraps of paper confirmed she'd called the station five times over a two-week period, starting with the morning Shannon had gone missing. The notes skipped a few days, but the statement indicated that Edith had also gone to the station on three separate occasions to inquire about her missing roommate. It didn't take a genius to see that no effort had been made to locate Shannon Randall. "Missing hooker reported three days ago, still missing" was the extent of the notes one officer had scribbled. Dorsey could only begin to imagine how frustrated Shannon's roommate must have been.

Room service was quick and good, and Dorsey sat cross-legged on her bed with her shrimp, which had been served with grits. She pushed the white mound to one side of her plate. Even after six years of living in the south, she had yet to develop a taste for grits.

When she finished eating, she left her tray outside the door, then tried her father's cell phone. When he didn't pick up, she left a message asking him to call her, then lay back against the pillows with her eyes closed. She tried to reconcile the sweet face of the young girl she remembered seeing in newspapers and on television all those years ago with that of the woman whose lifeless eyes had stared unseeing at Doctor Fuller's ceiling. What, Dorsey wondered, had forced her from her home without a trace?

It occurred to her, not for the first time, that perhaps Shannon had been kidnapped. But surely that possibility would have been considered back in 1983, when no trace of her had been found. And if she'd been kidnapped, but alive all these years, why had she not contacted her family? Why, if she'd been free to live and work in Deptford, had she never gone home?

Dorsey recalled several cases where kidnap victims never did contact their loved ones, even though they had many opportunities to do so. The explanations were as varied as the kidnappings themselves. None were ever exactly the same, the human psyche being what it is.

Then again, how could she be certain Shannon had never contacted her family?

She sat straight up in bed. Was it possible that someone in the Randall family could have known that Shannon had been alive all this time?

But who would keep such a secret, and why? And there was the matter of Eric Beale. Surely, if someone knew the girl had not been killed, they would have stepped forward before this, wouldn't they?

Wouldn't they . . . ?

A chill ran up her back and into her scalp.

Yes, of course. Of course they would tell. She shook off the obscene possibility that anyone could have had such knowledge yet kept it to themselves. A young boy's life had been at stake. Surely no one would have watched him go to his death and not said anything.

She closed her eyes again and thought about the role her father had played in this drama, of the irony that she had stood over Shannon Randall's dead body twenty-four years after the girl had supposedly been murdered. Twenty-four years after her father had arrested Eric Louis Beale for her death.

She thought about the Beale family, and wondered if word had gotten to them yet. As difficult as it must have been for the Randall family to learn that Shannon had been alive all these years, how much more terrible it must be for the family of the young boy who'd been executed for a murder that had never been committed.

Dorsey tried her father again, and was almost relieved when he didn't pick up. It would be difficult to speak with him tonight. It all weighed too heavily on her heart, Shannon and Eric, their parents, their siblings, along with so many unanswered questions.

She fell asleep with the light on, the possibilities playing free and loose in her head.

"Good morning," Andrew said when Dorsey walked into the lobby at two minutes past eight the next morning.

"Hi." She smiled and walked past the front desk to the door. "You driving or am I?"

"I'll drive, if it's all the same to you."

She shrugged and followed him out the door and into the parking lot.

"So. Did you have your eggs and grits this morning?" He unlocked the car with the remote and walked to the driver's side.

"I don't do grits." She opened the passenger door and got in, dropping her bag on the floor with one hand and slamming the door with the other.

Andrew laughed and started the car without comment.

"Do you know where we're going?" she asked as the car turned left at the exit.

"Got directions from the police department. Seems Shannon and Edith were no strangers to the locals."

"Their paths had crossed in the past?"

"On more than one occasion. Loitering, mostly. Solicitation a time or two." Andrew checked his rearview mirror, then pulled into the lane of traffic that was headed downtown. "I thought we'd spend some time with the roommate this morning, then I want to head up to Hatton, talk to the family."

"Sounds good."

They rode in silence for a few minutes, then Andrew said, "You read the file last night?"

"Several times."

"Then you know there's no love lost between Edith and the cops. She had to have been royally pissed when her friend went missing and she couldn't get the cops to give her the time of day."

"Hey, what's one less hooker in Deptford, right?"

"Exactly. So I was thinking, she sees us coming, she's going to try to bolt. Our best bet is to wake her out of a sound sleep; at least we'll know she's there."

"Maybe. Or maybe she won't answer the door at all."

"In which case, we'll have to resort to plan B."

"Which is?"

"I'm still working on it."

He drove into the city, past block after block of nondescript neighborhoods, some slightly nicer than others, before stopping in front of a tan brick building that might have been a fashionable address in the 1920s. Out front, there was a small patch of grass overdue for a cutting and a single white pot with some dried flowers that might once have been geraniums in cement-hard dirt. Andrew parked in a spot marked Reserved and turned off the engine.

"Agent Shields, you do take me to the nicest places." Dorsey stared out the window, taking it all in.

"Nothing's too good for a fellow agent." He unbuckled his seat belt. "Ready?"

She swung open her door and stepped out onto broken pavement. Candy wrappers and fast food bags lay on the ground close to the steps leading into the building, and chalked squares for hopscotch were barely visible on the sidewalk.

"Do kids still play hopscotch?" Andrew glanced down as he caught up with Dorsey.

"Guess so." She started up the steps.

"You play when you were a kid, Dorsey?"

"No." She pushed open the unlocked door. "Did you?"

"My sister played. She loved colored chalk, the brighter the better."

"We didn't have sidewalks where I grew up," she told him as she read the names on the mailboxes.

"No sidewalks?" He frowned.

"Hathaway Beach, where I was born, had sandy paths. No concrete."

"I thought you were from around Philly."

"How would you know that?" It was her turn to frown.

"I know that's where your father lives. He's on TV all the time, and he always mentions it. Besides, you have the accent."

"I do not have an accent." She tapped on one of the mailboxes. "Second floor, apartment 2G."

She headed toward the steps and Andrew followed.

"We'll knock on the door, and when she answers, you tell her you're here to talk about Shannon," he said.

"I thought I was supposed to stay in the shadows."

"Like you did yesterday at the ME's?"

She glared at him and went past him on the steps.

"Hey, that was the deal," he reminded her. "You do have a way of getting yourself right in there."

"Is that a problem for you?"

"Only if it gets you noticed by the wrong people." He reached the landing first and held the door for her.

The hall was narrow, the carpet old, and the padding bunched in several places. Dorsey tripped twice between the stairwell and the door with 2G painted unevenly in black.

"This must be hell at night after a few drinks," she muttered, looking down at the uneven floor covering.

Andrew pointed to the door, and Dorsey knocked three times and waited, listening for some movement behind the door. She knocked again, louder, then called, "Miss Chiong, are you in there?"

After a few moments of silence, they heard a shuffle from inside the apartment.

"Miss Chiong, are you there?"

"Who wants to know?"

"My name is Dorsey Collins. I'm with the FBI. I need to talk to you about Shannon."

"You got some ID?"

"Yes."

"Hold it up so's I can see it."

Dorsey pulled her badge from her pocket and opened it while a dead bolt was released on the other side of the door. A chain kept the door from opening more than three inches.

"Hold it closer," Edith demanded.

Dorsey did as she was told.

"What is it you want to know?" Edith asked.

"I want to talk about Shannon."

The chain came off and the door swung open.

"Better late than never, I suppose." The woman stepped back to let Dorsey enter, then began to close the door when she saw Andrew. "Wait a minute, who's he? I thought you were alone."

"Special Agent Andrew Shields, Miss Chiong. We spoke on the phone the other day," he reminded her. "I'm in charge of the investigation into Shannon's death."

"What got the FBI all fired up? That sister of Shannon's being a senator? Is that what it took to get someone's attention? Couldn't be bothered looking for her when y'all thought she was just a hooker. But ooh-wee, once it started getting out that her family was big shots, yeah, now you're interested."

Edith Chiong drew her pale yellow robe tighter around her, and tied it snugly. She was short and slender, with straight dark hair to her shoulders, and dark, uneasy Asian eyes that smoldered in a pretty face. Dorsey guessed she was in her mid-thirties.

"I understand how upset you must have been when you reported Shannon missing and the local police blew you off," Andrew said. "I'm sorry for the way you were treated."

Edith looked from Andrew to Dorsey and back again.

"Come in." She closed the door behind them and relocked the door.

They followed her into a small living room that was surprisingly neat and girly. The sofa was covered with quilts, and there was a worn hooked rug on the floor. On the top of a chest that had been painted white sat a small television, and a glass topped trunk served as a coffee table. On the table was a blue vase filled with daisies and a bottle of dark pink nail polish.

Edith gestured to the sofa and both agents sat.

"Miss Chiong—may I call you Edith?" Dorsey asked, and the woman nodded.

"Is it like I said, the FBI is interested because of that sister being a senator?"

"Actually, no," Andrew said carefully. "We were called in because there's a relationship between this case and an old case the Bureau handled a long time ago."

"What case was that?" She leaned against the doorway with one hand on her hip.

"How long had you known Shannon, Edith?" Dorsey asked.

"Six, seven years."

Dorsey stole a quick glance at Andrew. She knew he was supposed to lead, but they had agreed Edith would most likely respond better to her questioning, and now was as good a time as any to test that. Andrew sat back against the sofa cushions, and Dorsey took that as a green light.

"Where did you meet? Here in Deptford?" she continued.

"Savannah. We were both working Savannah at the time." Her voice softened and she seemed to debate with herself for a moment before walking into the small kitchen area. She returned with a wooden folding chair and placed it next to the coffee table, opposite Dorsey. "Both of us were on the street for the same guy."

"You worked for the same pimp?"

Edith nodded. "His name was Bass. He was one mean son of a bitch. There was just no pleasing that man. No matter how hard you worked, how much you made, it was never enough, you know?"

Dorsey nodded, but Edith appeared not to notice.

"Me and Shannon got to be friends. We were always talking about moving on, moving out. Getting a place of our own, saving some money so that someday we could do something else. Something better. But we knew there was no chance of that while we worked for scum like him."

"How did you get involved with him?"

Edith snorted. "The same way any girl gets into it. It's such a . . . what you call it, a cliché? You come to town thinking you're gonna get a nice job, and you get off that bus and realize those few dollars you got in your pocket aren't going to be near enough. Guys hang around the station, just waiting—you know that. You know the story." She looked directly into Dorsey's eyes. "You know you do."

"Young girl, no place to go. Nice looking guy promises you a job, he tells you he can get you a place to stay with a friend of his. . . ." Dorsey nodded. Edith was right. She'd heard it a hundred times before with minor variations.

"Yada, yada, yada." Edith finished Dorsey's sentence. "What can I say? I was stupid but I thought I was so grown-up, you know? I thought I was leaving something bad for something better. Thought I could handle the city, thought I could handle anything." She bit her bottom lip. "Well, I guess Bass showed me."

"And Shannon?"

"Same story." Edith nodded. "Way back when, some guy picked her out at the bus station, same as me. Same promises. Same job. Same yada yada. Then she comes to Savannah, same thing all over again."

"She arrived in Savannah before you? How much before?"

"She'd been working for Bass for maybe a year by the time I got there."

"Where had she been before Savannah, do you know?"

"Bunch of places." Edith shrugged. "I remember her talking about being in Tennessee for a while. Nashville. Knoxville. Memphis. She said how she used to go to Graceland and stand outside the gates with the tourists."

"Where'd you come from, Edith?" Dorsey asked.

"What difference does it make?" Edith snapped, then softened and told Dorsey, "Virginia. But that was a long time ago."

"You have family there?"

"I guess they're still around. Most likely." Edith licked her lips. "Let's stick to Shannon."

"Did she ever talk about why she left home?"

Edith shook her head. "Shannon didn't talk much about where she was from, except that it was called Hatton and it was in South Carolina. She talked some about her family—she said she had sisters—but she never said why she left."

"And you didn't ask?"

"She'd have told me if she wanted me to know."

"She have any contact with her family that you know of?" Andrew asked.

"No. None."

"So how do you know one of her sisters is a senator?"

"The cops said."

"When?"

"When they came to get her stuff. Day before yesterday."

"What stuff?" Andrew stopped writing and looked up.

"Just some stuff of hers they wanted," Edith told him. "They said her family was coming into town and that they wanted her things. That's when they said her sister was a senator. I heard them talking in her room."

"What did you give them?"

"Stuff." Edith's mouth curved in a half smile.

"Everything?" Dorsey asked.

"Sure," Edith replied flatly.

"So tell us how you got from Savannah to Deptford," Andrew said, changing the subject. There was no question in his mind that Edith had not handed over all of her roommate's possessions willingly.

"No way was Bass gonna let us go, just walk out, so we planned it. Went out one night like we always did, worked our way uptown a bit. Turned what we had to, had the johns drop us off at the bus station. Got on the first bus that was leaving, took us into

Charleston. From there we took the first bus out, that took us to Raleigh. We thought maybe we'd try to cover our tracks some, in case Bass sent someone after us. We worked Raleigh for a while, then worked our way down here to Deptford."

"Why Deptford?" Dorsey asked.

"Shannon liked that it wasn't far from the ocean. She liked the beach. We thought if we lived here, we'd go to the beach." Edith's eyes grew haunted. "We did go sometimes. Not as much as we planned, but we did go a time or two."

She got up and walked into the kitchen and ran water in the sink. When she came back into the living room, she held a glass of water in one hand. She did not ask the agents if they were thirsty.

"It's weird, don't you think? We moved here 'cause she wanted to be near water, and that's where she died. Out there someplace near the water."

"Well, we're not really sure where she died," Andrew told her.

"She wasn't killed out there on that island where they found her?" Edith looked surprised.

"It doesn't look like it. We're pretty sure she was killed someplace else and taken there by car," Dorsey explained.

"Damn cops tell me nothing." She was angry again. "Like I don't have the right to know what happened. Every thing I ask, they say, 'We're only releasing information to the *family*.'" She spit out the word. "I tried to tell them, I'm her family. I'm the one who cared about her. Where has her *family* been all these years, she's missing and they don't come looking for her?"

"I'd be happy to keep you informed of the arrangements, as soon as we find out when and where," Dorsey promised, noting that Edith didn't seem to be aware Shannon was supposed to have been dead for years.

"Like I'm really going to go?" Edith got up and began to pace. "I said my good-byes there in the morgue. I don't need to say good-bye again."

"You identified the body?"

"Well, yeah. It isn't like there was anybody else to do it." Edith sat back down again. "The cops called and said they'd found a body and I needed to come see if it was Shannon. And it was."

"What identification did she have?" Dorsey asked. Edith looked up at her curiously.

"Driver's license, what?" Dorsey probed.

"She didn't have a driver's license."

"What did she have that proved her name was Shannon Randall?"

Edith frowned. "What kinda stupid question is that? She said who she was. I never asked for an ID. She told me who she was and where she was from, and that's what I told the cops."

"Did Shannon keep a journal?" Dorsey changed the subject.

"A what?"

"A journal. Or a diary."

The answer came just a beat too quickly.

"No."

"Did she ever receive any letters while she was here?" Dorsey continued. "Or e-mail? Did she have a cell phone?"

"We don't have a computer. And the only thing the mail guy brought us was the electric bill. Mostly she used pay phones. Once in a while she'd pick up one of those disposable phones."

"Did Shannon ever talk about her past?"

"Not really. Like I said, she never seemed to want to talk about it, and I never pushed it."

Dorsey looked at Andrew as if to ask, Did we miss anything?

"Edith, we really appreciate your time. I know this has been really hard for you." Andrew stood, signaling the interview was over. He closed the notebook and tucked it under his arm.

Edith stared at the floor.

"What are you going to do now?" Dorsey asked as she, too, stood.

"Not sure." Edith shrugged.

"This might be a good time for you to think about . . ." Dorsey searched for a way to put it that would not offend. "About maybe moving on with your life."

Still staring at the floor, Edith nodded.

Dorsey opened her bag and took out a card.

"Look, if you remember anything you think might be important, or if you have any questions, you call me, okay?" Dorsey handed the woman the card.

Edith took it and folded it into the palm of her left hand.

They walked to the door and waited while Edith unlocked it and released the chain. Dorsey was into the hall when she remembered one thing she'd forgotten to ask.

"When did she start cutting herself?"

Edith looked out from behind the partially closed door, clearly surprised.

"We saw the marks on her arms and legs," Dorsey said softly.

"Just a few months ago. I came home one morning and Shannon was in the bathroom, leaning over the sink, cutting herself." Edith pointed to the upper part of her left arm. "I said, 'Jesus, Shannon, stop! You're going to hurt yourself.'"

Edith hugged herself, her arms over her chest, her face reflecting confusion.

"She say why she did it?" Andrew asked.

"Yeah, but it didn't make any sense. She said it was the only way to make the pain go away." Edith shook her head. "Crazy, huh? Like, what kind of person does that to themselves?"

"One more thing," Andrew said. "You said sometimes she picked up a disposable phone."

"Yeah. She used those prepaid things sometimes."

"Who'd she call?"

Edith stared at him, then shook her head from side to side.

"She never said."

7

"So what's your take on Shannon?" Andrew asked after they'd returned to his car and headed toward the highway. "Why do you suppose she did it?"

"Why did she do what?"

"Cut herself."

Dorsey shrugged. "Something in her life was hurting her. She cut herself, bled away the pain."

He stopped at the red light at the corner. From the corner of his eye he was watching her face. There was a lot he wanted to know, but wasn't sure how to ask. He figured he'd just toss it out there and see what he caught.

"You know, I've read about it, but I don't understand. How does causing pain make pain go away? The cutting hurts more than whatever the other pain is?" he asked.

"It's really not quite that simple."

"Then explain it to me."

"Girls who cut themselves—and it's almost always adolescent girls, by the way—mostly they're afraid. The fear is real, generally speaking, not imagined, and usually follows some type of trauma. Could be physical, could be emotional." Her voice was oddly detached.

Andrew tried to see her eyes, but she turned her face to the window. "Could be anything from abuse, incest, parental divorce or death, to fear of being inadequate, of being alone, of being a disappointment to her parents in some way."

"Sounds like the same things you read about that cause eating disorders," he noted.

"Many kids who cut are anorexic or bulimic. Not all, but some."

"So how does one of those events—say, the girl's parents announce they're getting a divorce—lead to the kid picking up a razor blade and slashing her arms or legs?" The light turned green and he proceeded to make a left turn.

"It's a means of seeking relief," she said flatly. "It allows the cutter to control the pain."

"Is it a prelude to committing suicide?"

"No, no. Cutting rarely leads to suicide. It's a temporary solution to a traumatic situation. Suicide is permanent."

"But isn't it a cry for help, like an attempted suicide might be?"

"No. If you attempt suicide with the intention of failing, you're hoping someone stops you so that you can get help. A lot of those kids—adults, too—know they need help but don't know how to ask. Most cutters, on the other hand, go to great lengths to hide it, even from their friends. They hide the scars, they hide whatever implement they use. It isn't always a razor blade, by the way, though that certainly is a popular choice. They don't talk about it. Cutters don't want to be caught. It's a sort of self-medicating, if you could think of it in those terms."

Andrew reflected on this as he drove. He'd already noted that Dorsey had been wearing shirts with sleeves that rolled to the elbow, or T-shirts with elbow-length sleeves, and thick silver bracelets each time he'd seen her. Was she hiding scars of her own?

The thought of Dorsey slicing into her flesh to relieve some greater pain unexpectedly made his heart hurt. He pushed it aside and turned his focus back where it belonged, on the case.

"So you think Shannon had some trauma as a child?"

"I'd bet on it." Dorsey turned back to him; she, too, all business again. "Something happened to make her need to take control, so she did, years ago. Judging by the number of scars I saw on her arms and legs, I'd guess that she continued this behavior into her late teens, maybe her early twenties, before she was able to come to grips with whatever was behind it, and she was able to stop. Except for the fresh cuts, most of the scars appeared to be at least ten years old or better. Then recently, I suspect something happened that brought it all back, and once again, she coped by cutting."

"You think whatever happened that caused her to start cutting in the first place, happened again lately?"

"I think that whatever had been hurting her as a child, was hurting her again—or threatening to hurt her again. Yes, I do."

"Guess that's a conversation to have with the family."

"If they knew."

"If your daughter was into self-mutilation, don't you think you'd know?" he asked.

"Yeah, I'd know." She nodded. "But sometimes the source of the pain is unaware of the means the child takes to alleviate it."

"So in other words, the source of the pain could be something or someone in the family?"

"It almost always is," she said simply. "There's the sign for I-95. Take a right."

He followed the signs and merged onto the interstate. They rode in silence for a while, then he asked, "So how do you think it's going to go with the Randalls?"

"Probably not very well." She closed her eyes and moved the seat to a slightly reclined position. "For one thing, we represent the same agency that concluded Shannon had been murdered twenty-four years ago. Christ, if any of them knew my father was the one who investigated this and was instrumental in charging Eric Beale, in concluding she'd been murdered . . ."

"From what I've read, everyone back then came to the same conclusion. It wasn't just your father. The locals asked the agency to come in because they believed Shannon had been killed, and they'd had very little experience dealing with homicides. There was nothing in the Bureau file or in the Hatton police file that indicated anyone had given any thought to any scenario other than Shannon's murder."

"Mistake number one, then, and don't you wonder why? If no one had considered that Shannon had been abducted, or that she'd run away, then there were never any leads pursued that led anywhere other than murder." She made a face. "If there was anything to be found back then, it's going to be a million times more difficult to find it now. It's just so unlike my father to jump to a conclusion without considering every possibility."

"You don't know for certain that he didn't, so let's not make that assumption. That's one of those things you might want to ask him. Someone must have steered him in that direction. In the meantime, I think we're going to have to take another look at the evidence they did have, maybe reevaluate it."

"What evidence was there?" She counted off on the fingers of her left hand. "They had Beale's shirt covered with Shannon's blood. Her assignment book was found in his car. They had his admission he'd driven her to the park where she cleaned up, and they found the bloody paper towels in the ladies' room there. They couldn't find anybody who saw Shannon after Beale said he dropped her off, but somebody saw Beale driving Shannon out of town around seven, according to the file I looked at last night. There were no other sightings of this girl. The evidence shows she got into Beale's car and was never seen alive again."

"Well, not in Hatton, anyway," Andrew added.

"And you have to admit that all seems to point to Beale."

"What are the chances he drove her someplace, helped her to run away?" Dorsey suggested.

"You'd think he'd have said something back then, when his life depended on it."

"Suppose Shannon convinced Beale that something terrible was happening to her at home, that she had to run away, and he helped her." Dorsey considered the possibility. "He was her friend, maybe she made him promise not to tell."

"Promise or not, he would have spoken up," Andrew insisted. "No matter how good a friend he was, no way would that kid have kept his mouth shut if it meant being executed."

"You'd think." She sat quietly again for a while, then asked, "So you've read the Bureau's entire file?"

"Yes."

"Fill me in on everything. I've only read bits and pieces."

"Where would you like to start?" A light rain started to fall and he turned on the wipers.

"Start with the family. I remember seeing a picture of the four girls in the newspaper back then. Shannon was the second youngest, I think."

"Right. The oldest is Natalie, now Natalie Randall-Scott, the state senator. She was twenty-one, away at college in 1983. They barely talked to her at all back then. The next sister is Aubrey—she's not married. She's the one who has the television show, sort of a Southern Martha Stewart, if I understand correctly.

She's rumored to be in line for a national show. She was seventeen, a high school senior, when Shannon disappeared. Shannon was the third child, and the last was Paula Rose, who was three years younger than Shannon. She's a minister in the church previously served by her father and grandfather."

"Mom and Dad are both still alive, I know. But what about the grandparents?"

"Martha and Paul Randall. Grandma's still with us, Reverend Paul passed on a few years ago."

"One of the sisters might know what it was Shannon was running away from," she murmured, "if in fact she ran and wasn't abducted."

They drove a mile in silence.

"Thank you," she said.

"For?"

"For not shutting me out of this. I know you're letting me closer than John wanted me to be."

He chose his words carefully.

"John didn't exactly tell me what to do here—he rarely does. I don't know that he's afraid anyone would recognize you—why would they?—or figure out you're Matt's daughter. Your last name is Collins, not Ranieri. No one connected with the case, outside a very few individuals within the Bureau, would know, which is why he doesn't want your name on any reports. You just don't know who might read them inside the Bureau."

"He doesn't think anyone would . . ." Dorsey looked confused.

"Your dad had a great career with the Bureau, and

left to have an even better one as a crime analyst, or whatever they're calling him on TV these days. There might be some who are jealous of his success."

"Jealous enough to call the media and tell them that Matt's daughter is secretly investigating the case?"

Andrew shrugged. "Hey, people can be unpredictable, you know that. The bottom line is, we just have to play this whole thing very smart. Like I said, Mancini doesn't want it out there that you're Matt Ranieri's daughter and he's right about you not signing reports. You're not assigned to the case. He certainly doesn't want the Bureau to be embarrassed.

"On the other hand, Edith Chiong obviously responded to you better than she did to me. It was in the best interest of the investigation for you to do the talking, and for me to observe." He took note of the highway sign directing them toward their exit.

"The notes will be in your handwriting and will go into the file," she murmured. "No need to even mention that I was there."

"For the record, I think Mancini knew going in that you weren't going to play silent partner." Andrew changed lanes. "And let's face it, there are going to be times when the interests of the investigation will best be served by you doing the talking."

"Because I'm a woman."

"Simple fact." He shrugged. "Some people relate better to women, some to men. We'll go with whatever best suits the circumstances."

"Fair enough."

Dorsey used the controls to bring her seat back up. "Why do you suppose he agreed so quickly to let me in on this?"

"I'm sure he had his reasons. Maybe he thought you'd try to investigate on your own, and that wouldn't have been good for anyone."

"So at least this way he thinks he can keep an eye on me?"

"I'm not reporting back to him on what you are or are not doing, if that's what you're insinuating." For some reason, the idea that he was spying for John annoyed the hell out of him.

"Sorry," she said after a few silent minutes had passed. "But you have to admit, the devil you know, and all that. . . ."

"I don't really know all of his motives, but I do know he'd declined to bring another agent into the case, so as long as you're not flaunting your pedigree and no one in the Bureau figures out you're here, I think he's just going to leave things the way they are. As long as it works."

"Do you think it's working?" she asked.

"You did a good job with Edith Chiong. The Randalls might be a little tougher. We'll play that by ear, see what kind of a read we get on them. They've gone through a lot in the past few days."

"About that." Dorsey turned in her seat to face him. "Have you seen any news reports about this?"

"No, but I haven't been watching television. The

newspapers I read at breakfast this morning didn't have the story, either."

"I totally expected this to be everywhere. I even told my dad not to answer his phone unless he knew for certain who was on the other end."

"Guess it just hasn't been put out there yet."

"But wouldn't you expect it to have been? This is a story. How is it that even the local papers haven't picked up on it? I mean, if this had been your daughter, or your sister, wouldn't you be screaming about the incompetence of the FBI or the police or something?"

"Maybe not if I was one of the Randall sisters, and my screaming announced to the world that my sister was a hooker."

"Still, it seems odd to me. My first thought was that this was going to be a bomb of a story, a PR nightmare for the Bureau. But then . . . silence."

"Has anyone from the press tried to get in touch with your father? Has anyone contacted him?"

"He had a call from Owen Berger the other day, but I told him not to return it."

"Are you sure that's why Berger was calling? Your dad does guest spots on his show a lot, doesn't he?"

Dorsey nodded.

"Well, maybe he was calling about a different case. There was that model that disappeared out in Oregon last weekend. Berger could have been calling about that."

"It's possible," Dorsey agreed. "You're probably right. It doesn't make sense that Berger could know

about Shannon and no one else in the media would
know. And he certainly wouldn't miss an opportunity
to break the story. As soon as I talk to my dad, I'll
ask."

"Then let's assume the story isn't out because the
family doesn't want it out there." He slowed for the
exit and eased into the far right lane. "Does that tell
you anything?"

She thought for a moment, then nodded slowly. "It
tells me that no one's told Eric Beale's family that
Shannon's been alive all these years. They're the ones
who would be doing all the screaming. They still
don't know. . . . God, what a horrible shock this will
be to them."

"John assured me that he's handling that. Let's just
hope he finds them before the story hits the wires."

The main street in Hatton, South Carolina, was decidedly Southern. The houses lining either side were
brick or clapboard, and most dated from the 1880s
or earlier, the town fathers having surrendered to
their Northern occupiers rather than see their homes
burned to the ground. In some families, this was still
whispered about, as it implied a level of cooperation
much of the South had disdained. But in retrospect, it
had been a damned good idea, Dorsey thought, since
most of the town had survived the invasion of their
Northern aggressors and now qualified as a historic
site.

Live oaks lined the wide boulevard on either side
and their moss-covered branches met in the middle to

form a canopy over the street. Large, gracious homes with porticos and porte cocheres sat well back on generous, lush green lawns, their drives long and winding. Andrew slowed the car to a near crawl. Somehow he felt speeding on this street would have been tantamount to running through a church yelling at the top of his lungs.

"Quite the place," Andrew remarked, watching for the Randalls' street.

"It's beautiful," Dorsey agreed. "It looks almost as if time's stood still here. The houses, the grounds, the gardens—look, there are even swans on that pond over there on the right."

"That's our turn. Swan Pond Road."

"Seriously, that's the name?" She turned in her seat to read the sign. "Damn if it isn't. How do you suppose they've managed to keep swans here since that road was put through?"

"They clip their wings, most likely, so they can't leave. Or they bring in new ones when the old ones fly away."

He turned right and continued the slow drive past the pond.

"They're pretty," she said, watching the swans float across the water. "Majestic. They go with the town."

"This part of it anyway. Let's see what the rest of it looks like. I'm betting it isn't all white columns and restored grandeur."

"What street are we looking for?"

"Sylvan Road. Three streets down." Andrew took

a right and continued driving slowly, taking in the town.

The houses on the side streets were increasingly modest in size. By the time they turned onto Sylvan, the architecture had gone from antibellum to sturdy American foursquares. The lots were still generous, but not stately, and the driveways made of crushed stone led to one- or two-car garages rather than handsome carriage houses.

"That's it there, number 717." Andrew slowed, then stopped on the opposite side of the street from the Randall home.

"Nice, tidy looking house," Dorsey noted.

"Doesn't look like there's a lot going on," Andrew observed as he got out and slammed the car door. In the quiet of Sylvan Road, the sound almost seemed to echo.

Dorsey got out as well and stood on the sidewalk, taking in the neighborhood. All the homes were well-kept, the lawns and flower beds well-tended.

"All very respectable, wouldn't you say?" Andrew asked when he joined her on the walk.

"Looks very solid. Late-model car back there near the garage, flower pots on the front steps, even a porch swing. Think there's an apple pie in the oven?"

"Let's go find out."

They followed the walk to the front door, where Dorsey stood back while Andrew rang the bell. Somewhere in the house a dog barked and seconds later footsteps could be heard crossing a hardwood floor.

The inside door opened, and a women in her fifties holding a small white dog asked, "Yes?"

"Mrs. Judith Randall?" Andrew asked. "Special Agent Andrew Shields, FBI." He held up his credentials, and she leaned close to the screen door to study them.

"Well. I suppose this is about Shannon," she drawled flatly. "You could have called first."

"Yes, ma'am, I should have. I apologize for not having done so."

"I suppose I should let you in," she said, as if thinking aloud. She unlocked the screen door and ushered them in. The dog began to wiggle in her arms, its nose sniffing furiously.

"Bebe, you behave yourself, now." Mrs. Randall placed the dog on the floor and it immediately jumped around Andrew as if begging to be picked it. "You can come on in—you just ignore her and she'll stop." She paused a moment. "Eventually . . ."

She led them into the living room, which appeared to be one of those rooms used only on holidays and at times like this. The furniture was mostly antique and highly polished, and the mantel was adorned with a tall vase of flowers. She gestured to the sofa and said, "Please have a seat."

Andrew moved to the far end of the sofa to allow Dorsey to sit to his left. "Mrs. Randall, I know how difficult a time this must be."

"Well, we just do not know what to make of all this," Mrs. Randall said as she sat on a high-back wood chair opposite the sofa. "I simply do not know how such a thing could happen. All these years, we believed Shannon was dead—killed by that boy—and now they tell us she's been living down in Georgia, working as a . . ."

She shook her head, unable to say the word.

"I cannot imagine what ever could have possessed that child to do such a thing. Clearly, she'd been forced to leave, someone took her and did God only knows what to her, and made her do these terrible things. Imagine, her being kidnapped and held against her will all these years." Mrs. Randall's voice was shaky. "I knew my daughter, Agent Shields. She was a good girl. An honor student. Played on the high school softball team from the time she was in seventh grade, she was that good, did you know that?"

"No, I didn't," Andrew replied. Dorsey had yet to open her mouth.

"Oh, she was quite the star. She had so much here, so much to live for here. Everyone loved her. Why would she have stayed away?" The woman's eyes now filled with tears. "That's what I don't under-stand. Why would she have stayed away all this time? Her father and I just can't understand that. So you see, she must have been held against her will. Forced into slavery, like you read about nowadays."

"Mrs. Randall, did Shannon ever try to run away from home, or give you any indication that she'd thought of doing something like that?"

"Good heavens, no." She appeared slightly indig-nant. "Shannon came from a very good home, Agent Shields. She was loved. She was happy. She had everything. What on earth would she have been running away from?"

"Is your husband home?" Dorsey broke her silence.

"He's in the back room. He was in an accident a few years back, Miss . . . ?" She tilted her head slightly to the right, looking at Dorsey as if she hadn't noticed her before.

"Agent Collins," Dorsey told her.

"My husband had a terrible accident about three years ago, run off the road one night coming back from a home visit—he took over his daddy's church when Father Randall passed on—and was just left for dead. He's been in a wheelchair ever since. It's made him . . . a bit bitter." She lowered her voice. "This thing with Shannon has just about killed that man now. He's been sitting in the back room staring out the windows ever since Chief Bowden came down here and told us about that girl's body being found on that island and it turnin' out to be Shannon."

She swallowed hard and stood, her arms across her chest, staring at Andrew.

"Now, you just tell me how that could be."

"Mrs. Randall, I promise you we're doing everything we can to find out," he replied.

"Can you find out how my baby girl could have been alive all these years, and I didn't know?" Her voice grew husky. "Can you tell me how it could be that her mother's heart didn't know she was still on this earth?"

"No, ma'am, I can't." He shook his head. "I am

very sorry—I cannot imagine what you must be feeling right now."

"Right now, I'm mostly feeling numb," she told him, "so if you have any questions you want to ask me, better ask them now, before the numbness goes away. I'm afraid that once they bring her back here, once I see her, I'm not going to be of much use to y'all."

"I understand that." He nodded.

"So you haven't seen your daughter yet, is that correct?" Dorsey had waited an appropriate moment before asking.

"Yes, that's true." She fussed with the rings on her left hand. "Only our oldest girl, Natalie, has seen her. When Chief Bowden came here and told us they'd found Shannon—I still find it hard to speak of it, you're going to have to forgive me—why, we just all thought he was crazy, that those folks down there in Georgia were all just crazy, too. He wanted to know if we had anything that might still have her fingerprints on it, and of course, I did. I had everything of hers up there in the attic."

She looked from Dorsey to Andrew and back again, as if needing to explain. "You just don't throw everything away, you understand. You need to keep the things that meant the most."

They both nodded.

"So I gave him her things—her Bible, her hairbrush—things she'd mostly touched, and he put them in plastic bags and took them down to Georgia himself. Came back the next day and told us the fingerprints matched.

Well, you just can't imagine . . ." Nervous fingers scratched the back of her neck.

"But we wanted to make sure there wasn't somehow some mistake, so Doctor Ellis, he's been our dentist forever, he sent her dental records down." She sighed heavily. "They matched, too. They said they'd try to get DNA from the hairbrush, but it would be weeks before those results would be back. Doesn't matter, though. We know it was her, Natalie saw her. Natalie saw the birthmark on her shoulder. She knew it was Shannon."

She patted her lap, and the dog jumped onto her from his spot on the floor. She petted him with shaking hands.

"When we first heard, we were thinking, well, mistakes are made every day, but there was that birthmark on the back of her left shoulder the police officer down there described, so one of us had to go to Georgia to look. My husband . . . well, that was out of the question, and I just couldn't . . . even if it wasn't her, it was somebody's baby girl, do you see? So Natalie said, don't worry, Momma, I'll go. And she did, bless her heart."

"Were Natalie and Shannon particularly close?" Dorsey asked.

"Not so much as Shannon and Aubrey, due to the age difference. Natalie was in college, and Shannon was just a high school freshman when all this happened."

"And your youngest?"

"She was just everyone's baby, you know how that

is with the baby sister. She was too young to be too close to any of the others, I'm afraid." She wiped tears from her face. "I'm sorry, it's just so hard to understand. So hard to accept . . ."

"I'm sure it is. We respect what you're going through, Mrs. Randall," Dorsey said sympathetically, "and we're sorry we're going to have to ask you to relive that all over again. I'm sure looking back is going to be very painful."

"It isn't that"—Judith Randall shook her head—"as much as realizing that all these years we've spent grieving for her, we should have been searching for her instead. . . ."

8

"Judith, who you talking to out there?" a man's voice called from the back of the house.

"Some FBI folks, come to talk about Shannon," Mrs. Randall replied.

The sound of rapidly approaching wheels on the wooden floor preceded Franklin Randall's appearance in the doorway, where he sat for a very long moment, his dark angry eyes boring holes through the agents he found sitting in his living room.

"Well, of course the FBI would show up," he said without emotion. "Gotta cover your tracks from last time, right? I'm surprised they didn't send that fool who told us all back then Shannon was dead. Lost no time arresting that Beale boy. Gettin' him convicted. Gettin' him the death sentence."

His stony glare focused on Dorsey, and she held her breath, as if expecting him to *know*.

"Sir, I respect what you've gone through, and I'm really sorry for everything," Andrew told him.

"Sorry isn't going to make up for all those years—twenty-four goddamn years—when we thought our daughter was dead. And instead of being here, with her family, where she belonged, she's out doing the devil's work for someone." He shook his head. "You sorry about that, too?"

"Yes, sir, we are. We don't know what happened back then. We're trying to find out what went wrong with the investigation, and get to the truth," Andrew said solemnly, adding, "and yes, we are sorry, but we do have to ask some questions of you and your family."

"You got questions, why don't you just ask Agent Hot Shot Ranieri? Or is he too busy with his TV appearances to talk to the FBI these days?" Randall spit the words out, and Dorsey felt a deep flush creep up from under her collar and spread clear up to her scalp. "He had all the answers back then, didn't he? Bet he doesn't have a lot to say now. Bet we won't see him on TV admitting he'd jumped to the wrong conclusion, left my baby to be forced into a life of sin all these years, sent that Beale boy to his grave. Much as he did come from the wrong side, he still didn't need to die back then."

Randall looked as if he was about to jump from the chair and attack them both.

"I understand how terrible this must be—" Andrew began.

"You don't understand jack-shit, boy." Franklin Randall turned in his chair and wheeled from the room as quickly as he'd entered it, leaving his wife and the two agents locked in an embarrassed silence in his wake.

"He's terribly overwrought," Judith finally said. "He's feeling the guilt of not having found her before this happened to her. The past few years, since the accident, his focus has been on himself, on his . . . condition. Having to step down as minister at his daddy's church was just one more blow. He just didn't have the stamina anymore. It's more than he can stand."

Andrew nodded. "We're not here to add to your pain, Mrs. Randall, but if we're going to find out what really happened to Shannon, we're going to have to speak with everyone in the family. Including your husband."

"Of course. Maybe leave him till last, if you could? Maybe by the time you get to him, you'll have learned something to share with him that might help." She was fiddling with her rings again. "Maybe you should start with me."

"We appreciate that, Mrs. Randall," Andrew told her. "Maybe we can start with you telling us a little about Shannon."

"I don't know what more I can tell you. A top student. Top athlete. Popular," Mrs. Randall began, her bottom lip quivering.

"Could we have the names of her friends, the ones she spent the most time with?" Andrew asked.

"Heather Whalen, Carrie Harrison, Kimmie White. The four of them were always together."

"Do you have any idea where those girls might be now?"

"They're all still around," Mrs. Randall replied. "I can get their addresses and phone numbers for you before you leave."

"Thank you," Andrew said. "What about boyfriends?"

"No, no, Shannon didn't have a boyfriend." The girl's mother shook her head vehemently. "She was only fourteen years old, for heaven's sake. Much too young for boys."

"Mrs. Randall, very often, girls have friends who are boys, not boyfriend, girlfriend. Just . . . friends." Dorsey told her. "Were there any boys she was just friends with?"

"Not that I know of. Shannon mostly hung around with her girlfriends. She just didn't pay any attention to boys at all." She fell silent, as if recalling how her daughter had been making a living for these past years—how many, they still didn't know for sure. "She just had no interest at all in boys, Agent . . . I'm sorry, I forgot your name."

"Collins."

"Agent Collins, right." Judith Randall wet her lips. "Shannon loved school, she loved teaching Bible at her granddaddy's church. She loved playing softball. She liked to read. That was all, pretty much. She was just a very good girl. I don't know what else I can tell you about her that you don't already know."

"Let's go back to that last morning, if we could," Andrew suggested gently. "How did the day start? Was there anything bothering her? Did she seem to be preoccupied with anything?"

"No, no more than usual." Judith Randall tried to smile but failed. "You know how teenagers are, Agent Shields. Upbeat and happy one minute, moody and sulking the next."

"Was Shannon moody that morning?" he continued.

"I don't remember she was," Mrs. Randall said thoughtfully. "I remember her being late leaving for school because she had to run upstairs to get something for some project she was working on—whatever project that was due at the end of the week, she and her friends were all working together on it. That's why she was at Kimmie's after school instead of coming right home."

"Did she usually come right home from school?"

"Not always. Shannon was a busy girl, Agent Shields, like most girls at that age. If she didn't have softball, she'd have Bible class or choir at the church. She was real active in her granddaddy's church. All our girls were."

"The reports in the Bureau's file indicate that Shannon left her friend's house and went to the church around 4:30," Andrew recalled.

"That would be about right." She nodded. "We know she was there, her grandmother saw her. Shannon had stopped there to put the programs together for choir practice later that night. I don't remember what time my mother-in-law saw her, though, you'd have to ask her. I can give you directions to Mother Randall's home. I expect you're going to want to talk to her, as well."

"We will, yes," Andrew told her. "When did you realize that Shannon hadn't come home?"

"Unfortunately, not until the next morning." Mrs. Randall's eyes filled again. "I'd gone down to Charleston with my sister, Andrea, to see a movie and have dinner. We didn't get back until close to 11:30, and I just assumed that everyone else was in already. All the lights were off except the front hall so I locked up the house. Shannon was never later than nine getting back from church, and if she used her study halls, she often finished her homework early. I assumed she'd gone to bed sometime before I got home."

She bit her bottom lip and added, "I didn't check on her that night. I was tired from the trip, and just figured she was sleeping." She looked at Andrew, then Dorsey, with haunted eyes. "I was just too tired to walk up to the third floor to check in on her and Aubrey. If I had, I would have known, I could have called the police sooner, they could have started looking for her, found whoever took her before it was too late. . . ."

"Mrs. Randall, it's not your fault," Dorsey told her gently. "Whatever happened was beyond your control. If Shannon had been abducted after she left the church, she would have been long gone. Please don't blame yourself."

"It's hard not to. We all blame ourselves. My husband also blames himself for not checking, but he thought she was up in her room studying when he arrived home from church that night. He'd gone straight into his study, so he wasn't aware she wasn't home. And Aubrey figured Shannon was still at choir practice when she went to bed a little before ten. She turned in early that night because she had to get up early in the morning. So you see, we all were neglectful, and Shannon slipped out of our lives because of it."

"Mrs. Randall, take us through the next day. When did you realize Shannon was gone?" Andrew resumed his lead in the questioning.

"When she didn't come down for breakfast. I told Paula Rose to run upstairs and tell Shannon to get a move on. She came back down a few minutes later and said Shannon wasn't there." Mrs. Randall rose and began to pace, in an effort, Andrew thought, to relieve her anxiety. "Well, I said, that's just crazy—she's not down here and she's not up there—I sent Paula Rose back up to look in Aubrey's room and the bathroom they shared. Aubrey had a class trip that day, so she left the house very early, close to six, I think."

"Aubrey's room was on the third floor as well?" he asked.

"Yes. She and Shannon were both in high school that year, and Natalie was away at college, so we put the two older girls who were still at home upstairs together."

"Aubrey must have been shocked when she came back from her trip and found out that Shannon was missing," Dorsey spoke up.

"Yes, she was. And she's been devastated by this latest news. I swear, she just has not been the same since."

"Where would I find her now?" Andrew asked.

"She'd be back at her little house in Stephens. About halfway between here and Charleston. She has her own television show down there, you know. Does all sorts of things—cooking and baking and gardening. Just like Martha Stewart." Judith's expression softened.

"I'm sure you're very proud of her," Dorsey said.

"I am very proud of all my daughters." She leveled her chin. "All of them. I don't know who or what led my God-fearing child to a life of sin, but I know she did not go willingly. And I know she would have come home if she could have."

She turned to Andrew.

"Twenty-four years ago, the FBI sent a man down here to investigate my daughter's disappearance. We all believed him when he said that Eric Beale killed her and hid the body someplace where we couldn't find it. A jury believed that as well, and Eric Beale was sentenced to death for killing my girl." She took a deep breath before continuing. "Now we find out that none of it was true. She had not died. That Beale boy did not kill her. He went to his death knowing he was innocent when everyone else believed he was guilty. I cannot imagine the pain that family went through."

She looked from Andrew to Dorsey, then back again.

"You find out the truth this time, hear? Whatever the truth might be, you find it. We've all been living with a lie all this time. It's about time we all knew what really happened to my girl, and why that poor boy had to die for a murder he did not commit."

"We'll do our best," Andrew said, and rose from the sofa. "I promise you we will do all that we can."

"You do that, Agent Shields, then you come back here and tell me what really happened. No mistakes this time. No jumping to conclusions. You bring me facts."

"Mrs. Randall, do you know where I can find the Beale family?" Andrew asked.

"I surely do not. I don't know if they're dead or alive. They moved right after their boy was executed. People in town . . . well, let's just say people in town here were less than charitable to them after their son was arrested." She covered her face with her hands. "God forgive me, I said such harsh and terrible things to Jeanette Beale. . . ."

"Under the circumstances, I'm sure—" Andrew began, but she cut him off.

"No." She held up one hand as if to ward off his words. "Don't say it was understandable. The things I said about her boy were unforgivable. It's all I can think about, him dying for no cause at all."

She stared at the floor for what seemed like a long time, then looked up at Andrew and said in a steady voice, "Now then, you wait right here and I'll get you those addresses I promised you."

She disappeared into the back of the house, leaving both agents in the front hall with the dog, who circled around Dorsey and pawed at her until she knelt to pet him. Andrew stared out the front door, all the while pretending he didn't hear the muffled conversation— and occasional raised voice—between Judith Randall and her husband. When Judith returned several minutes later, she handed a sheet of notebook paper to Andrew.

"I've written it all down for you, names, addresses, and phone numbers of everyone you'll want to speak with. My daughters, Shannon's friends, Mother Randall—everyone I could think of. I imagine as you speak with them, the list may grow. Chief Bowden can help you there, as well." She bit her bottom lip. "He might even know where the Beales are living. Maybe even contacted them, I don't know. Someone should do that."

"It's being taken care of." Andrew extended his hand and she took it and squeezed it. "We thank you for your time, and for the list of contacts."

"You just find out what happened to my girl, Agent Shields. We'll be burying her probably by the end of the week. We'd like to know why before we put her in the ground."

"We'll do our best," he promised, then opened the front door and followed Dorsey out after she'd said her good-byes to Mrs. Randall.

Andrew stood on the porch, holding the screen door open, when he turned to Mrs. Randall and said, "There is one more thing I need to ask. At any time over the past twenty-four years, did you receive any contact that could have been from Shannon? Can you think of anything at all, no matter how insignificant it might have seemed at the time, that could have made you think, even for a second, she might be alive?"

The warmth she'd offered in her handshake disappeared before their eyes. Judith Randall leveled a stony gaze, and in the coldest voice imaginable, told him, "If I'd had any cause to think my girl was still alive— if there'd been anything, anything at all that would have had me thinking she was out there someplace— by God, I'd have found her, and I'd have brought her back home where she belonged, and this evil thing never would have happened."

With one last hostile glance in his direction, Judith Randall slammed the door in his face.

9

"Wow, who'd have figured you to be so smooth," Dorsey muttered as they walked back to the car. "Way to turn off the witness."

"I had to ask. I knew there was a chance I might piss her off, but I had to get her thinking." Andrew stuck his hand in his pocket for the car keys and unlocked the doors with the remote. "I had to make her start looking back. Maybe there was something she didn't totally understand at the time."

"She's thinking, all right," Dorsey told him. "She's thinking she never should have opened the door in the first place."

"Look, if you'd been Shannon, you've been away from your home for God knows what reason or how you got there—let's put the whys and the hows aside for a moment. Wouldn't there be some point when you'd at least try to contact your mother? Wouldn't you want to hear her voice again? No matter the circumstances, wouldn't you at some point miss her so much that you had to hear her voice just one more time?"

"Probably." Dorsey nodded. "Yeah, I probably would."

"So maybe Shannon did. Maybe her mother just didn't realize it at the time. Maybe it will come back to her."

"You could be right. Maybe she will remember something. And with any luck, she'll even tell us about it." Dorsey rolled the window down to let out the steamy summer air before she fastened her seat belt. "Where first?"

"I think maybe we'll start by working our way through the sisters." He started the car and handed the list of names and phone numbers to Dorsey.

"Well, we know Paula Rose is still here in Hatton." She glanced down the list that Judith Randall had prepared. "Just three blocks away."

Andrew put the car in gear and made a U-turn in the middle of the street. "We'll stop there first, but before we leave town today, we'll pay a call on Granny Randall. She was the last person to see Shannon that night."

"The last person who admitted to seeing her, anyway, other than Eric Beale." Dorsey looked up from the sheet of notebook paper. "The three friends are all still living in Hatton. It's tempting to stop by to see them while we're here, but I'm thinking we should probably keep this within the family for as long as we can."

"Which probably won't be more than another twenty-four hours. I still can't believe the story isn't out there, locally, anyway. At the very least, I'd expect the cops to be discussing it."

"Maybe this Chief Bowden that Mrs. Randall mentioned hasn't spread the word through the troops yet."

"Well, that's all going to end the minute word gets out that Shannon Randall's body has arrived at the local funeral home," he reminded her. "Let's get what we can before the media storm hits Hatton."

"Third Street is right up there." She pointed off to the left.

"He's really bitter," Andrew said as he turned the corner. He didn't have to tell her who he meant.

"Wouldn't you be?"

"Yeah. I'm sure that bitter would be the very least of it. And he sure didn't talk like any preacher I ever met."

"The man's been through a lot. His faith has been tested. He lost his daughter, believed she'd been murdered. Then the accident, that not only took his legs, his mobility, but cost him his position in his church as well. You can see why he'd be pissed off. And now this . . . this has to have been a bombshell for him," Dorsey said.

"And toss into all that the fact that his wife said he feels guilty about not having saved Shannon, and you have one very unhappy man. You have to wonder how much more he can take."

"I would have liked to have asked him a few questions, but I figured that would have gotten us tossed out even sooner."

"He sure wasn't in a friendly frame of mind," Andrew said, as he parked the car. "Listen, the comments he made about your dad—"

She stopped him with a wave of her hand.

"I have to expect that. Actually, I expected to hear a lot worse."

"And you well may, before we're finished."

She shrugged. "There are going to be a lot of people who blame my father for the way things turned out, and they'll probably be right. He's my dad and I love him, but he obviously screwed up big time and a lot of good and innocent people were hurt very badly because of it. Why the investigation went the way it did . . . I don't know. But he was in charge of it, and things went horribly wrong. People's lives were destroyed."

"Still, it has to be hard for you to hear it."

"He has a lot to answer for." She unfastened her seat belt.

Andrew merely nodded and got out from behind the wheel. He knew all too well how heavy the burden of someone else's sins could be. He'd been carrying plenty of weight this past year. Time to change the subject.

"Nice, they painted the manse to match the church," he observed.

They stood in the center of a wide driveway that divided the church property in half. On one side stood the church, a modest structure with little embellishment other than the bell tower above, and the beds of brightly colored flowers spread out in front. A sign stood among the flower beds.

THE CHURCH OF THE RESURRECTION AND THE LIFE
REVEREND PAULA ROSE RANDALL WELCOMES YOU

On the other side stood the clapboard house that, like the church was painted a light gray. Black shutters framed the windows and red impatiens in white pots hung from the porch roof. Four white rocking chairs stood on the porch and a wreath of flowers hung on the front door. Next to the front steps, a sign announced WELCOME in dark blue letters on a pale blue background.

"Pretty." Dorsey nodded. "Welcoming, like the signs say."

"Well, let's see if that welcome extends to us," Andrew said as they walked up the porch steps. A pile of mail held together with a thick rubber band sat on the top step. Andrew picked it up, then rang the doorbell.

Moments later, the door was opened by a young woman wearing a white blouse and a tailored black skirt. Her brown hair was pulled back in a ponytail gathered low on the nape of her neck, and tortoise-shell glasses sat atop her head. She was of medium height, and seemed to carry most of her weight between her hips and her knees. Carefully applied makeup gave her face interest, but her features were too uneven to be called pretty, the nose too sharp, the pale brown eyes too small and set too close together to highlight her face. Nothing, Dorsey thought, distinguished her in any way. She appeared . . . average.

"Reverend Randall?" Andrew asked.

"Yes." She opened the door. "And you're Agent Shields."

He raised an eyebrow and she smiled as she reached for the bundle of mail. "I know you're not the mailman."

"And you know I'm with the FBI because your mother called." He returned the smile.

"Just hung up the phone." She beckoned them inside. "Come on in out of that heat. It's just been terrible these past few weeks, hasn't it?" She turned to address Dorsey. "And you're the lady agent whose name Momma couldn't remember. Starts with a C."

"Collins," Dorsey said as she stepped into the foyer behind Andrew.

"Agent Collins. I will remember," Paula Rose told her. "Now, shall we sit for a few minutes in the parlor? It's nice and cool in there, relatively speaking. These old houses can sure hold the heat, but all these trees give a bit of shade. I'll get us a cold drink—I just made iced tea and was about to pour myself a glass when Momma called to tell me you were on your way. You just have a seat and I'll be back in a minute."

Dorsey stood near the window facing the church and said, "I would have thought 'Momma' would tell her not to talk to us."

"I suspect she probably did." Andrew sat on a wing chair on one side of a round table holding a large, ugly lamp. "Either Reverend Paula Rose is going to ignore Momma, or she's got a point of her own to make."

"I just turned the air conditioning up a notch; it's still a bit warmer than I like." Paula Rose returned with a tray holding three tall glasses, frosty with condensation. She held the tray out for her visitors to help themselves, then set it on the coffee table. She took the last glass, seated herself on the sofa, and gestured for Dorsey to sit as well.

"Now. You wanted to talk about Shannon." She looked from one agent to the other. "What exactly is it that you want to know?"

"We're trying to go back over the night your sister disappeared—" Andrew began.

Paula Rose cut him off. "I know all that. Momma told me. I'm asking, what do you want from me?"

"Just what you remember from that night, the following day," Andrew told her as he took his notebook from the inside pocket of his jacket.

"I don't remember much at all. I was only eleven years old. My bedtime was 9:30, and my parents were pretty strict about it."

"Who else was home when you went to bed that night?"

"My daddy was there, in his study. He was working on his sermon for Sunday. He came in from choir practice and went straight to work."

"I thought your grandfather was still the pastor then," Andrew said.

"Well, he was, but Daddy was his assistant. He didn't take over full-time preaching until Granddaddy retired. He founded this church, you know. Helped raise every dime that went to building it."

"You're very proud of that," Dorsey remarked.

"I surely am," Paula Rose assured them. "Proud of

the legacy he left behind, proud of all the good works he did for the people in this community. Whether they followed him to the church's door or not, he did what he could for anyone who asked for his help. It's a privilege and an honor to be carrying on in their footsteps."

"None of your sisters had an interest in the church?" Andrew asked.

"Good heavens, no. Now, Natalie, I must say, does her best to do what's right for others. She's one of those mythical creatures that you sometimes hear about but never see?" Paula Rose smiled. "An honest politician. Yes, she really is. Aubrey, on the other hand, well, let's just say she's more worldly than we'd like her to be. All that time spent on TV, showing people how to make wreaths and dry flowers and bake meringues."

Paula Rose laughed indulgently. "Well, she isn't harming anyone, but she's not exactly doing God's work, either. I can't say she ever had much of a calling, though."

"And Shannon? Did she ever have a calling?" Dorsey found herself asking.

"Well, apparently not." Paula Rose all but sniffed indignantly. "Look at how she ended up."

"If Shannon had been out after you'd gone to bed, wouldn't you have heard her come in?" Andrew jotted down some notes and changed the subject.

"Not necessarily. Most nights, I'd read for a while in bed, then Momma would call upstairs to tell me to turn the light out and go to sleep. Momma wasn't home that night, and I don't remember if Daddy was still at the church when I turned out the light. I think I may have heard Aubrey come in after I'd turned off my light, but I was falling asleep right about that time. I don't know if I thought it was Aubrey or Shannon, but if Shannon had been out late, I'd have been sleeping soundly by the time she got home."

"So you didn't realize she hadn't come home until . . ." Andrew continued.

"Until the next morning. When Shannon didn't come down for breakfast, I went up to get her and she wasn't there." Her face darkened. "She wasn't anywhere. Not in her room, not in Aubrey's. Not in the bathroom."

"And Aubrey was where?"

"Aubrey had to be at school really early that day. She left the house before I woke up. There was a class trip down to Savannah, some cultural thing for a class she was in."

"What did you do after you realized Shannon was gone?" Andrew asked.

"I went downstairs and told Momma that Shannon must have gone to school early with Aubrey, 'cause she wasn't there. Momma went upstairs and looked for herself. She looked everywhere in that house—outside, down in the basement, up in the attic." Paula Rose shook her head. "She was just calling all over the place."

"And your father?"

"He was already over to the church. He and my granddaddy had breakfast with the church's senior-citizen group on Wednesday mornings. He didn't know Shannon was missing till Momma ran over there and asked him where she was. Well, he didn't know, either." Paula Rose's fingers tapped on the side of her glass. "So they started calling everyone—all of Shannon's friends, the girls she'd been with after school the day before, but none of them knew where she was. Turned out nobody'd seen her since she left the church the day before. Nobody, apparently, except for Eric Beale."

"Whom we now know did *not* murder your sister," Dorsey reminded her.

"He did something to her, didn't he? Even though they found her dead just a few weeks ago, that was still her blood they found on his shirt, right? And that was her notebook they found there in his car, wasn't it? And didn't he admit he picked her up after she left the church?" Paula Rose set her glass on the tray and folded her arms across her chest. "He may not have killed her back then, but he did something to her. Maybe something that made her feel she needed to run away."

"What do you think happened, Reverend Randall?" Dorsey casually sipped at her tea.

"I think—and please call me Paula Rose, I'm not in the pulpit right now—I think he took her to the park, like he said he did, and then I think he raped her. I think she was so upset about what he did to her, she ran away."

"Why would she run away?"

"It would have been very hard for her to come

home and face Momma and Daddy and tell them what he'd done to her. I think she was too ashamed."

"So she ran away and stayed away for twenty-four years?" Dorsey raised an eyebrow.

Paula Rose shrugged her shoulders. "That's how I see it. Makes sense."

"But once she found out that Eric had been arrested for her murder, once the papers carried the story that he'd been tried and was going to be executed, wouldn't she have come home? Wouldn't she let someone know she was still alive?"

"If he hurt her . . . if he raped her . . . she probably thought he deserved it, after he defiled her," Paula Rose said righteously. "Then again, maybe wherever she was, she didn't hear about him being sentenced to death. Didn't know he was executed. Maybe if she'd'a known, she would have come back and let people know she was alive."

"Did Shannon have a boyfriend?" Andrew asked. "A boy she liked, or one who liked her, maybe someone who called the house a lot?"

"We weren't allowed to date until we were sixteen, so no one would have been calling, unless it was for homework or something like that."

"Any names come to mind, anyone who called for homework assignments a lot?"

"No."

"Do you recall if there was anyone back then who paid more attention to her than he should have? Maybe someone who followed her, or showed up where she was when she wasn't expecting him?" Andrew followed on with his line of questioning.

"No." Paula Rose shook her head. "I don't remember her ever mentioning someone like that. There was just Eric. I know he brought her home from school a couple of times, like when it was raining or stormy or something, he'd drive her home."

"He ever come into the house? Did you ever see them together anywhere other than in his car?"

"Oh, goodness, no. He'd just pull into the driveway, close up to the porch, I guess so she wouldn't get wet, and he'd drop her off. She'd get out of the car and come right inside. That was all."

"So the police were called when?" Andrew asked, moving the interview along.

"I'm not sure when, exactly. Before Momma left for the church, she told me to get on down to the school bus and she'd take care of finding Shannon, so I did. I left for school. It wasn't until I came home that afternoon and saw the police cars around the house I knew something was wrong." She took another swallow of tea. "I knew something bad had happened to Shannon."

"Does anything else stand out about that day? Was there anyone around the house who maybe seemed out of place?"

"Not that I can remember. After I got home from school, I got sent right over to my grandparents, so I don't know who all was here or hanging around. I was only home for a minute, and my parents told me Shannon was missing but they were doing everything

they could to find her. I stayed with my grandparents
for a few days because my parents were just too upset
to deal with me, I guess. And I think they didn't want
me at home in case she was found, you know. It was
a very sad, very scary time for all of us. Especially me,
being so young and not really knowing what was
going on."

Paula Rose sighed heavily.

"At first, the police didn't seem sure if she'd been
kidnapped or murdered, so they brought the FBI in,
several agents and that one who figured out Eric had
killed her, he was in charge, I think. Then Eric was arrested, and went to jail." She took another sip of tea.
"Which seemed right at the time. Everyone thought it
had been him all along."

"Everyone like who?" Andrew asked before Dorsey
could.

"Everybody." Paula Rose shrugged. "Soon as everyone knew she'd been in his car and they found that
bloody shirt, everyone figured he'd killed her. The police, my father, my grandparents—everyone in town
thought it was him. Hearing that FBI agent say it just
made it so."

"Except that it wasn't," Dorsey pointed out.

"True. But I still say that if she ran away, it was because of what he did to her."

"Can you think of any other reason Shannon would
have wanted to leave home? Was she unhappy? Had
she been having any problems?"

"None that I knew of. Then again, like I said, I was

only eleven. If there was something going on with her, she wouldn't have told me about it."

"Who would she have told?" Dorsey asked.

"Aubrey. Or maybe Kimmie White."

"Did you ever hear her talk about running away? About leaving home?"

"No. But I'd have been the last person she'd tell, if she was going to do something like that. She'd have been too afraid I'd tell Momma."

"So, I guess we should schedule a visit with Aubrey." Andrew stood, as did Dorsey. "I'm sure she's expecting us by now."

Paula Rose laughed. "I'm sure she got a phone call, just like I did. Natalie, too, most likely."

"And Kimmie? Do you think your mother called Shannon's old friends to give them a heads up?" Andrew took the half-empty glass from Dorsey's hand and placed it along with his on the tray.

"Undoubtedly. She was pretty heated up when she called me. She did not appreciate you asking if she'd known Shannon was alive all this time."

"Actually, what I asked was if there was anything that might have happened over the years that might have made her think that Shannon might not be gone. Something that might have made her think Shannon was trying to contact her."

"Well, however you phrased it, she didn't care for it one bit." Paula Rose began to walk toward the door, obviously intending for the agents to follow her.

"I'm sorry for that. But while we're on the subject, how about you? Was there anything that might have

happened years ago that, looking back, you might
wonder if your sister might have been reaching out to
you?" Andrew stood his ground, watching her face.
"Phone calls where the person on the other end did
not speak? Hang-ups? Something in the mail that
came anonymously?"

"No. Sorry." She opened the front door and stood
waiting for them to walk through it. "But if anything
comes to mind, I'll certainly give you a call, Agent
Shields." Outside, Andrew turned back.

"I expect you'll need one of these, in that case."
Andrew held out one of his cards. "You can call my
cell phone and—"

"I surely will do that." She snatched the card from
his hand and closed the outer door. "You both have a
nice day, now."

10

"Well, we've certainly scored big with the Randall family today, haven't we?" Andrew drove to the end of Paula Rose's street and made a right.

"We? I'd say you. I was doing just fine."

"And here I always fancied myself a lady's man."

"We all have our little delusions." She rested back against the head rest, a tiny smile playing on her lips.

"So what do you think of the Randalls so far?" he asked. "Any impressions you'd like to share? Other than the fact that they're a strange group?"

"You thought so, too?"

"Definitely. Let's start with the mother. She's devastated about her daughter, yet when it comes time to make a positive identification, she sends her eldest daughter—alone—to do the deed."

"Maybe, like she said, she just couldn't face it. It had to be a shock, after all these years, to find out that Shannon could have been alive, only now she's been murdered for real. Maybe she couldn't face Shannon's death twice."

"All I know is, if Shannon had been my sister, my mother would have walked barefoot over hot coals to get to her. And we'd have all been walking with her."

"I can't relate." Dorsey looked out the window. "I have no siblings and my mother died when I was young."

He glanced over at her as if he was about to say something, then thought better of it.

"And Paula Rose—you get the feeling she's played that baby-of-the-family role for all it's worth?" he asked.

"Definitely." She nodded. "And I think I'd bite my tongue off before I went to her for guidance for any problem I was having. I noticed a definite lack of charity in her attitude toward her long-lost sister."

"You're referring to her comment about 'the way Shannon turned out'?"

"Yeah. Very cold. Turned on her sister like that." Dorsey snapped her fingers. "I didn't get any 'judge not' vibes from her."

"I can hardly wait to see what Grandma brings to the mix."

"Well, let's see if we—that would be you, actually— can strike out as thoroughly with the matriarch. Shall we bet on how long it takes you to piss her off? I'm thinking fifteen minutes, tops."

"What's the wager?"

"Loser buys lunch." She looked at her watch. "Make that dinner. And the winner gets to chose the place."

"You're on. I should warn you, though. I'm planning on winning the elder Mrs. Randall over with my charm. I'm going to be a model of sensitivity."

"Plan on finding a place that serves great barbecue,

then, because that's what I'm going to want as my winnings." Dorsey took her cell phone from her pocket and checked for messages. There were none. She bit the inside of her lip, and wondered where her father was and why he hadn't returned her calls.

"I was actually thinking along the lines of some good old-fashioned Southern comfort food."

"We'll see who gets to—oops!" Dorsey referred to the directions Judith Randall had given them. "I think you should have gone straight instead of making a turn at that stop sign. Mrs. Randall lives around the corner on the next street."

"I just wanted to take a look around the back of the church property." He reduced his speed to a crawl as they approached the wide drive that marked the rear of the church's parking lot. "You never know what you might find."

"Like that blue van parked behind the church?" she asked.

"Yeah. Like that."

He turned into the lot and parked next to the dark blue vehicle. THE CHURCH OF THE RESURRECTION AND THE LIFE was painted on the both front doors in white block letters. Andrew parked the car and got out, but before he'd taken three steps, a man emerged from the stairwell leading up from the church basement. He was tall and broad and—though he looked to be in his late sixties—vigorous. He eyed Andrew suspiciously when he saw him standing close to the van.

"Help you with something?" He took a key ring from his pocket and unlocked van's side door.

"You work here?" Andrew smiled and tried to look friendly and nonthreatening. He wished he'd taken off his tie and jacket when he'd left Reverend Paula Rose's house. He was pretty sure his attire didn't lend itself to casual questioning around Hatton.

The man nodded. "I am fortunate enough to offer my time in service to the church, yes sir."

"You drive this van?"

"Right again." The man wiped sweat from his forehead with a handkerchief that he pulled from a pocket and turned to watch Dorsey round the back of his vehicle. "Hot as blazes today, isn't it?"

"Sure is." Andrew nodded. "May I ask what you use the van for?"

"May I ask why you're asking?"

"We're investigating something for the Randall family."

"I use it for church business, whatever Pastor Paula wants me to do. On Sundays I pick up members who don't have a ride to services, either 'cause they're too sick or too old to drive themselves, or maybe 'cause their car broke down or something. Use it during the school year to pick up folks for choir and such. Starting next week, I'll be using it to pick up kids for Bible camp. Church runs camp every year, two weeks in June, two weeks in July."

"Anyone else drive it?" Andrew asked. "Reverend Paula, for example?"

"Nope, she hasn't driven it once that I know of. No one else drives it, either. Just me." He returned the damp cloth to his back pocket.

"Where is it garaged at night?"

"Garaged? Ain't no garage. It goes home with me, every night, sits in my driveway until I drive back over here in the morning."

"Weekends, as well?"

"Every day, seven days a week. Like I said, I pick up people for Sunday services, drive 'em back home again."

"Thanks for your time." Andrew started back to his car, then turned to ask, "This van hasn't been painted recently, has it?"

"Nope. Always been dark blue, far as I know."

"Thanks." Andrew waved and got behind the steering wheel just as Dorsey got in her side and rolled down the window.

"You suspicious of Reverend Paula?" she asked.

"I'm suspicious of everyone right now."

"The van spotted on the island that night was a light color, right?"

"That's why I asked if it had been painted." He circled around to the exit. "But you know that would have been too easy."

"Right. And it never is." She snapped on her seat belt.

"It would have been nice though. There's the sister with the motive—God forbid anyone should find out the minister's sister not only did not die twenty-four years ago, but ran away and has been doing the dirty for money all this time. Here's the van the minister used to dispose of the body. And of course, as soon as we question the good reverend about it, she'll break down and confess."

"I've never had it happen like that, all wrapped up and tidy with the first suspect on the list." She added wistfully, "Though I've heard about such things happening. Might be nice, just once, just to see how it feels. The very thought of a murder confession . . . well, it's always been a fantasy of mine."

"You've never had anyone confess? You're kidding, right?"

"Not to murder." She shook her head. "Everyone is always innocent. You can catch someone at the scene with the murder weapon in hand and they'll tell you they were just holding it for someone. You forget, I've been in Florida for six years. That's a death penalty state. Nobody admits to anything."

"You've been in Florida for the entire time you've been with the Bureau?" Andrew drove slowly to the corner, then asked, "Which way?"

"Right, then right again at the next corner. Then straight for a block." She folded the paper and stuck it in the top of her handbag. "I was in Cincinnati for a few years before I was transferred to Florida."

"Cincinnati was your first assignment?"

"Yes. That's where I worked with Aidan. He was only there for my first few months, though." She smiled wryly. "Then he went off to play with the big kids."

"The big kids?"

"John Mancini's unit." She turned in her seat. "I think we passed it."

He pulled to the curb and parked. "We can walk back. Which house is it?"

She got out of the car and checked the number on the nearest house. "I think it's that gray bungalow about four or five houses back. The one with the black shutters and the red geraniums out front."

The house they'd parked in front of looked vacant, and a sale sign had been placed at the edge of the unkempt lawn. The sidewalk was cracked and uneven in spots. By the time they arrived at Martha Randall's home, Dorsey was wishing she'd opted for low-heeled shoes.

"This is it." She nodded in the direction of the low-slung house with the wraparound porch. On one side, a trellis supported a trailing vine heavy with red-orange flowers. "Cute, but you'd have thought the family would have moved her into a better neighborhood."

She glanced at the houses on either side of the house, then at those across the street.

"It does seem a bit run-down," Andrew agreed as they walked to the front door. "Think she's heard from her daughter-in-law by now?"

"Her daughter-in-law and her granddaughter, no doubt." Dorsey rang the bell.

A moment later, a plump, unpleasant-looking woman in her thirties answered. She was dressed in a white blouse with stains under the armpits and a straight denim skirt. Her hair was secured into a tight bun in the back, and rhinestone trimmed glasses dangled from a beaded chain worn around her neck.

"Yes?" She gave each agent the once-over.

"We're here to see Mrs. Randall," Dorsey told her.

"She expecting you?" the woman asked.

"By now?" Andrew glanced at his watch. "Probably." He held out his I.D.

"I'm going to have to check with her." The woman closed the door in their faces.

"Did we expect otherwise?" Andrew asked.

"All things considered, no." Dorsey grinned.

"For the record, annoying the housekeeper, or whatever she is, does not count as pissing off a family member."

Before Dorsey could respond, the woman returned and pushed open the door.

"Miz Randall will see you." She held the door for them and sighed deeply as they passed into the narrow foyer, as if their unexpected presence was a personal intrusion into her life. "She's in the back room, right on through here."

She directed them down a hall leading into the kitchen, and from there, to a screened porch overlooking a surprisingly pretty backyard. The room was filled with white wicker furniture. An elderly woman, white hair pulled back in a bun, sat in a rocking chair near the window.

"Mrs. Randall, thank you for seeing us like this," Andrew said as they entered the room.

"If 'like this' means not calling first to see if this might be a convenient time, you needn't worry. My daughter-in-law took it upon herself to announce your intentions." The woman rocked gently, assessing them with cool blue eyes.

"Kind of her."

"I'm sure." Mrs. Randall pointed at the sofa positioned against the one long wall. "Please sit. I'm going to be getting a crinked neck from looking up at her." She gestured at Dorsey. "You're certainly a tall one, aren't you." It wasn't a question.

"Yes, ma'am, I am." Dorsey sat where she'd been instructed.

"Those high heels make you even taller," she observed with more than a trace of the South in her speech. "Your mamma a tall lady?"

"Yes, ma'am, she was." Dorsey nodded.

"Was?" The old woman leaned forward slightly. "Meaning she has passed on?"

"Yes, ma'am."

"Recently?"

"When I was nine," Dorsey told her.

"Who raised you, then?"

"My aunt and my father."

"They did a fine job." Mrs. Randall nodded approvingly. "You're a well-mannered, polite young woman. You tell your daddy I said so."

"I'll do that. Thank you, Mrs. Randall." Dorsey smiled.

"Now, what is it that you two expect to learn from me that you haven't learned from my daughter-in-law or my granddaughter?" Before either could answer, Mrs. Randall called out, "Dorothea? You bring some

lemonade on out here for our guests. And turn on
that ceiling fan."

She turned back to Andrew. "You were about to
say?"

"My name is Andrew Shields. I'm a special agent
with—"

Martha Randall waved her hand impatiently. "I
know who you are and where you're from. You
wanted to ask me questions about our Shannon?"

He nodded. "I'm sure it was a terrible shock to find
out she'd been alive all these years."

"Oh, my land, yes. You simply cannot imagine
what we've all been going through these past few
days." She placed a hand over her heart. "It's been
most unexpected, to be sure. Not just that she's been
alive, but where she's been. *What* she's been. And to
find she's been murdered, after all."

Her small hands continued to flutter about the
middle of her chest.

"Doesn't this just beat all? Who'd have thought
that girl could have been alive all these years. And to
never let us know. Well, like I told Judith and Franklin,
it must have been amnesia."

"Amnesia?" Dorsey asked.

"That kept her from coming home." Mrs. Randall
stopped rocking in her chair. "She obviously didn't
know who she was or where she was from. Otherwise, she'd have come home long ago."

"Actually, Mrs. Randall, the police were able to
identify her and locate her family here in Hatton be-

cause she'd told her roommate her name, and where she was from," Andrew told her.

"How is that possible?" The old woman frowned. "How could she have known who she was, and not tell us she was alive?" She looked at Andrew, wide-eyed, as if the mere suggestion was ludicrous. "And for her to have been doing what she was doing down there in Georgia. . . ." She visibly shivered. "No, no, Agent Shields. No granddaughter of mine would have lived a life of sin the way that poor girl had been doing. If she'd known who she was, she'd have come on home, and gone to college, just like she'd planned."

She looked at Dorsey and added, "She was going to be a nursery school teacher, you know."

"I didn't know," Dorsey said softly. "Shannon gave her name—Shannon Randall, of Hatton, South Carolina—to her roommate. How could Edith Chiong have known, if Shannon hadn't told her?"

"Edith Chiong?"

"Her roommate for the past several years," Dorsey explained.

Shannon's grandmother thought this through, then said, "She must have had something with her that had her name on it when she developed amnesia. Perhaps that boy hit her over the head with something and she lost her memory. Then when she looked at the . . . driver's license, perhaps—"

"Shannon wasn't old enough to drive when she disappeared, Mrs. Randall," Andrew reminded her. "She didn't have a driver's license."

"Her school identification card, then. She saw her

name on something," the woman said triumphantly. "I'm sure that was it. She knew her name, but not *who* she was. That would explain it."

"But wouldn't she have tried to come back to Hatton?" Andrew asked.

"Well, not if she couldn't remember it. If she couldn't remember *being* from here, why would she want to *come* here?" Mrs. Randall said as if it were a given. "It's as plain as the nose on your face, Agent Shields. If my granddaughter had known who she was, she would have come home, not gone to who knows where, doing who knows what." She shook her head adamantly. "Our Shannon was a good, God-fearing girl. She was baptized in the church by my husband, and she was raised in his church. She would never have chosen a life of sin. Never. If she was up to . . . to what they're saying she was up to, it has to have been because someone forced her."

Mrs. Randall folded her arms across her chest in a manner that clearly indicated the matter was closed.

"About the night she disappeared, Mrs. Randall," Andrew ventured.

"You wanted to know what I recall of that."

"I understand you saw Shannon at the church shortly before she disappeared," he said.

"I did indeed." Motion from the doorway distracted her. "Dorothea, don't stand there like you don't know where to put that tray. Right there on that table, just like always. Thank you. You may go back to what-all you were doing."

When the woman left the room, Mrs. Randall muttered, "Listening at the doorway, no doubt."

To Dorsey she said, "Would you mind, dear?"

"Would I mind?" Dorsey asked.

"Pouring the lemonade. Made it fresh this morning. I'm sure you and Agent Shields could use a cold drink on a day as warm as this one. And you know the weather people are saying it's just going to get warmer."

Dorsey did as she was told, and passed glasses to Mrs. Randall and to Andrew, then poured one for herself. She took a sip and told her hostess, "Delicious."

"An old recipe of my mother's. The trick is to boil the lemon juice with the water and add just a bit of lemon zest."

"I'll remember that." Dorsey smiled to hide her indifference. The last thing on her mind was the fine art of making lemonade.

"So, you were saying?" Andrew tried to steer the conversation back to the night in question.

"Yes, yes. The night Shannon disappeared. My husband and I arrived at the church right around 4:45."

"You arrived with him?"

"Yes. He was supposed to meet with someone in his office at 5:00, and I had to pick up the proceeds from the church's winter carnival to take to the bank the next day."

"Doesn't the church treasurer do that?" he asked.

"Back then, I was the church treasurer, Agent Shields. On Sunday night, I locked the money in a drawer in my husband's office, but when I went to get it on Wednesday evening, it was gone. I looked everywhere for that envelope—I'd put it in a brown envelope for safekeeping—but it was nowhere to be found. I looked upstairs, I looked in the church. Why, I even drove home and looked all around the house, thinking maybe somehow I'd picked it up without thinking, but I could not find it."

"The church didn't have a safe?" he asked.

"No, not back then."

"And it didn't occur to you to take the money home with you?"

"Of course not. We never had a break-in at a church in all the years I've lived in Hatton, but homes had been robbed, now and then. It never crossed my mind that someone would steal from a church."

"Why wasn't the money deposited in the bank?" Andrew wondered.

"Because Thursday was my banking day. I went once each week, on Thursday morning. My sister, Gloria—she worked in the bank back then, rest her soul—and I met at noon every Thursday. I did my banking business, she took care of the deposits and such for me, and then we would have lunch together. We used to go to a little teahouse down on Montgomery. They had the loveliest little sandwiches and fruit tarts."

"On that Wednesday, while you were looking for the missing money, your husband was in a meeting?" Andrew steered the interview back to the night in question.

"I believe he was." She nodded.

"Who was the meeting with?"

Her hands fluttered again. "Truthfully, after all these years, I cannot recall. Goodness knows there are days when I can barely remember my own name, but I believe it was someone from the congregation, someone who was having problems of one sort or another. In any event, I searched for an hour or better at the church, then I went home thinking maybe I'd stuck it into the purse I had with me on Sunday. I was so tired by the time the carnival was finally over, you know, that when I didn't find the envelope in the drawer, I thought perhaps I'd only *imagined* I'd put it in there. So I went home and looked in that purse, but of course it wasn't there. So I searched the house, then went back to the church and searched some more. Missed choir practice that night, I was so busy searching for that envelope."

"And you never found it?"

Her head moved slowly side to side. "Never did. I finally had to accept the fact that someone had gotten into the church and stole it."

"So you're pretty sure you had locked it in Reverend Randall's desk," Dorsey asked.

"I am. Which means that sometime between Sunday night and Wednesday afternoon, my husband must have unlocked the desk and either he forgot the money was there, or I'd forgotten to tell him—it was all so long ago, and you know, as much as I hate to admit it, the truth is, my memory isn't what it used to be. Had I just said that?" She sighed with resignation.

"In any event, someone must have gone into his office and taken the envelope, because it was never found."

"You reported it to the police?" Andrew resumed his questioning.

"I did. But not until we got home that night. Maybe, oh, 10:30 or so. I spoke with Chief Taylor himself."

"Did he send someone out to investigate?"

"Oh, yes," she told him. "First thing in the morning, the chief showed up himself, along with one of his officers. I believe it was that nice young Brinkley boy—what was his first name? Margaret and Ted's middle boy, I believe he was. He married one of the Connelly girls? Kathleen, maybe?

"Anyway, they met me over at the church around 8:30, and we were downstairs in the office—they took fingerprints all around my husband's office and around the doorways as well—when I heard a commotion over near the church hall. Well, we went on upstairs, and there was Judith, ranting something fierce at Franklin about Shannon not being in her bed this morning and where was she?"

"Your son was there early that morning for a breakfast meeting," Andrew read from his notes.

"That's correct. The senior citizens' weekly breakfast. Franklin was there in the community room over in the church hall with my husband and a few others. So Chief Taylor and Officer Brinkley picked up the investigation from there and took over. Talked to Judith for a while, talked to Franklin, then the chief called up another officer—Bob Donohue, that was—to take the two of them on home in case Shannon showed up, or called. Of course, they were of no earthly use at that point."

"I'm sure they were very upset," Dorsey said.

"You just cannot imagine. Why, we were all just beside ourselves. Nothing like that had ever happened in Hatton before, it was just too hard to believe."

"What had you believed at the time, Mrs. Randall?" Dorsey asked. "What did you think had happened to Shannon?"

"Well, I thought what everybody thought. I thought that boy had taken her and killed her."

"You mean Eric Beale?" Andrew resumed his questioning.

"Why, yes, of course." Mrs. Randall nodded.

"Who first brought up his name, do you remember?"

"I think it must have been Chief Taylor. I vaguely recall one of Shannon's friends saying something about how the Beale boy was always offering Shannon rides in his car. And then someone said they'd seen Shannon in his car that afternoon."

"Do you remember who that was?"

"I'm sure I do not, but maybe someone down at the police department might know. Chief Taylor's been gone now for about seven years—the cancer, you know—but maybe Jeremy Brinkley might remember. He's retired now, but he lives somewhere nearby. Simpson's Creek, I think, about six miles outside Hatton on the way to Charleston."

"We'll check with him, thank you."

"And maybe you can talk to that FBI agent who

came down here and arrested the boy. He was so sure that boy was guilty. I know he convinced me and my husband that the boy had killed her. That's who you want to talk to, that FBI man." She shook her head. "He was so sure, he made us all so sure. Now, looking back, looks like he didn't know squat. Maybe he was just wanting to finish up his job quickly. If he'd worked a little harder, maybe we'd have found her. Way things were, with him telling us Shannon was dead and that boy had killed her, we never bothered to look for her."

She shook her head again. "You ask me, he's the cause of all this. Our girl missing all these years, and that boy convicted and executed. All his family went through . . . such as his family was. It was still a terrible thing. So I think you should look within your own house, Agent Shields. I'm thinking that's where the answers lie, if you're asking why we all believed Shannon was dead."

"We will be speaking with former agent Ranieri about that," Andrew assured her.

"I would certainly hope so."

"Mrs. Randall, do you remember what Shannon's state of mind was when you saw her at the church that night?" Dorsey asked.

"What on earth do you mean?" Alert blue eyes narrowed and focused on Dorsey like lasers.

"I mean, did she seem as if something was bothering her? Did she appear upset about anything?"

"Oh, goodness, no," the woman said. "Why, she was just her usual happy-go-lucky self."

"Were you and Shannon very close?"

"I am close to all of my granddaughters."

"So if something or someone had been bothering her, she'd have confided in you," Andrew said.

"I feel certain she would have, yes. But she did not."

"By the way, how much money had the carnival taken in?" he asked.

"Almost three thousand dollars between Friday and Sunday night." She smiled. "Most we ever made. It was a rousing success. We had raffles and carnival rides and concessions going practically nonstop for three days. Everyone was so pleased. We'd planned on using the money for a community center. We did eventually build it, but it was a few more years before we could afford to."

"Did Shannon know the money was in the drawer?"

"I believe she may have been with me when I placed it in there." Mrs. Randall stared at Andrew for a long moment. "Agent Shields, are you implying that my granddaughter was a thief?"

"I think we have to consider that she might have taken the money. In retrospect—"

"Shannon was not a thief, Agent Shields. She would not have stolen from her church." The old woman's gaze could have turned him to stone on the spot.

"Mrs. Randall, I think in light of what's happened over the past week, we need to consider—"

"I believe our little chat is over, Agent Shields." Mrs. Randall raised her chin and called out, "Dorothea? You may show Agents Shields and Collins to the door, please."

"Mrs. Randall . . ."

The old woman turned her face to the window.

"My apologies, Mrs. Randall," Andrew said softly.

"Thank you for your time, Mrs. Randall," Dorsey added.

Still looking out the window, Mrs. Randall waved a hand dismissively.

"Twenty-five minutes on the nose," Dorsey calculated the time after Dorothea had closed the front door behind them. "Who'd have thought it would have taken so long?"

"And I'd been doing so well up to that point."

"Well, never let it be said I'm a sore loser. Looks like dinner's on me."

11

"So, shall we compare notes?" Andrew rested his forearms on the edge of the table in the small restaurant where he and Dorsey had stopped for dinner.

"First things first. I'm famished. Do you remember what time it was when we last ate? I can't, and I can't think until I eat." Dorsey read from the menu, "Barbecued ribs, barbecued chicken, barbecued pork. Slaw. Hush puppies. Okay." She folded the paper menu over and slapped it onto the tabletop. "One of each, please."

"I'd pay to see you eat all that." He laughed.

"You might want to think twice about that." She grinned. "I'm ravenous."

She signaled the waitress, who looked like a high-school girl on her first job.

"Are you ready to order?" The girl, whose red-and-white name tag identified her as Jessie, appeared immediately when summoned.

"I'll have the chicken barbecue with all the fixings," Dorsey told her. "And a diet Pepsi, please."

The girl began to write down the order, then looked up and asked, "Did you want the small, medium or—"

"Large," Dorsey nodded. "Definitely large everything."

"Okay." She scribbled and turned to Andrew.

"I'll have the same. Iced tea, though."

"I'll be right back with your drinks," Jessie told them.

"Doesn't it seem that no matter where you go, the summer help gets younger every year?" Andrew asked.

"They do get younger every year. Because we get older. The older you get, the younger sixteen or seventeen looks." Dorsey smiled at Jessie who returned with their drinks.

"I'll have your dinners in just a few minutes," the young waitress told them.

"Just another thing Shannon didn't get to do," Dorsey observed after Jessie had walked away.

"What's that?" Andrew asked.

"Get that all-important first summer job as a waitress."

"Was that your first summer job?"

"Yes, but I didn't last very long." She chuckled, remembering. "I lasted ten whole days. Only job I ever got fired from."

"Dropped a lot of meals, did we?"

"Dropped things, got orders mixed up, spilled things on customers." She leaned her elbow on the table, and rested her chin in the palm of her hand. "I learned at the tender age of sixteen that I was not good at waiting on other people. Which limited my future career choices."

"When did you decide you wanted to get into law enforcement?" he asked.

"Ironically, when my dad 'solved' this case." She smiled ruefully. "Watching him then, seeing how he was so focused on this girl, how dedicated he was. How important it all seemed back then, finding the killer. Finding the truth."

"Those things are still important," he said. "They always will be."

She eased a long lock of hair behind her ear. "I guess."

"No, not you guess. You know." He looked almost as if he was about to scold her, then thought better of it. Instead, he said, "You know how important it is to find the truth. Otherwise, you wouldn't be here."

"I do know," she admitted. "But what about you? When did you decide you wanted to be a special agent for the FBI?"

"I don't remember ever deciding." Andrew shrugged. "It was just always assumed."

"Because of your family."

He nodded. "You know that my dad and my uncle were both agents. Then my cousin Connor joined . . ."

"Connor. International man of mystery."

He laughed. "You know him, then."

"No, actually, I've never met him. But he's sort of a legend, you know. The man who always seems to move through the shadows. People talk about him in hushed voices," she wiggled her eyebrows, "but you never really meet anyone who's met him, so you wonder if he's real, or a fictional character someone at the Bureau invented to lend a bit of mystery to the job."

"Oh, he's real enough." Andrew laughed again. "And as for what he does, or where he goes, no one seems to know except John Mancini and the director. And I'm not sure John always knows, to tell you the truth. Connor just sort of appears and disappears."

"There was a woman in my class at Quantico who said she went out with him a few times, but no one believed her."

"Oh, she could have. He's been known to play the field. And he has spent some time teaching covert skills at the academy."

"*Covert skills,*" she repeated with a grin. "That sounds so dangerous. Makes those classes on investigative techniques seem so mundane."

"Yeah, well, Connor's a hard act to follow. It's all that tall, dark, and handsome stuff, combined with that air of mystery and touch of danger."

"You left out sexy. I've heard he's really sexy."

"Gets the girls every time. Like I said, he's been known to play the field."

Dorsey looked across the table. Was he not aware he could as easily be describing himself? Without the dangerous element, of course. Andrew didn't seem to Dorsey to exude danger in the way Connor was reputed to.

"I don't think he's ever had his heart broken, or been the one left holding the bag when a relationship ended. I don't even know that he's ever *been* in a long-term relationship, come to think of it." Andrew rubbed his chin. "He's always been a bit of a loner. Dylan always used to say he wanted to be around when Connor finally fell for someone, because it was bound to be headfirst."

Andrew paused. "Of course, Dylan won't be around when that happens."

"But I'm thinking the rest of you will probably enjoy watching him take a header."

"Without question." Andrew nodded. "I can't remember ever seeing him with the same woman more than once or twice. God only knows what it is he's looking for."

The waitress appeared at the table with a large tray and proceeded to serve their meals.

"So did you join the Bureau because you felt you were expected to, or because you wanted to?" Dorsey asked after Jessie had moved on.

"Both. I felt I had to—everyone else in the family already had, or was planning on it—but I also wanted to. It was exciting as well as ordinary, if you know what I mean. I'd seen the excitement firsthand, with my dad, and later with my older brother and cousins—Connor's brother, Dylan, was older as well, and he'd joined right out of college. There always seemed to be something going on. But I saw the other side of it, too. The days on end when my dad would be gone working a big case, as well as the days when it almost seemed to be a nine-to-five job."

"I don't recall it ever seeming ordinary to me," she told him. "It always seemed exotic and thrilling. Then again, I always thought there was a touch of the exotic about my dad, though maybe a better word might be dramatic. There was a bit of drama around everything he ever did."

"I'd say recent events bear that out."

They ate in silence for a moment.

"Dorsey, I didn't mean—" Andrew began, and she silenced him.

"Don't apologize. It's true. I know. It's true." She sighed. "His role in this case has complicated things. I thought I could look at this as though he hadn't been involved, and I'm finding I can't. I keep thinking there must have been a reason why he zeroed in on the Beale kid and wouldn't let go, wouldn't look for other suspects. I haven't seen anything that would have convinced me that the only option was that this boy had killed her. I want to see it through my father's eyes, so I can understand, but I just don't seem to be able to. I'm just not seeing Beale at all."

"Maybe because we already know that Shannon was alive, but no one knew that back then."

"*Someone* knew, Andrew," she told him solemnly. "Someone knew. We just have to find out who it was. Maybe then we'll know how my father could have messed up so badly."

"Do you think someone could have deliberately led him in the wrong direction?"

"I don't know. Maybe. If he'd had all the facts, would he have assumed Eric Beale was guilty?"

Andrew put his fork down and appeared to be considering what she'd just said.

"You're thinking maybe I'm not being objective, aren't you?" she asked.

"The thought did cross my mind, yeah."

"If at any time you feel my actions are not objective, or might compromise the investigation, you can tell me to leave."

"I wouldn't have a choice," he said softly, "but I'd hate for that to happen. You've been helpful so far. You have good instincts, good skills. I'd hate to have to ask you to leave."

"I'll do my best to make certain you're not put in that position."

"I'll hold you to that."

They ate in silence for a few more moments, then Andrew said, "So, what are your thoughts at the end of day two?"

"It seems like it's been more than two days, doesn't it?"

He nodded. "We've covered a lot of ground in a short period of time. Anything stand out?"

"Yeah. The more I see of the Randalls, the more screwed up they seem." She chewed a bite of chicken thoughtfully. "I mean, here you have their daughter, sister, granddaughter back from the dead, so to speak. But definitely dead this time. Wouldn't you expect more emotion? Wouldn't you have thought the daughters would have been at their parents' home? Did you see any sign that the family was gathering together to mourn?"

"Nope. Everyone seems to be off doing their own

thing. Business as usual," Andrew agreed. "Paula Rose certainly didn't appear heartbroken."

"I haven't even heard anyone mention a word about a funeral, not even Paula Rose. Did she seem like she was immersed in preparing a service for her beloved, long-lost sister?" Dorsey picked at the cole slaw on her plate. Before he could respond, she went on. "And another thing. Everyone so far seems to think she was kidnapped. Forced to leave. Even back then, they all knew this money was missing from the church. How come it never occurred to anyone that she might have taken it and run off?"

"You know, if she took the money from her grandfather's desk on or before Wednesday afternoon, it means she knew she would be leaving home Wednesday night." Andrew looked up at Dorsey. "Would she have gone home to pick up clothes and maybe some more money? Would she have left Hatton with nothing but the clothes on her back?"

"She might if she was running away from something. But she could have packed some things in her backpack before she left for school that morning. It wasn't found in Eric's car, remember. They only found her assignment book. So let's assume she had that with her when she left. She could have had at least one or two changes of clothing in there, maybe whatever money she had saved up in a bank or something at home."

"So maybe she had it planned, knew about the money from the carnival, and decided to take that too." He paused. "So who smacked her around? And how did she get out of town?"

"Someone had to have driven her. Maybe the same person who smacked her."

"But everyone connected to her had an alibi," he reminded her. "Except Eric Beale, and I don't believe he helped her run away. He'd have said so. And if he'd taken her someplace, like the bus station here in town, someone would have seen her, right? All the publicity this case got back then, if she'd been there, someone would have said so. But no one did."

"True. Same thing if she tried to hitch a ride. Someone would have had to have seen her." Dorsey nodded. "But again, no one's stepped forward to say they did, and as you point out, that wouldn't follow, in a case like this. It's hard to imagine someone not reporting having seen her, or having picked her up."

"What about Dad?" Andrew took another bite of his dinner, and barely seemed to notice. "We don't know what time he got back to the house that night. The report said he was at the church until 7:30 or 8:00 that night—then he went home and went directly into his study."

"Paula Rose said her father was in the study all night, working on his sermon for Sunday."

"I don't think she said she saw him, though."

Dorsey drew small circles on the table with the tip of her index finger. "The most common reason for girls to cut is because they're being abused, and most abusers are someone in or close to the family. Same with girls who run away—look hard enough, and you'll probably find she was running away from someone who was hurting her."

"It's no secret that most girls who turn to prostitution have been sexually abused," Andrew noted. "Doesn't look too good for Reverend Dad, does it?"

"He's at the top of my list." Dorsey appeared thoughtful. "You know, if he was abusing Shannon, chances are he had been abusing one or both of the older sisters. Or still was. He might not have moved on to Paula Rose just yet, but I'm betting Natalie and or Aubrey knew what was going on."

"So we're going to have to talk with him sooner rather than later. Which I'm guessing he won't like."

"If he doesn't cooperate, we could ask Chief Bowden to invite him down to the station for a chat."

"He'll like that even less," Andrew told her. "We have a meeting with Bowden first thing in the morning. With luck he's found the PD's file and we'll see exactly what Franklin said back then."

Dorsey looked across the room to the clock on the wall.

"It's really late. I think we need to get back to the inn. Our meeting with Bowden is at what time?"

"Eight."

Dorsey groaned. "I'm thinking we should probably be staying here in Hatton after tonight. We still have a pretty good drive ahead of us."

"That's not a bad idea. We passed a motel out on the highway, coming into town. Maybe we can stop there on our way in from Deptford in the morning and get a couple of rooms. Plan on driving your car and we'll meet up there in time to be at the police station by eight." He signaled for their bill. When it arrived, Dorsey reached for it.

"That's mine. Dinner's on me," she reminded him. "Never let it be said I'm a poor loser."

He laughed and handed it over, just as his cell phone rang.

"Shields."

He listened for a minute, then said, "We have an appointment first thing in the morning and I don't know how long we'll be tied up. But if we could meet with you later in the afternoon . . . yes, four would be fine. The address?" He fished a pen from his pocket and scribbled on a paper napkin. "Thank you. Yes, I'll see you then."

He snapped the phone closed and returned it to his pocket. "That was Senator Randall-Scott. She and her sister Aubrey would like to meet with us tomorrow."

"Really. Fancy that." Dorsey counted out bills and handed them to the approaching waitress. "I'm not real happy about interviewing them together, though."

"I agree. But unfortunately, that's the invite. Maybe we'll find a way to separate them." Andrew pushed back his chair. "Ready?"

"I am." She stood.

"Thanks for dinner."

"You're welcome. I'll bet more carefully next time." She walked toward the door and Andrew followed. Once outside, she paused.

"You go ahead to the car," she told him. "I need to make a call."

"Okay." He continued walking.

She took her phone from her bag and checked her voice mail. Nothing. She hit redial.

"Come on, Pop. Answer."

The phone continued to ring and ring. Voice mail picked up, but she didn't bother to leave another message. She'd left three over the past two days. If he was checking his phone, he already knew she wanted him to call.

She slipped the phone back into her bag and walked across the lot to Andrew's car, wondering where her father could be.

12

Hatton's police department was housed in a two-story restored clapboard house smack in the middle of the town's only commercial district. Smart shops sat on either side—gourmet goodies on the left and a women's boutique on the right—an odd juxtaposition given the fact that the other shops in town were much more mundane. Strip malls out on the highway were home to national chains—home-supply stores, bookstores, supermarkets, clothing. But here in downtown Hatton, there was an ice cream shop spelled with the obligatory *ppe* at the end that still boasted the same chipped Formica counter and red leather seats topping stainless-steel stools that had been installed in the 1950s. The newsstand still sold men's magazines from under the counter, the postal clerks knew the name, address, and history of everyone in town, and the old-fashioned grocery store at the very end of the block still delivered and sent a monthly bill.

Chief Ryan Bowden ushered Andrew and Dorsey into his office in the back of the building. Judging from the corner cupboards and the fireplace mantel adorned with carved wooden fruit, Dorsey guessed this room had served as the dining room for the family who'd once lived there.

"Nice office," Andrew was saying as they were seated in uncomfortable-looking chairs with high wooden backs.

"Thanks." Chief Bowden nodded amicably and lowered himself into his own cushy leather seat. "Coffee? Tea?"

"None for me," Andrew declined.

"I'm fine," Dorsey said.

"So you want to talk about the . . ." Bowden glanced at the doorway. From the next room came the sound of early-morning office conversation. The chief got up and closed the door. "You're here to talk about the Randall girl."

Without waiting for an answer, he shook his head side to side. "Who'd ever thought she'd be alive all these years? Doesn't that just beat all?"

"That pretty much sums up everyone's reaction," Andrew said.

"Everyone who knows"—Bowden pointed to the door—"and I'm not sure just how many people that would be at this point. I've been keeping a lid on it, out of respect for the family, but that doesn't mean someone doesn't have loose lips." He waved a pink While You Were Out message slip and said, "This here's a call from one of the TV stations in Charleston. Want to bet they're not calling to ask about Aubrey Randall's driving record?"

"Does she have one?" Dorsey asked.

"Nah. Oh, she's been stopped a time or two

lately—mostly for driving a little too fast—but I figure I owe the girl some slack, you know, her sister turning up alive . . . well, dead . . . and being a hooker and all that." He shook his head again. "If anyone'd ever told me years ago that Shannon Randall would end up hooking. . . ."

"You knew her?" Andrew asked.

"Sure. I knew all the Randall girls back then. 'Cept Paula Rose, she was just a little kid."

"So you grew up in Hatton." Andrew leaned back against the seat and tried unsuccessfully to get comfortable.

"Oh, yeah. Lived here all my life."

"How well did you know the Randalls?"

"About as good as I knew anyone else in town. I knew Aubrey the best. She and I were in the same homeroom. I asked her out once, but the reverend gave me such a third degree I never asked her out again, figured it wasn't worth the interrogation."

"Would you say Reverend Randall was strict with the girls?" Andrew continued.

"Pretty much, yeah. They were all about appearance, you know what I mean? Most of the girls' social activities centered around the church, at least until they turned sixteen. After that, they were allowed to date, but only in a group. They could go to dances, but only at the school or at the church, and they had to be home right after the dance ended."

"And before that?" Dorsey asked. "Before they turned sixteen?"

Chief Bowden grinned. "I don't think life began in

that family until you reached your sixteenth birthday. Up until then, it was all about the church. Everything centered around the church. Those girls had to leave home to have any kind of life at all." He paused to reflect on what he'd just said. "I guess maybe that's what Shannon did, right?"

"Did you ever get the feeling that their father was maybe too involved with their lives?"

"No more than most fathers were around here back then, I guess. Tragic what-all happened to him. Losing his daughter, losing the use of his legs and all." He shook his head sympathetically.

"So I guess you remember when Shannon disappeared?" Andrew asked.

"Oh, yeah. That was the biggest thing ever to happen around here. No one could believe it, you know?" Bowden stared into space for a moment, remembering. "We'd gone on a class trip that day. The first thing we heard when we got off the bus was Shannon Randall was missing. I thought Aubrey was gonna fall over and die right then and there."

"What were people saying, that first day? Do you remember?" Dorsey asked.

"No one was sure what happened, not that first day. By the next night, though, the story was going around that she'd been murdered and Eric Beale had killed her."

"Right off the bat, they were talking about Beale?" Andrew slanted a look that said *I'll take it from here* in Dorsey's direction. "Were there any other names tossed around?"

"None that I recall. Pretty much it was all Eric Beale."

"I guess you knew Eric, too?"

"Sure I knew Eric. He was a senior that year. We didn't have any classes together, and I didn't know him real well. I knew his sisters and his brother, though."

"Was Eric on that class trip, too?"

"I don't think so. We went to see a play we were studying in English, and he wasn't in that class." Bowden rubbed his chin. "You know how they always say, you make your own luck? The Beales made their own, all right, but their luck was all bad."

"Give me a for instance."

"The father was a mean drunk, drank himself to death even before Eric was executed. Some said it was because everything that happened with Eric, but tell you the truth, I'd seen that man on a bender. He didn't need an excuse to drink, know what I mean? I don't think Eric's situation had anything to do with that."

"By Eric's situation, you mean him being arrested, tried—"

"Convicted, yeah, the whole thing." The chief nodded. "Timmy, Eric's older brother, he was in prison for assault, he'd been in some bar fight. Mrs. Beale, she had her hands full, what with a drunk for a husband and four kids to keep track of. She got into fights with her husband a couple times a week, or so they said. He beat up on her a lot, her and the kids." He glanced from Andrew to Dorsey and said, "That was back in the days when no one ever interfered with the way a father raised his kids. Nowadays, you beat up on your wife or your kids like that, you end up in jail.

"Anyway, yeah, Mr. Beale was not exactly father of the year. Both girls dropped out of school as soon as they were legal. Funny thing was, Eric was the only one in the family who looked like he'd amount to anything. He got himself a job at the gas station in town and I heard he was saving up to go to college. Ironic, isn't it? He might have actually made something of himself, if he hadn't been arrested for murdering Shannon."

"Do you have any idea where Mrs. Beale is living now?"

"No, she moved from Hatton years ago. I have no idea where she went," Bowden said, "but I can ask around. Seems to me people were happy enough to see her go. Her being here while Eric was on death row, and after—well, it just made some people uncomfortable, you know? Like the whole town just sort of breathed a big sigh of relief after she left." He rubbed the back of his neck with his right hand. "She had a sister who lived out on Camp Hill Road down around Pebble Run. She'd know, if she's still there."

"How about the brother? The sisters?"

"Timmy, I think I heard was living in one of those trailers out by Naylor's Marsh, fifteen, sixteen miles from here. The sisters, I don't know. They both got knocked up before they were sixteen—apologies, Agent Collins, but that's the truth. Maybe some in town might know where they are. I can ask and let you know."

"We'd appreciate it," Andrew said. "By the way, were you able to find Sheriff Taylor's file?"

"I was not. I was just going to tell you that. I'm sorry, but it's not in either of the file rooms." Bowden did his best to look apologetic. "You have to understand, the police department here in Hatton has been in about three different places since 1983. Files were dragged around from here to there and back again. I did search, but I'm afraid I don't have a clue to where it could be. Could have been it was in the boxes that were stored in Chief Taylor's garage when it caught on fire 'bout ten years ago."

"Any chance you overlooked someplace?" Andrew asked.

"I don't think so, but if anything comes to mind, I'll be sure to let you know."

"Can't ask for more than that." Andrew glanced at his watch, stood, and offered his hand to Bowden. "We appreciate your time. If you think of anything, anything at all, even if it's just rumors you recall. . . ."

"I'll be sure to call you, Agent Shields." Bowden stood to shake Andrew's hand, then Dorsey's, before walking them out to the front door. "Where you off to now?"

"We have an appointment with Jeremy Brinkley."

"He'd have a better recollection of what was going on, I'm sure. I was just a kid back then." Bowden shrugged again, as if his shoulders were loose and he had to hitch them up every once in a while. "But Jeremy was with Chief Taylor on that case. He's likely to have some insights I don't have. No tellin' what he might know."

"Thanks again," Andrew called over his shoulder to the chief who now stood on the top step, watching them walk away.

"Well, that wasn't much help," Dorsey said when they got into the car.

"At least now we know where to find one member of the Beale family." Andrew started the car and shifted into reverse. "I'd sure like to hear some of this tale from the Beales' standpoint."

"I'm wondering what part we're missing. You know the old, if two people witness an accident, there will be three versions of the same story, what each witness saw, and what really happened."

"I'll ask John if he's been able to get through to anyone in the family. He said he'd be handling the Beales, and I don't want to step in if he hasn't been able to locate them yet."

Andrew made a U-turn and headed out of town while he searched a pocket for his phone. He dialed, then left voice mail.

"I guess we're still standing down as far as Tim Beale is concerned, but I'm sure John will get back to me on that." He looked around for landmarks, then said, "Brinkley's home isn't too far down from here. He said we'd come to a fork in the road about eight miles outside of town, and to take the left toward Simpson's Creek. There should be a sign and then it'll be another mile or so before we come to his house."

"He tell you what to look for?"

"He said the house is made of logs and sits back a bit on the right. There's a mailbox with some kind of viney thing growing around it."

"We should be able to find that." Dorsey watched out the window as they passed the remnants of the old rice fields on either side of the road. "Interesting, don't you think, that even Bowden, who was just in high school at the time, knew by the next evening that Beale had been the only person pulled in for questioning?"

"Only one he knew of, anyway."

"You see anyone else's name in the Bureau's file?"

"No," he admitted.

"Well, think about it. According to Bowden, approximately thirty-six hours after Shannon was discovered to be missing, Chief Taylor declared her dead and named Eric Beale the sole suspect in her murder. No body? No problem. You have to wonder why he jumped on that so fast." She pointed straight ahead. "There's the fork in the road. And the sign for Simpson's Creek."

Andrew made the left.

"And for reasons I don't understand, my father was brought into it, just like that," she murmured.

"Maybe he didn't accept it all that quickly. We don't really know how much investigating he and the other agents actually did here. That's something we need to talk to him about."

"I would, if I could find him. I've been trying to get him to return my calls since I arrived here."

"You haven't spoken with him in three days?"

"No."

"Any idea where he could be?"

"No. He always has his phone with him. If he's not calling me, it's because he's avoiding me."

"Is that unusual?"

"Very."

"What do you think's behind that?"

"I don't know. Maybe"—she paused for a moment—"maybe he's off somewhere with Diane, this woman he's dating. Maybe he just doesn't want to discuss his love life with me."

"You think that's it?"

"No, but it sounded like a good rationalization."

"Look, if you're worried, you can take off a few days and go—"

"Nope. Pop's a big boy. Yes, I'm worried, but I'm not in constant communication with him under normal circumstances, and frankly, I don't know that he doesn't just take off sometimes, alone or with a friend. Maybe he's done just that. Maybe this whole thing has played on his mind so much, he's just gone off somewhere to work things out in his own head. I don't know what he's thinking. And I guess that's what's bothering me."

"We could ask John to send someone to—"

"Uh-uh. The last thing he needs right now is to think the Bureau is looking for him. For whatever reason. I think I just have to let it be. For now."

She turned her head to look out the window. "There's the log house."

Andrew pulled to the right and parked alongside the rustic post-and-rail fence. The small house was set back from the road, sheltered beneath a stand of live oaks.

"You think he has the file?" Dorsey got out of the car and waited for Andrew.

"It's certainly possible. Big case—probably the biggest case of his career, file shifted around from place to place, it's easy enough to explain how it could get misplaced." Andrew stopped to roll up his shirtsleeves. "Make one hell of a souvenir. Bloody shirt and all."

"Let's go see if he has it."

"*If* he admits to having it. I'm betting he won't."

"That's one bet I won't make."

They walked up the dirt driveway and followed a path made of cut slices of tree trunk. They knocked on the front door, but no one answered. Back behind the house, a dog began to bark.

"Maybe around back." Andrew motioned to the right. They followed the path to its end near an open porch, where a man slept on a hammock.

Andrew cleared his throat, and the old dog on the porch rose reluctantly and made a show of barking some more.

The man jerked in his sleep and opened his eyes.

"Jeremy Brinkley?" Andrew asked.

"Yeah." The one-time police officer ran a hand over his face as if to wipe the sleep away. "Sorry. Must have dozed. Blood pressure medication. Makes me drowsy. You Shields, the guy who called?"

"Yes."

"You got some ID?" Brinkley was fully awake and standing.

Andrew met him halfway to the hammock and handed over his badge, which Brinkley scrutinized. He handed it back, then looked at Dorsey and said, "Yours?"

She took it from her bag and handed it over. Brinkley gave it a quick glance, then returned it.

"Too hot out here. Come on inside." He motioned to the two agents to follow him. "Not you, Barney. You stay," he told the dog, who then lay down in a grassy patch near the back steps.

"Water?" he offered before turning on the spigot in the narrow, dark kitchen.

"No thanks," Dorsey and Andrew both responded at once.

Brinkley filled a large glass for himself, then gestured toward a closed door. "We'll talk in there."

He led them into a small room that smelled of damp wood and cats and was cooled by an ancient air conditioner. There was one armchair and a loveseat in desperate need of a slipcover. He pointed to the loveseat, and the agents sat. Brinkley took the armchair and turned it to face them.

"You said on the phone this had something to do with the Shannon Randall case." He directed the question to Andrew. "What's up with that after all these years?"

"Officer Brinkley—" Andrew began.

"Not Officer Brinkley anymore," he corrected. "I've been retired for several years now."

"Once law, always law," Andrew replied.

"Hey, you're right on about that." Brinkley nodded. "In my heart, I'm still wearing the badge. I watch those TV shows—shit, CSI?" He laughed, shaking his head. "Never seen a case worked the way they work theirs. Not in this little town, anyway. Christ, the biggest case we ever had was the Randall case, and we didn't even have a body. No DNA testing back then, though we could test for blood type. We had to solve every case with good old-fashioned detective work."

"That's still the best way," Andrew said.

"Oh, yeah." Brinkley nodded his enthusiasm, a broad grin on his face. "Now, Agent Shields, tell me why you're interested in Shannon Randall after all these years."

"Officer Brinkley—"

"Hey, it's Jeremy." Brinkley leaned forward in his chair, his forearms resting on his thighs.

"Jeremy, the story hasn't broken yet, so I'm going to have to ask for your confidence. We're trying to learn as much as we can as quickly as we can, before the media grabs on to it."

Brinkley looked from one agent to the other. "What's the big mystery? The case was solved twenty-four years ago."

"Not exactly," Andrew told him.

"What are you talking about? I was part of it, I was there when we picked up Eric Beale for questioning, I was there when—"

"Whose idea was it to question Beale?" Andrew interrupted.

"Chief Taylor's," Brinkley replied without hesitation.

"What put him on to Eric, do you remember?"

"Yeah. He was the last person seen with Shannon that night. He left town with her at least an hour after he said he'd dropped her off. Kimmie White saw them. The chief called her and the other two girls Shannon hung around with as soon as school was over to see what they knew. The other two didn't have much to say, but Kimmie gave a statement to the chief that afternoon."

"Did anyone else claim to have seen them leaving town?" Dorsey asked.

"No. Just Kimmie. But that was enough. It placed him with her after he said he'd let Shannon out on Montgomery Street. Showed he lied. Shot his story to shit."

"Kimmie was credible?" Dorsey asked.

"Hell, yes. She was one of Shannon's best friends. They'd grown up together. Her dad's the doctor in town, one of the deacons at the reverend's church." He was looking more and more perplexed. "She wouldn't have said she'd seen them if she hadn't."

Brinkley warily watched them both.

"You want to tell me what this is all about? Why's the FBI sending two agents down here to talk over an old case?"

"There's been a bit a development," Andrew told him.

"What kind of development?" Brinkley frowned.

"This is going to come as a bit of a shock, Jeremy, but Shannon Randall's body was found a few weeks ago on a small island off Georgia," Andrew told him.

"No shit? After all these years?" Brinkley's smile returned. "But hey, that's good, right? Now the family can have some closure, right?"

"When she was found, she'd been dead less than eight hours."

Brinkley's smile faded slowly as Andrew's words began to sink in.

Finally, he said, "That just ain't possible."

"It's not only possible, it's true. Blood type, fingerprints, dental records, all matched. She's been positively identified by one of her sisters," Andrew assured him.

"But how the hell . . ." Brinkley got up and began to pace the length of the small room. "I don't understand this. How could she have just died now?"

"The obvious answer is that she wasn't dead then," Dorsey stated.

"But how?" He jammed his hands into the pockets of his cutoff khakis. "I just don't understand. . . ."

"Twenty-four years ago, Shannon left home, apparently voluntarily, though we're still looking into that," Andrew explained.

"But Eric, he had that shirt with all her blood on it. He had her stuff under the seat of his car. . . ." Brinkley was still trying to come to terms with the fact that things were not as they had seemed.

"That's right, he did." Andrew nodded. "Do you recall how he explained that?"

"He said she was beaten up when he picked her up and he gave her the shirt to clean herself up with."

"Looks like he was telling the truth."

"I can't believe this, man." Brinkley ran a shaking hand through thinning hair. "Eric Beale . . . he was charged with her murder. He was fucking *executed!*"

"We're trying to understand how that happened, Jeremy. Obviously, your recollections will be crucial to helping us figure it out," Dorsey told him.

"Shit. Yeah, yeah, sure. Whatever I can tell you." Brinkley sat back down, still dazed, still visibly shaking.

"After Kimmie White said she'd seen Eric and Shannon driving out of town, Chief Taylor brought Eric in for questioning." Andrew started the ball rolling.

"Yeah. Right after the chief talked to Kimmie, we went straight on down to the gas station where Eric worked, picked him up, brought him in. Chief questioned him himself."

"You weren't in the room with them?"

"No. After we brought him in, the chief took him into a small room off the lunchroom in the old station. Closed the door, they were in there most of the afternoon. When the chief came out, he said Eric had all but confessed."

"Then why call in the FBI?" Dorsey asked. "If you already had a confession, or close to one, why call in the Bureau?"

Brinkley shrugged. "I asked Chief Taylor that very thing. He said since it was a murder case, and Shannon being so young and all, and us being such a small department and none of us having much experience with homicide, we'd best let the Feds take over, 'specially since there was no body. I never did understand it myself, no offense to either of you, but it just seemed unnecessary to bring the FBI in. But Chief Taylor, he was pretty firm on wanting the Feds in."

"When did he tell you that, do you remember?" Andrew asked.

"Must have been pretty soon after he talked to Kimmie and brought Eric in, since it seems like the FBI agents were there the next day. Couple of 'em."

"That soon, Taylor had decided it was a homicide and Eric Beale was the killer?"

"Best I recall, yeah."

"Did that seem odd to you at the time?" Dorsey couldn't help but ask.

"At the time, no, not really. I mean, since Kimmie saw them together and him having that bloody shirt in his car and all, it didn't seem odd." Brinkley crossed his legs, one foot pumping nervously.

"And now?" Andrew prodded him.

"Now . . . I don't know, man." He uncrossed his legs, then recrossed them.

"We were told that sometime before Shannon disappeared, there'd been some sort of bad blood between Eric and the chief's nephew," Andrew said.

"Oh, Jeff Feeney." Brinkley nodded. "Yeah, they did get into it a few times. Last time might have been sometime before Shannon was kill . . . disappeared."

He exhaled loudly.

"Where's she been all this time?"

"She's been around. Here and there," Andrew told him. "She had a hard time of it."

"She been on the streets all that time?" Brinkley searched Andrew's face.

"It's all going to come out soon enough." Andrew nodded. "Yeah, she's been on the streets since she left Hatton."

"Son of a bitch." Brinkley shook his head. "Son of a bitch."

He rubbed his chin thoughtfully for a moment. "How'd she die?"

"Shot through the heart at close range," Andrew replied.

"Someone wanted to make damn sure she was dead."

"It appears that way, yes."

"Wow." Brinkley got up and paced, his hands in his pockets. "Wow. All this time, she's been . . . wherever she was. And Eric . . . Jesus, man, that poor son of a bitch."

"You can understand why we want to get a handle on what went on back then."

"Yeah. Yeah." Brinkley continued pacing.

"So if you can think of any reason why Chief Taylor might not have considered anyone else for Shannon's murder. . . ."

"I don't know." He shook his head. "Maybe that thing with Jeff . . . I don't know."

"You know what that was all about?" Dorsey asked.

"I don't. All I know is that there was no love lost between the two of them, but what was at the bottom of that?" He shrugged.

"Could the chief have been influenced against Eric because of bad blood between Eric and the nephew?" Dorsey pressed.

"I want to say no"—Brinkley dropped back onto his chair—"but truthfully, I don't know. I don't know what it was about, but whatever it was, it had been going on for a while."

"Is Jeff Feeney still around?" Dorsey asked.

"Yeah. I saw him a few weeks ago at the Little League field, coaching one of his boys."

"You got an address for him?"

"No, but he's usually down at the hardware store, Feeney's, right on Main Street. He took over from his father. And the chief's widow is still around. Jeff is her nephew, her brother Jed's oldest boy. She's still pretty active around town, still living in that big house she and the chief bought and fixed up after her old man died and left her all that money."

Brinkley stared at the floor for a while as if lost in thought, trying to comprehend it all. Finally, he looked up and said, "That agent they sent down here back then to head up the investigation. . . ."

"Agent Ranieri." Andrew tensed.

"Yeah. I see him on TV sometimes. Seems like he made a big career for himself after this case was over." Brinkley scratched the side of his face. "Anyone tell him about Shannon?"

"He's been told."

"What's he got to say?"

"He was as surprised as you are," Andrew said simply.

"I'll just bet he was. Ranieri. Yeah, I remember him." Brinkley nodded. "Seemed like a decent guy. Course, I didn't have much contact with him, but he seemed like a nice guy. Guess we won't be seeing him much anymore."

"What do you mean?" Dorsey frowned.

"On the TV. After this, who's going to want to have him come on and talk about how the cops should investigate a case?"

"Jeremy, do you know what happened to the police file?" Andrew changed the subject swiftly.

"Is it missing?"

"Chief Bowden can't locate it."

"Miz Taylor might know. I think for a time they kept some stuff in the garage, back when the department was being moved." He shrugged and averted his eyes.

"To the best of your knowledge, was there ever another suspect?" Dorsey asked. "Anyone else who maybe should have been a suspect, anyone who might have had something to do with Shannon disappearing that night?"

"Not as far as I know, uh-uh." Jeremy paused, as if reflecting. "You know, everyone thought Eric did it, just accepted it. Looking back, I'm thinking maybe because his family was such trouble, people expected him to be trouble too. Funny thing, though, Eric always seemed to be different from the rest of the Beales, you know what I mean? Smarter. But maybe people didn't know that. Maybe that's why no one really questioned that it was him. It was just, Eric did this. Eric killed her."

"And the case was built from there," Dorsey said.

"Pretty much, yeah. Everyone was talking about how Eric used to follow Shannon around, but she was just a freshman, you know? All her friends said how he had a thing for her but she was only interested in him as a friend. So it wasn't a secret, you know, that he had the hots for her." Jeremy got up and took a sip from the glass of water. "Then, when Kimmie swore she saw them heading out of town and no one ever saw her again, well, that pretty much sealed it."

"There was a break-in at the church the night Shannon disappeared." Andrew changed the subject.

"Right. The money from the carnival was stolen." His head bobbed up and down. "When I got in to work on Thursday morning, the chief said he'd gotten a call from old Mrs. Randall—Mrs. Randall, senior, I mean—after he got home the night before. Said there'd been some money stolen, but we could wait until the morning to come out to make the report."

"Is that usual?" Dorsey asked.

"Not *un*usual. Mrs. Randall said her husband had already locked up the church after choir practice and she didn't want to disturb him to go back over and open the church back up again. It wasn't a big deal."

"Do you remember what you did the next morning?" Andrew backed Dorsey off with a glance.

"Sure. We met Mrs. Randall at the church around eight thirty. She showed us around the reverend's office, showed us the drawer."

"You take any prints?"

"Yeah. As I recall, they were pretty blurred. Nothing distinct, there were just too many of them. Some were the reverend's, some were Mrs. Randall's, we knew that, but if there was someone else's prints there, we couldn't have told you back then who they belonged to."

"What areas did you dust for prints, besides the office?"

"None, that I recall. We were just finishing up on the desk when we heard screeching and yelling from the community center where the senior citizen's breakfast was taking place. We ran down and there was Mrs. Randall, Shannon's mom, yelling at her husband that she couldn't find Shannon anywhere." Brinkley shook his head. "At first, there was so much screeching, I couldn't understand what she was saying. Then she talked to the chief, and they started searching for her. They searched around the house, the church, all around the town. Mrs. Randall had called all Shannon's friends but no one had seen her since the night before."

"Anyone question Franklin Randall at the time?"

"About what?"

"About the fact that his daughter had gone missing and no one seems to recall seeing him between the time he left the church and eleven thirty or so when his wife arrived home from an evening out with her sister."

"I'm sure we did question him, we questioned everyone. Did we at any time think Reverend Randall had anything to do with Shannon's disappearance? No." He paused and looked at Andrew long and hard.

"Are you saying you think the Reverend had a hand in whatever happened to her?"

"I'm saying someone did and it looks like it wasn't Eric Beale. I was just wondering if anyone talked to him."

"Yes, we talked to him."

"What was his demeanor?"

"His demeanor?" Jeremy repeated sarcastically. "His demeanor was that of a man who'd just found out his daughter was missing and probably had been since the night before and he hadn't known it. What the hell do you think his demeanor was?"

He continued to glare at Andrew. "Look, we had an eyewitness who placed her in Eric Beale's car—Eric's speeding car—on the road out to the lake. We searched the lake, we searched the woods, we searched the park. The FBI had their team out there with us, even had a few divers. We had better'n half the town searching for that girl for two, three days. She was nowhere to be found. The only trace of her was in Eric's car."

He rubbed his chin thoughtfully, and softened just a little.

"Look, not trying to make excuses now, but back then, no one gave more'n a passing thought to the possibility that Shannon might have run away. She just wasn't the type to do that, you know what I mean? Everyone in town knew her, everyone knew she was a happy kid, a good kid from a good family. She never got into any trouble, she was a good student, she played sports, she didn't hang with a bad crowd. She was an all-around solid kid. So for a kid like that to be gone, someone had to have taken her. And for her not to be found, we just all figured she had to be dead. And with her blood in Eric's car and him being seen with her, it just followed that he'd done something really bad to her. No one ever figured it had been any other way than what Chief Taylor said it was."

"That Eric had killed her and hidden her body in a place where it couldn't be found?" Andrew stood. There was nothing else to be learned here.

"Even the FBI believed it." Brinkley stood as well. "That made it so, far as everyone around here was concerned. No one ever doubted that Eric was guilty. The chief said he was. Said he'd all but confessed to him. Why would he have told us that if it wasn't true?"

"Good question," Dorsey said.

"Yeah." Brinkley rocked back and forth on his heels thoughtfully.

"Sure makes you wonder what was at the bottom of all that, don't it?"

13

"So, what do you say we stop at the Widow Taylor's and see if she has any thoughts on where we might find that file?" Andrew made a U-turn and headed back toward Hatton.

"Good idea. We have a few hours before we meet with the sisters. Bowden said Aubrey's house was about a half hour from Hatton, so there's time."

"The more answers we get, the more questions we find," Andrew said thoughtfully. "It almost seems Chief Taylor deliberately steered the investigation toward Eric Beale, but why would he do that?"

"Would it be a stretch to think it might have something to do with whatever was going on between Eric and Jeff Feeney?"

"Not to my mind." Andrew slowed to round a bend in the road. "But I don't expect Feeney to admit to anything."

"It would have to be something really big for Taylor to have knowingly framed Eric, and let an innocent man be executed."

"You'd think, but who knows what goes on in these little towns."

"And who's going to tell, all these years later?" Dorsey wondered aloud.

"So far, maybe only Jeremy Brinkley and Chief Bowden. Unfortunately, neither of them seem to know. And I think Brinkley was really rattled by this."

"I think so, too. I think he was a good cop, and I think he liked to think Taylor was, too." She gazed thoughtfully out the window. "But I also think that if he believed his chief pulled something back then, he'd be shocked, but he'd do what he could to make it right."

"Well, I gave him my card. I hope he uses it."

The drive back to Hatton proper took less than ten minutes. They drove along the main street where the renovated houses stood like newly polished jewels.

"Oh. Taylor." Dorsey turned in her seat to look back at the mailbox they'd just driven past. "Slow down. Back two houses."

Andrew checked his rearview mirror, then pulled to the side of the road.

"Shall we make a cold call?" he asked.

"Why not?"

They walked up the neatly trimmed sidewalks to the house where the pale blue mailbox announced the Taylor home.

"What a place." Dorsey stood at the end of the driveway. "It looks like something out of a magazine."

"Is there a magazine called *Antebellum*?" Andrew observed the house and the grounds. "It's not all that big compared to some of the plantation houses you see in this area, but it's clearly the same era and the same style. Interesting, don't you think, this whole row of mini-mansions, all renovated?"

"It takes a lot of money to do this kind of restoration," Dorsey told him as they walked the length of the drive.

"Brinkley said she'd inherited a lot of money from her father," Andrew reminded her. "Her money. Her nephew . . ."

"So maybe Miz Taylor might have been holding a lot of the cards back then." Dorsey stepped onto the flagstone walk that led to the front door and Andrew followed.

"Hold onto that thought." He reached past her and rang the doorbell.

Moments later, a woman who looked to be in her mid-seventies appeared and opened only the inner door.

"May I help you?" she asked.

"I'm Special Agent Andrew Shields, FBI." Andrew held his badge to the door. "Are you Mrs. Taylor?"

"I am." She remained motionless on the other side of the screen.

"We'd like to talk with you for a moment, if that's all right."

"About?"

"We're trying to track down some old files of your husband's. Chief Bowden said files had been stored here at one time."

"They were all sent to the new police department."

"Mrs. Taylor, if we could just have a minute of your time." Dorsey put on her best manners. "We'd like to ask you about an old case that your husband handled."

"I never involved myself in my husband's work. I'm sure I'd be of no help at all."

"Mrs. Taylor, if you don't mind—" Andrew started to plead with her, but he didn't get far.

"Oh, but I do. You all have a nice day, now."

The inner door closed.

"Well, was it something we said?" Dorsey asked.

"Apparently. I'd say we've been dismissed."

They turned to walk back to the car.

"I'm feeling overwhelmed by all this hospitality," Andrew told her.

"Me, too. That was so strange."

"Do you think she's just an inhospitable, cold, ornery bitch, or do you think she knew why we were here and wasn't having any of it?"

"Both. I think she's a cold and ornery bitch and I think she knew why we were here and doesn't want to talk about the Randall case."

They reached the car and got in.

"Word has to be starting to get around town. No doubt it's reached the chief's widow that the FBI is questioning the old investigation," Andrew said.

"She could just be protecting her husband's name," Dorsey suggested, "or she could be protecting something—or someone—else."

"You think her nephew?"

"I think it's a possibility."

"Me, too. Let's see what Chief Bowden knows about Jeff Feeney." Andrew took out his phone and dialed the chief's private line. After several minutes of conversation, he snapped the phone closed and slid it into his pocket.

"So, what did you find out?" Dorsey asked.

"Jeff Feeney was three years older than Eric Beale, and had the reputation of being a bully."

"Three years older, that makes him about the same age as Eric's brother Tim, doesn't it?"

"Yeah." Andrew appeared thoughtful as he started the car and pulled onto the roadway. "He said there was definitely bad blood there, but he didn't know why."

"That's all he said?"

"That, and the fact that Jeff Feeney was one of the witnesses in the assault case that sent Tim Beale to prison."

"We need to talk to Jeff Feeney."

"And in about another minute, we will."

Andrew made a left onto the street that led to the town's center, then parked in front of the hardware store. He pointed to the sign above the door. FEENEY'S HARDWARE EST. 1886.

"Let's go see if the proprietor is here." Andrew got out of the car and dropped a quarter in the meter.

They walked from the oppressive heat of the afternoon into the air-conditioned cool of the old building.

"Nice." Dorsey observed as they looked around. The store had wide-planked oak floors and old-fashioned displays and fixtures, but the lighting and the cooling system had obviously been updated.

"Something I can help you find?" a young clerk asked them.

"We're looking for Jeff Feeney," Andrew responded.

"Jeff's right back there near the office." The boy pointed toward the rear of the store. "Blue shirt."

"I see him, thanks." Andrew motioned to Dorsey to follow him.

Jeff Feeney looked up from his conversation and watched the pair approach. He was a tall, burly man of around forty, and his arms, chest, and neck broadcast that he still worked out on a frequent basis.

"Mr. Feeney?" Andrew had his badge out of his pocket, and Feeney's eyes were on it.

"That's me." Jeff Feeney's smile was clearly disingenuous. "Help you with something?"

Even as Andrew held up his badge, he had the distinct feeling that Feeney knew exactly who he was. Feeney took the badge and pretended to look it over. He gave Dorsey a long look, top to bottom.

"And you, pretty lady? You have something to show me?"

"It's Agent Collins." Dorsey passed her credentials to him. He took a long time studying them before handing them back.

"We can step into my office." He turned and walked through an open door to his left.

He closed the door after the agents and folded his arms across his chest.

"What can I do for you?"

"We're in town—"

"I know why you're in town. I suspect by now,

everyone else does, too." He waved off Andrew's explanation.

"Word travels fast," Dorsey remarked dryly.

"Not really, pretty lady, it's taken—"

"Agent Collins," she repeated coldly. "My name is Agent Collins."

"Ahhh, right, of course. My apologies," he drawled without sincerity. "I was going to say, word has actually traveled a bit slowly, by Hatton's standards. You've been here, what, three days now, and people are just starting to talk? Why, that's near unheard of."

"What exactly have you heard?" Andrew asked.

"Well, they're saying you're looking into the Shannon Randall case because somehow she's been alive all this time, but turned up dead for real a few weeks back down in Georgia." He shook his head. "Imagine that. Alive all these years, and no one knowing. And that kid being executed and her not even being dead."

"Eric Beale," Dorsey said pointedly.

"What?" Feeney frowned.

"Eric Beale. The boy who was executed was Eric Beale."

"Oh, right. Beale." He nodded.

"We understand you had a run-in with him not too long before he was arrested for Shannon's murder."

"Did I?" He rubbed his chin thoughtfully. "I may have. It was a long time ago. I don't really remember."

"You remember having been involved somehow in a bar fight with his brother sometime before that?" Andrew asked.

"Agent Shields, that was a long time ago. I'm afraid when I was younger, I did more than my share of hell-raising and got into more than one barroom brawl. It may be one of them involved this kid's brother—Tim, was it?—but like I said, it was a long time ago."

"You were a witness in the case against him. He went to prison for assault. Served time."

"Oh, *that* fight." Feeney nodded as if a light had just gone on in his head. "That was out at the Past Times. I do remember that. Tim Beale got into it with a buddy of mine."

"Do you remember what the fight was about?"

" 'Fraid not." Feeney perched casually on the edge of his desk.

"Where's this buddy now?" Dorsey asked.

"In the churchyard, First Baptist of Hatton," he said smugly. "Motorcycle accident. Knoxville, nine, ten years ago."

He stared at Andrew. "Anything else I can help you with, Agent Shields?"

"I think we're good for now."

"Well, then, I hope you find what you're looking for." Feeney reached out one long arm and opened the door.

They left without thanking him for his time.

"I swear I feel his eyes burning a hole right through the back of my head," Dorsey mumbled as they stepped back into the sunshine.

"I don't think it was the back of your head he was

staring at." Andrew unlocked the car with the remote.

"What an asshole," Dorsey said when they were in
the car. "Creepy and arrogant."

"Yeah, but that just makes the picture more clear."
Andrew checked the time. "We have time to get a
quick bite before we head out to Aubrey's. Let's grab
something at that diner across from the post office."

"Fine. What do you mean, the picture's more
clear?"

"We have two cases to solve here. The first one
being what happened twenty-four years ago, the second being who killed Shannon. Let's just look at the
first one for now."

He drove to the municipal parking lot and took a
spot.

"Let's assume that whatever happened to put Tim
Beale behind bars had something to do with Jeff
Feeney."

"That feels right." She nodded. "So Tim's behind
bars, then something's going on between Feeney and
Tim Beale's little brother."

"Okay, hold that thought." Andrew turned off the
car but didn't move to get out. "Not too long after
whatever confrontation there was between Feeney
and Eric Beale, Shannon Randall runs away from
home. Kimmie White tells Chief Taylor that she saw
Shannon in Eric's car. Eric's picked up and questioned, and when the bloody shirt is found in his car,
Taylor concludes that Eric killed Shannon."

"To get back at Eric somehow for having gotten into something with his nephew?" Dorsey frowned.

"With his wife's nephew." Andrew let that sink in. "Is there any doubt in your mind that Taylor's wife held the reins in that house? The house bought and restored with money she inherited?"

"So, you're thinking that after Eric appeared to be a suspect, his wife leaned on Taylor to turn it on full blast, to get Eric out of the way for some reason?"

"Think about it. Both Beale boys get into seriously hot water with the law, after each of them had a run-in with Jeff Feeney."

"Maybe Tim and Eric had something on Jeff, or maybe knew something that Jeff—and his aunt—didn't want anyone else to know." Dorsey thought for a moment. "Or it could have been the other way around."

"Could be either. Having Eric arrested for Shannon's murder was the way Taylor shut him up."

"But why wouldn't Eric have spoken up back then?" Dorsey frowned. "Why didn't he say something at the trial? It doesn't make sense that he'd keep quiet and let them execute him if he knew why he was being railroaded."

"I agree. It doesn't make sense at all."

"And how would Shannon's disappearance be connected to that?"

"I don't think it is. I think her disappearance was just a convenient way for Taylor to get rid of Eric the same way he got rid of Tim."

"I find it hard to believe that Taylor would have let them execute Eric, knowing he was innocent."

"Maybe he didn't know. Maybe once the story was concocted, he believed it. Maybe it all made perfect sense to him, once all the little bits of evidence starting falling into place. You know you can talk yourself into just about anything, if the stakes are high enough."

"Let's suppose you're right," Dorsey said. "Let's suppose that's how it happened. Eric gets onto Taylor's radar somehow, he believes Eric is guilty, Eric is convicted and he's executed. Now fast forward to 2007. Shannon Randall's murdered. You're saying you don't think the two events are connected?"

"I think there's a thread of a connection, but I don't think that thread has anything to do with Eric Beale. I think he was an unfortunate victim of something else, something to do with Taylor's nephew. I think Shannon's disappearance was merely an unfortunate coincidence as far as Eric was concerned. A convenient means of getting rid of him."

"Do you see a connection between Shannon's disappearance in 1983 and her murder in 2007?" Dorsey turned to face him. "I feel there has to be something that ties one to the other. I just don't know what that something is."

"Neither do I, but I agree there's something there, and there are a whole lot of pieces to this puzzle." He opened his car door and started to get out. Over his shoulder, he added, "I'm hoping sooner or later we'll be able to put them all together and see the whole picture."

"Wow, those white columns really stand out against those redbrick walls, don't they." Dorsey rolled down the window to get a better look at the home of Aubrey Randall, the self-styled Southern version of Martha Stewart.

It wasn't a question.

"She certainly does seem to like that antebellum look." Andrew parked in front of a tidy boxwood hedge. "I could swear I heard the theme from *Gone With the Wind* while we were driving up that long drive from the road."

"You too? I thought it was just me. Eleanor Taylor's got nothing on Aubrey."

"Except of course, Eleanor's got the real thing. Aubrey's is all new construction. A mere copy of the real thing."

"Well, copy or no, I'm impressed."

Andrew turned off the engine and stared at the house.

"It looks like she's home. Assuming that's her Mercedes over there."

"The license plate is AGR. Aubrey some-middle-name-that-begins-with-G Randall." Dorsey opened her door. "I don't see another car, though, so maybe the senator hasn't arrived yet. Which would be good, because I'd rather we have some time with Aubrey alone."

"If they've concocted a story, for whatever reason, it's already done. They know what they're going to say." Andrew got out of the car and took a good look around. "Nice gardens. Nice horses out back. Very nice."

"I'd say Miz Aubrey does quite well for herself."

"She's a local star on her way to the big time, right?"

Dorsey looked around at the lush grounds and the beautiful house that stood before them.

"I'll bet it would hurt like hell to give up all this. I'll bet someone who had all this would fight tooth and nail if they thought they were in danger of losing it."

"Your point?"

"Just that if this were mine, I'd feel really anxious if something threatened to take it from me, that's all."

"Something like a sister who's supposed to be dead turning up with a record of numerous arrests for prostitution."

"Yeah. Like that."

"How do you think those network folks would feel about giving Aubrey a shot at the big time with a scandal like that just beginning to break?" Dorsey said.

"I'd say it would be pretty unfortunate timing."

"Unfortunate enough that you'd do something really desperate?"

"You know what they say." Andrew glanced around as they walked. "Desperate times call for desperate measures."

The path they walked along was red brick to match the house, laid out in a herringbone pattern that led right to the front door. Breezy daylilies grew around the steps in clumps and vied with huge puffs of hydrangea for attention.

"Nice," Dorsey said again. "Very nice. Tasteful, even, and—"

"Agents Shields and Collins?"

The woman who opened the door was tall and willowy, her features as finely chisled and delicate as her younger sister's were sharp. Her blond hair curled around her face in a short and charming cut. She wore a pale pink T-shirt tucked into the waist of a slim denim skirt, lots of silver jewelry, and a welcoming smile.

"I'm Andrew Shields, this is Dorsey Collins." Andrew smiled back as warmly. "Miss Randall?"

The woman barely glanced at Dorsey. Andrew had her total attention.

"Aubrey."

"Aubrey," he repeated with a smile meant to charm. "This is quite a place you have here."

"Well, thank you." Aubrey Randall beamed as she stepped out onto the small square that served as the front porch. "Would you like a quick tour while we wait for my sister?"

"We'd love it. Thanks."

"Where would you like to start?" She folded her arms over her chest, her eyes never leaving Andrew's face. "We have the stables, the pond, the gardens. . . ."

"I noticed some horses out in the pasture there," he said. "How about we start there?"

"Sure thing," she drawled and stepped between Andrew and Dorsey. "Are you a horseman, Agent Shields?"

Aubrey sidled up to Andrew and touched his arm in a follow-me gesture. The two of them walked side by side down the walk, leaving Dorsey to roll her eyes and tag along, Aubrey chatting incessantly, Andrew occasionally nodding agreeably. Aubrey was playing the Southern belle, and Andrew was playing along.

"You, there, Sugar Plum. You come on over here and be sweet," Aubrey called to the chestnut mare that pranced inside the fence. "Come say hello to our new friend, Andrew."

The horse leaned over the fence just as a car sped up the drive. State Senator Natalie Randall-Scott parked her sedan next to Andrew's and jumped out. She wasted no time in hurrying over to the fence.

"Natalie, honey, you're just in time. This is Agent Shields—" Aubrey began the introductions and her sister cut her off.

"I know who he is. Agent Collins, Agent Shields." Natalie offered her hand first to Dorsey, then to Andrew. "Natalie Scott."

Before either of them could respond, she turned to her sister and said, "So much for keeping this whole mess under wraps."

She pointed toward the end of the drive. "I've had two news vans following me since I left my office. I had to call the state police to send a few troopers over to block off the drive here and to limit access to my home."

"So the story's out," Dorsey said.

"Apparently," the senator responded dryly. "Out with a vengeance."

"Then I suggest we warn Mother and Paula Rose," Aubrey said.

"I've already called everyone. Chief Bowden is on

his way over to Sylvan Road. He'll do the best he can
to keep things under control there. I'm wondering if
we should move Mother and Father here until this
blows over. I think we need to . . ." Natalie stopped
herself, then turned to the agents and said, "I'm sure
you can appreciate how difficult this has been for our
family. I don't want our parents unduly harassed by
the media. This entire thing has been simply . . ." She
sought the right word.

"A mess," Aubrey said. "It's just a damned mess."

"Aubrey," Natalie chided her.

"Well, it is. There's just no other way to describe it.
It's a damn mess and it's got Momma and Daddy just
beside themselves." Gone was the Southern lady
who'd been trying to sweet-talk the hunky FBI agent
into forgetting why he was there. "If she was alive,
she never should have gone away, and she never
should have stayed away all this time. She should
have come home."

"Aubrey, you and I both know Shannon wouldn't
have taken off on her own," Natalie interjected. "You
know she had to have been forced. Kidnapped, maybe
by someone involved in white slavery. You hear about
that all the time now, but it's nothing new. Whoever it
was who took her forced her onto a path she never
would have followed willingly."

Spoken like a true politician, Dorsey thought.

"Well, of course she was forced, Natalie. Of course
she wouldn't have done those terrible things if she'd
had a choice. But she could have come home before
this. She could have escaped and come home *long* be-

fore now." Aubrey crossed her arms over her chest. "I don't blame her for leaving. I know she didn't have a choice being abducted back then. But I do blame her for staying away as long as she did, making us all suffer all these years . . . making Momma so sad and Daddy so bitter." Aubrey's eyes welled with tears.

And coming back from the dead at a most inconvenient time, Dorsey was tempted to add. Instead she said, "I'm sure this has been incredibly distressing for all of you."

"You have no idea, Agent Collins," Aubrey addressed Dorsey directly for the first time.

"Do either of you remember if Shannon had been upset or depressed in the days before she disappeared?" Andrew signaled Dorsey that the time for his interrogation had come.

"Not that I noticed, no." Aubrey continued to dab at her eyes with the tissue she'd pulled from a pocket in her skirt. "If she was, she hid it well. And she was sort of private about things, you know? She wouldn't have said anything. She was big on writing in her diary, but she wasn't much for talking about things."

"Any idea where that diary is now?" he asked.

"No. I don't remember ever seeing it after . . . well, after Shannon was no longer with us," Aubrey told them.

"Natalie, had Shannon confided in you about any problems she might have had?" Andrew turned his attention to the senator.

"I was away at college that year and didn't get home much. I'm afraid I wasn't there for her, if she needed me," Natalie said solemnly. She turned to Andrew and asked, "There's obviously something going on here that we're not being told. You've been here what, three days, and yet you're still here asking questions. Why?"

Before Andrew could answer, Aubrey asked, "What do you think happened back then, Agent Shields?"

"Our investigation has concluded that Shannon had not been kidnapped but ran away on her own accord."

"What?" Aubrey gasped.

"That's preposterous." Natalie's face went stony, much as her mother's and grandmother's had. "Why, even your own FBI man back then believed Eric had killed her."

"For the past six years or so, Shannon was living with a roommate in Deptford," Andrew told them. "She told the roommate she'd been traveling around the South on her own for years. There's no question she hadn't been kidnapped, she'd told her roommate she was a runaway. The question is, what was she running from?"

"Were either of you aware that your sister was a cutter?" Dorsey asked.

"A what?" Aubrey frowned.

Dorsey explained.

"No, of course not." Aubrey shook her head. "That's the sickest thing I ever heard. Shannon was not crazy. She never would have done something like that."

"Girls who cut aren't crazy," Dorsey said. "They're

in pain, and they're trying to find a way to make the pain go away."

"So they inflict more pain on themselves?" Aubrey snorted. "That makes a lot of sense."

"It does to those who cut," Dorsey said softly.

"The point," Andrew said, breaking in, "is that girls who exhibit this behavior are suffering, most likely from some sort of abuse or trauma."

"You're suggesting that Shannon was being abused." Aubrey's emotion was gone in a snap, replaced with a cool composure. "That she ran away because she was being abused."

"I'm suggesting that something happened to her that made her run away. That same something may have been the reason she turned to self-mutilation," Andrew told her.

"How do you know that my sister engaged in this . . . cutting herself thing." There was no trace of Aubrey's earlier warmth.

"We saw the scars on her arms. And her shoulders, and her legs," he told her. "They couldn't have been caused by anything else. We've established the behavior. We're trying to find out what trauma caused it."

"The trauma of being kidnapped and forced into prostitution would have done it," Aubrey snapped.

"Aubrey, I think Agent Shields has established that was not the case," Natalie said calmly. "Shannon ran away—and stayed away—for a reason."

The sisters exchanged a look that was difficult to read.

"Aubrey, Natalie, I have to ask," Andrew addressed

both sisters, causing them to look at him instead of each other. "What are the chances your father was abusing Shannon?"

"Ridiculous," Aubrey snapped. "How dare you!"

"Most often the abuser is someone close to the victim," Andrew explained. "Usually a family member, or a trusted family friend."

"Daddy never would have laid a hand on any of us that way," Natalie told them.

"Can you think of anyone close to the family who could have?"

"No," Aubrey said curtly. "No."

"I guess we'll have to ask your father if he has any thoughts on that," Andrew added.

"Please, don't." Natalie touched his arm. "He's been through so much these past few years. I'm sure my mother told you that he's never forgiven himself for what happened with Shannon, that he wasn't able to find her, to save her. If you accuse him of something like this"—Natalie's eyes filled—"if he thought for one minute that anyone would suspect him of doing such a thing, it would just about kill him."

"But surely if he understands that someone was hurting her, he'll want to help us to figure out who it was, don't you think?" Andrew glanced from one sister to the other. He could not gauge what either of them was thinking.

"Of course he would," Natalie said crisply. "We all would."

"By the way, we believe that at some point over the years, Shannon might have tried to get in touch with someone in the family. Did either of you notice a lot of hang-ups coming to your parents' home, for example? More than what might be considered normal."

"Everyone gets hang-up calls," Natalie replied. "I don't think we had more than our share."

"No," Aubrey agreed. "No more than most people have, I suppose."

"About the funeral services for your sister," Dorsey said as if it had just occurred to her. "When will they be held?"

The sisters looked as if they each expected the other to answer.

Finally, Natalie said, "I believe Paula Rose is in charge of the funeral arrangements."

Andrew gave them each a business card. "Call me if you remember anything you think might be important. We'll be around for a few more days."

"Ladies, thanks for your time." Dorsey made brief eye contact with the women, then she and Andrew walked back across the drive to the car, leaving the two sisters standing still as statues next to the pasture fence.

"They know," Dorsey said when they got back into the car. "They know who abused Shannon back then."

"You still think it's Dad?"

"I think he's the most logical suspect. But neither hesitated for a second to deny it."

"Let's stop off at the Randalls' on our way back to the motel. Let's see how he reacts when we start giving him our version of what happened that night back in 1983."

"I think this time, you should call. I don't think Mrs. Randall is going to be happy to see us show up twice uninvited."

"Good point." Andrew slipped the phone from his pocket. "Do you have the number?"

She took the phone from his hand and reached into her purse for the small notebook she'd been keeping phone numbers in. "You drive, I'll dial."

She entered the number on the keypad and hit send, listened for the phone to ring, then passed it over to Andrew. His conversation with Mrs. Randall was short and not so sweet.

"Reverend Randall is resting under doctor's orders right now and is not to be disturbed," Andrew said once he hung up. "Mrs. Randall will be sure to let him know I called as soon as he awakens."

"I say we go over anyway."

"I say you're right."

"Know what I thought was odd?" Dorsey said after a moment. "That neither Natalie nor Aubrey expressed any concern that Eric Beale was executed."

"What's that tell you?"

"Maybe they're more worried about something else right now."

Andrew drove slowly down the long winding allee.

"Shit," he said when they reached the first bend.

Dorsey craned her neck to look ahead. At the end of the drive, a state police car blocked access to the house. News vans and cars lined both sides of the road beyond the barricade. A trooper walked up the drive toward them, and Andrew stopped and rolled down his window.

"Identification, sir?" he asked.

"Special Agent Andrew Shields, Special Agent Dorsey Collins," he said as he pulled out his badge and Dorsey handed over hers. The trooper looked them over and returned them promptly.

"I'll clear the way for you," he told Andrew. "You're going to have to be careful. We haven't allowed anyone out of their cars—they'd be trespassing, and we've already made it clear we'd arrest anyone caught trespassing—but I don't know how they're gonna react when they see someone leaving. You're likely to be followed, sir."

"I can deal with that."

"In that case, sir, have a good night." The trooper walked away, and motioned for the car blocking the entrance to move.

Andrew slipped past the patrol car and onto the road. Several cars that had been parked began to follow him. He removed his phone from his pocket and used the speed-dial.

"John, I'm afraid we're beginning to draw a crowd. . . ."

14

The waves licked against the side of the boat, rocking it gently in the wake of a passing cruiser. Matt Ranieri sat on one of the deck chairs and stared out at the setting sun. The bay was quiet tonight, the silence broken by the engine of the occasional boat or a fish breaking the water's plane. Overhead a heron glided toward its rookery, across the bay a family of swans sought their own shelter.

"Matt, can I bring you a beer?" the boat's owner and skipper called from the cabin. "Wine? More coffee?"

"Nothing, thanks. I'm fine," he called back.

Moments later she appeared on deck, a glass of wine in one hand and an unlit candle in the other.

"I thought a little soft light might be nice." She placed the candle on the small table. "It's supposed to have something in it to keep the mosquitoes away." She smiled. "One could hope."

She took a seat in the chair opposite Matt's and pretended to watch the emerging stars. She was petite and blond—her natural color required more help these days to stay that way, but she didn't seem to mind—and athletically built. She'd played tennis and field hockey back in school, had excelled at archery and water-skiing, and knew her way around the Chesapeake and the rivers that fed into it like an old bayman. She was tanned even this early in the season, was a gourmet cook, and had been widowed almost as long as Matt had been a widower. She was totally head over heels about Matt and made no bones about it.

She knew he'd been dating someone named Anna on and off for several years but, as she told Matt, if Anna couldn't hold his interest, it was her own damned fault. Diane Coleman was in her late fifties, old enough, she told Matt, to make a stand when she wanted something. At this stage of her life, she wanted Matt. Her candor both amused and flattered him, and he'd found himself seeking out her company more and more. Lately, he'd been thinking about making the relationship permanent.

"So." She crossed her legs and sipped her wine. "Have you solved your puzzle?"

"I think so." He nodded slowly. That he'd told her about the case had surprised him, that he'd actually discussed it with her surprised him even more. "I think I know what went wrong back then. And I know what I have to do."

"Good." She smiled and took another sip. "Where will you start?"

"I already did," he told her.

"That phone call earlier?"

"Yes."

"Then you'll be wanting to head back to shore."

"In the morning, yes."

"Have you called your daughter?"

"Not yet."

"Matt, you know she's worried about you."

"You're right." He took his phone from his pocket and speed-dialed her number.

"I can go below if you want privacy," Diane offered, though she made no move to leave.

"It's not necessary." He listened for another few seconds. "She's not picking up."

"Just leave her a message. Let her know you're okay, let her know what you're going to do."

"Hey, honey. Sorry I missed you. I'm with a friend on her boat, just needed a little time to think things through, hoping to find some answers before the shit hits the fan." He tried to make a joke, but even to his ears, the joke fell flat. "Anyway, I just didn't want you to worry. I'll be in touch." He paused for a moment, then added, "Love you, Dorse."

He closed the phone and slid it back into his shirt pocket.

"You didn't tell her what you were going to do," Diane said pointedly.

"No. I did not." He started to repack his notebooks and files into the box that sat on the floor near his feet. "I don't want her to worry."

"Should I be worried?"

"You're a big girl."

"So's your daughter. She's been in the FBI for . . . how many years? Twelve? She's hardly a babe in the woods, Matt," she reminded him.

"Did you drop anchor here for the night?" He changed the subject without further comment.

Diane sighed. She got the point. He didn't want to discuss his next move with his daughter. Diane wouldn't push. She'd speak her mind, but she wouldn't push.

"No. I thought we'd go back to that cove up near the Sassafras again tonight."

"Sounds good to me." He stood and lifted the box. "I'll take these down below, then come back up and give you a hand."

"No need." She drained her glass and sat it on the table. "I've been pulling up anchors by myself for years."

He glanced back over his shoulder and wondered if the double meaning had been intentional or if he was just reading something into her comment that wasn't there. He knew Diane had been on her own for a long time, just as he had been. And, she'd just reminded him, as his daughter had been. He wondered what Dorsey would think of this woman, what she'd say if he told her he was thinking of marrying Diane. He'd never even mentioned Diane's name to her, and now he couldn't remember why.

Just one more thing he hadn't told Dorsey. He just hoped that he'd get the chance, and that his next move wouldn't be his last.

15

Andrew snapped on the light in his motel room as he came through the door. Outside it was still sunny late afternoon. Inside, with the drapes covering the windows, it was midnight.

He'd really wanted to push for some time with Franklin Randall, but John suggested he back off for tonight after Andrew filled him in on the interviews with the Randall sisters and Jeff Feeney. John also reminded Andrew that with the press beginning to sniff around, he needed to make sure Dorsey kept a very low profile.

"Especially now," John had said.

"Why especially now?" Andrew had asked, but the question had not been answered.

"Just tell her to keep her head down for a little while longer."

Andrew knew better than to push. If John wanted to say more, he would.

"What do you want me to do about the reporters?"

"Talk to them. Sooner, rather than later. Keep everyone under control. Say as little as possible at this point, but make sure everything you say is true. Don't say anything you'll need to apologize for later. God knows we're going to be doing enough backpedaling on this case as it is."

"You think maybe you should send someone down to handle this? Maybe someone from PR?"

"No, you'll be fine," John assured him. "Besides, there's no one who knows what's going on better than you. I don't want anyone thinking we're spinning this. It is what it is."

"I'll type up my reports later tonight and e-mail them in the morning." Andrew pushed aside one edge of the drapes and peered out through the window. The news vans that had followed him were parked in the lot where their drivers would have clear view of his door. Shit.

This was the last thing he needed.

"Listen, John, about Eric Beale's family . . ."

"It's covered, Andrew."

"Something was going on between this Jeff Feeney character and both the brothers. We're going to need to talk to someone in the family, and soon. Preferably Tim Beale, though if we could track down the mother—"

"Not yet."

Andrew frowned. It wasn't like John to be evasive when it came to a case one of his agents was working on.

"When, then?"

"I'll let you know. For now, just let me handle them from this end."

"All right," Andrew said slowly. He was feeling sandbagged and he didn't like it. No point in mentioning it, though. John obviously had an agenda he wasn't in the mood to discuss.

"How's Agent Collins doing?" John changed the subject.

"Fine. Good."

"Think she'd fit in with the rest of the unit?"

"You thinking about bringing her on?" Andrew watched as one of the cameramen got out of his van and began to chat with a reporter from another station.

"She's expressed an interest, and everything I'm hearing about her is good."

"Yeah. She's good, John. Real good. She'd fit in just fine."

"Then I'll have a talk with her when this is all over, see what we can work out. For the time being, just keep her out of the public eye. Any idea how much longer before you'll be able to wrap this up?"

"A few more days, at least. We have a picture emerging but it isn't clear yet." Andrew filled John in on the theories he and Dorsey had tossed around. "It's like a big puzzle, and we're still missing a lot of the pieces."

"Sometimes too many possibilities can be worse than too few," John said, "and I'm referring to the old case as well as the new. That many possible motives, you can make yourself crazy trying to figure it out. Of course, there's an upside to that, too."

"What's that?"

"When you get that many people involved, sooner or later someone is bound to step out from the crowd

on their own. It doesn't sound as if any of these people are professional criminals," John told him. "Sooner
or later, someone's guilt is going to get the best of
him. Or her."

"I can only hope." Andrew let the curtain fall back.
"So you'll get back to me on the Beales?"

"Soon as I have something to tell you," John assured him. "Good luck with the press. Gotta run."

Andrew disconnected the call and dropped the
phone on the bed wishing he'd pushed John a little
more about the Beale family. But he knew better.
When John had something to say, he said it. If he was
keeping something to himself, he had a reason and he
wouldn't be sharing that until he was ready.

He hung his jacket over the back of the chair and
debated whether to order a pizza or take a shower. If
he called for pizza, chances were there'd be a reporter
in his face when he opened the door. For a moment he
wished they were still staying at the inn. At least they
had room service and the rooms were nicer. This
motel room was anonymous, too much like every
other motel room he'd ever been in. It made him feel
displaced, and he'd had plenty of that over the past
year. Now he realized he'd traveled so much just to
keep himself moving, to keep from thinking too deeply
about too many things. For a while, it had worked.

Maybe shower first, he thought, then slip out when
it was dark. Maybe Dorsey could meet him somewhere. He'd really been enjoying her company these
past few days. She was smart. Had a good sense of
humor. Took the job seriously. Not to mention the

fact that the woman had some depth, and that put her head and shoulders above a lot of the women he'd known. She seemed to have it all. Including, he suspected, scars on her wrists and who knew where else.

His cell phone rang and he thought—hoped—it might be her.

"Agent Shields, this is Chief Bowden."

"Hey, Chief, how are—"

"I'm over here at the Randall place, and they got a truckload of reporters out there." Bowden had no time for pleasantries. "Miz Randall, she's awfully upset about the whole thing, didn't know what she should do, so she called me. I personally don't mind going on out there and talking to those folks, but frankly, I don't have a damned thing to say to them. I don't know where y'all are going with this thing. Now, Miz Randall did call the daughters, but they don't want to speak with the press either right now, so I'm asking you to come on over here and do the talking. I just don't know what to say."

"You're right not to say anything, except maybe that the FBI is handling the investigation, Chief. Thanks for the heads-up," Andrew said. "I'll be there as soon as I can."

" 'Preciate it if you'd hurry."

"Ten minutes, tops," Andrew promised. "Oh, Chief? You can tell Mrs. Randall that I'll be wanting to speak with her husband after the press conference. I'd appreciate you setting that up for me."

"Do what I can," the chief replied. "He's not in a good way right now, from what I understand."

So much for a shower and time to type up some reports for John, Andrew thought as he grabbed his jacket from the chair. He knew he looked a little shopworn, but there wasn't much he could do about that. He wasn't as adept at speaking to the media as some others in the unit were, and he'd assumed that John would send in someone from the Bureau who was proven at handling the PR aspects of the job since this was such a big case. But John had declined that as quickly as he'd declined to discuss the Beales. Andrew would have only the ten-minute drive from the motel to the Randalls' to figure out what he wanted to say and the best way to say it. He just hoped the network hadn't picked up the story.

The last thing he wanted was to face any of the reporters who'd covered the story about Brendan. They'd be compelled to ask about that situation, and Andrew wasn't ready to talk about it in public. Hell, he could count on one hand the number of times he'd spoken about it in private. Once or twice with his sister, Mia, and once with Dorsey, and that had barely skimmed the surface. He still wasn't able to face his cousins Connor and Aidan. The tragedy had left a hole inside him big enough for a small child to walk through.

He knew he should call Dorsey, but decided to do that from the car. He grabbed his phone and headed outside, where he was promptly approached by several reporters.

"I'm on my way to the Randalls' home." He held up both hands as if warding off their questions. "If you'd like to meet me there, you'll hear everything I have to say on the matter."

Ignoring their protests, Andrew got into his car and locked the doors. He dialed Dorsey's number, knowing she wasn't going to like what he was going to say.

"Hey," he said when she answered, her voice sounding somewhat groggy. "Did I wake you?"

"Yeah. But it's okay." She yawned quietly. "Sorry. You thinking about trying to sneak out past the gathering crowd for a bite?"

"Too late for that," he told her. "Listen, I got a call from Chief Bowden. He's asked me to come to the Randalls' to deal with the press."

"You're going now?" Suddenly she was wide awake. "You're on your way?"

"Yes. Look, I'm sorry, but you know we have to keep any involvement on your part from becoming public knowledge."

"It's your case," she said somewhat stiffly.

"That's not what this is about. No one wants a camera picking up your face so that everyone in the Bureau knows you're here. I wouldn't leave you out if I didn't have to." He paused. "I hope you know that."

"Will you give me a call when you get back?"

"Of course. But you know I wouldn't do this if I didn't have to, right?" He wanted to hear her say it. For some reason, it was important to him to know that she didn't think he was deliberately cutting her out.

"I do." She sighed. "Yeah, I understand. You did the right thing. And it's not your fault."

"It's no one's fault, Dorsey. It's just what is right now. But as soon as I get back, I'll fill you in on whatever I can drag out of Franklin."

"You're going to talk to Franklin?"

"I'm thinking a little quid pro quo here. I'll handle the press for them, but only if Franklin agrees to talk to me after."

"Why not make it before? What if he weasels out?"

"I'm not going to let him do that. They're going to understand up front that he talks to me, or I don't talk to the press for them. Which means either they talk—which you and I both know, no one in that family wants to do—or they'll have reporters camped on their front lawn until they do."

"So I guess I should tune in the eleven o'clock news to get the official version."

"I'm hoping to be back before then," he told her. "I promise to fill you in on everything."

"Anything I can do?"

"Well, you could sneak out and pick up pizza and some beer after the news vans leave."

"I'd be glad to, but by the time you get back here, the beer will be warm and the pizza will be cold."

"Hey, anyone who can't deal with cold pizza has no place in law enforcement."

"I trust the same cannot be said for warm beer."

"Good point. Beer's always better at the proper temperature."

"I'll see what I can do."

"I'm here." His eyes scanned both sides of the

street for a parking spot on Sylvan. "I'll call you when I'm on my way back."

"Good luck. With the press and with Franklin," Dorsey said as she hung up.

Andrew found a spot at the end of the block and parked the rental car. He walked toward the house, thinking about what he'd say once the microphones were turned on and the cameras began to roll. And he thought about what he wanted to ask Franklin about his relationship with Shannon. Dealing with reporters was going to be far easier than accusing a man of molesting his own daughter.

He was halfway up the Randalls' driveway before anyone noticed him. He quietly made his way to the front porch, where the door opened before he had time to knock.

"Agent Shields, we are so grateful that you agreed to come over here and deal with those people for us," Judith Randall said immediately. "I apologize for having cut you off so rudely the other day."

"Perfectly understandable, Mrs. Randall," Andrew told her as she closed the door behind him. "You've been under enormous strain."

"I appreciate your kindness." She led him into the living room where Chief Bowden sat talking quietly with Franklin.

"Agent Shields, I'm real happy to see you." The chief stood but seemed not to know what to do next. "You saw the crowd outside. . . ."

"I did, and I'll be out to talk to them in a moment. Would you mind going out and letting them know I'll have a statement for them? I just need a moment with the Randalls."

"Be glad to." The chief excused himself.

Once the door had closed behind Bowden, Andrew turned to Franklin. "I'm willing to give you a hand with this, but first, I want your agreement to meet with me as soon as I finish up outside."

"Agent Shields, my husband is not well," Judith protested. "The doctor said he should not be agitated. Perhaps tomorrow—"

"Tonight," Andrew told her, though he continued to look at her husband. "Or I leave now, and you can face whatever questions the media wants to ask by yourselves."

"Oh, for crying out loud," Franklin spoke for the first time since Andrew had entered the house. "Go tell them whatever it takes to make them go away, and I'll give you as much time as you need. Just make them go away."

"I have your word?" Andrew asked.

"Of course you have my word. I just said so, didn't I?" Franklin shot back.

Andrew opened the door and joined Bowden on the porch. The chief stood with his hands on his hips, looking over the crowd that had grown since he'd arrived several hours earlier. Where there had been only reporters, now neighbors of the Randalls' stood on the sidewalk and the curb, speaking softly among themselves. Their collective murmur created a low-pitched hum.

"I got you some microphones set up here." Bowden pointed to the end of the porch where several mics stood waiting for him.

"Thanks." Andrew walked to the stand of mics as the cameras were turned on. Some of the reporters weren't quite sure who he was, but he looked as if he was about to speak, and after several hours of waiting, that by itself made him worthy of their attention.

"I'm Special Agent Andrew Shields, FBI. I'll answer whatever questions I can, but in return, once we're finished here, you'll leave, and let the Randall family have some peace. Anyone who has a problem with that can leave now or face being arrested by Chief Bowden once we're done."

He paused and looked at the crowd, which had grown silent.

"Okay, then. I know there are a lot of rumors going around right now, so let me set the record straight." Andrew cleared his throat as lights flashed on from different parts of the front yard. "Twenty-four years ago, Shannon Randall disappeared and was presumed dead. Though a body was never found, a young man from Hatton, Eric Beale, was arrested and convicted of first-degree murder on circumstantial evidence." He paused for effect, then added, "Strong circumstantial evidence, but circumstantial all the same. Eight years after his conviction, Eric Beale was executed."

He glanced around the crowd. It was easy to spot the neighbors amid the reporters. The neighbors stood stock still, as if waiting for a bomb to drop. The reporters were taking down every word.

"Today, in June 2007, we've learned that everything we thought back then was wrong. Shannon Randall did not die in 1983." There was a soft gasp from one of the neighbors at the back of the crowd. "Eric Beale was telling the truth when he said he was innocent. The Hatton Police Department and the FBI both deeply regret the errors that were made that resulted in Eric Beale's execution. Any time an innocent person pays the ultimate price for a crime he did not commit, we all are diminished by justice not having been served." Andrew paused for a moment before continuing.

"Several days ago in Georgia, the body of a young woman was positively identified as that of Shannon Randall." This time there was more than one gasp. Andrew waited until the first wave of buzzing started to subside. "She was killed by a person or persons unknown. Our information is very sketchy at this time, so I'm asking that you be patient with us while we unravel this mystery. We'll tell you what we know when we know something definitive. Right now, all we know for certain is that the body is that of Shannon Randall. I'll take a few questions. . . ." He pointed to the reporter nearest the porch.

"What happened to Shannon Randall in 1983? Did she run away? Was she abducted?"

"We believe she was a runaway, but we have no other information at this time." Andrew cut her off and turned to the left side of the yard. "Next question."

"Where has she been all these years?"

"We have reason to believe she lived in several different cities throughout the south. Next."

"Any idea who killed her?"

"No. That's what 'person or persons unknown' means. Next question."

"How was she killed?"

"She was shot." No need to add *and stabbed,* Andrew decided, since it was the gunshot that killed her.

"About the family of the executed man—"

"They're meeting with someone from the Bureau." Andrew hoped that was true. "I'm not involved in that aspect of the case, so I can't answer any questions pertaining to Eric Beale's family. Next?"

"Was Shannon Randall involved in prostitution? Can you comment on that, Agent Shields?"

Andrew hesitated. John had told him not to utter any words he'd have to eat later. At the same time, he didn't want to feed the fires of lurid speculation, either.

"Whatever Shannon did or did not do in the time she's been away from her family is not at issue here. Right now, we have a family who is dealing with the death of their child, grandchild, sister—for the *second* time. They're also dealing with a lot of unanswered questions, and I'm going to ask you to respect their privacy. This is a very difficult time for this family. Please allow them to grieve in peace, to bury her in peace. Try to put yourself in their place and respect what they're going through right now."

"The FBI was part of the investigation in 1983," someone toward the back called out. "Is that why you're here now? To do damage control for the Bureau?"

"I'm here to help find out what happened back then that caused a lot of people to believe that an innocent man was guilty. And I'm here to make sure that whoever is responsible for Shannon's death is apprehended and punished."

"This is a big case," the reporter added. "How many other agents are involved in this investigation?"

Andrew hesitated briefly before answering as truthfully as he could. "For the time being, I'm the only agent assigned."

"What about Agent Collins?" Chief Bowden asked from the side of the porch.

Andrew turned to him hoping that his response would not be picked up by the microphones. "Agent Collins isn't officially assigned."

Chief Bowden looked at him blankly.

"How does Senator Randall-Scott feel about her sister being a hooker?"

"I'm not going to comment on that." Even as he spoke, he knew this same crew would be camped out in front of Natalie Randall-Scott's home within the hour.

"Thanks for your time, everyone. As soon as we know anything else, we'll be sure to let you all know." Andrew cut the conference short. The pertinent information had been given. He wasn't going to feed into speculation.

Ignoring the protests and the rush of questions that followed his announcement, Andrew stepped back inside the house, then looked behind him. Chief Bowden was leaning over the porch rail, talking to a reporter. Andrew walked over in time to hear the chief say, "Dorsey Collins, I'm pretty sure her name is . . . yes, she's definitely with the FBI. Maybe she got called out to work another case, maybe that's what he meant. Maybe he's waiting for someone to replace her—"

"Chief," he said pointedly from the doorway.

"I'll be right there."

Andrew took a deep breath and closed the door behind him. Hopefully the reporter Bowden was talking to wouldn't make anything of his remarks. He had briefly thought of asking Bowden not to mention Dorsey's name, but decided that would make her presence there seem more mysterious than he wanted it to be. Besides, what were the odds someone would have asked?

Apparently better than he'd suspected.

"Thank you, Agent Shields, for handling everything so delicately." Judith met him in the hallway, tissues clenched in each hand. "For your sensitivity. We still don't know what to think, what to believe, about Shannon. And the speculation is just going to be more than I can bear. . . ."

Andrew patted her gently on the shoulder. "We'll do everything we can to find the truth, Mrs. Randall, and to make certain you and your family hear it before anyone else does."

"We appreciate that." She dabbed at her eyes.

"Now, where might I find your husband?" Andrew asked.

"He's back in his office, waiting for you," she said. "The first door on the right."

"Thank you." Andrew started down the hall just as the police chief came back through the door.

"Agent Shields, about Agent Collins—" Bowden called to him.

"She's not officially on the case," Andrew told him truthfully.

"Could have fooled me."

"She's here as a special observer only. But that information doesn't need to be shared."

Andrew debated whether to offer more of an explanation, then decided against it. Maybe later. Right now, he wanted to get on with his questioning of Franklin while the man was still willing.

"Are the reporters leaving?" Andrew asked.

"Some have, some are taking their time," Bowden told him. "I'll keep an eye on them."

"What if they come back and start asking more questions?" Judith said. "Agent Shields said you'd arrest anyone who didn't leave. . . ."

"And I will, Miz Randall. But let's give 'em a few more minutes to pack up their cameras and get themselves moving. Nobody's answering any more questions until Agent Shields is ready to call another conference, so just don't you worry about that."

Andrew started off for his meeting with Randall, wishing Bowden had thought of that before he'd started answering the inquiry about Dorsey. He was hoping that cat wasn't too far out of the bag.

At the first door on the right, he stopped and knocked lightly on the half-closed door.

"Come in, Agent Shields. And close it behind you."

Franklin Randall sat behind his desk in his wheel-chair. He pointed to a dark green leather club chair and said, "Sit there."

Andrew did as Randall requested.

"Thank you for what you said out there. They all gone yet?"

"Chief Bowden is keeping an eye on the stragglers. He's making sure the last of them leave."

"What is it you wanted to know that you didn't already learn from my wife, my mother, or my daughters?" Franklin said, cutting to the chase.

"I want to know what Shannon was running away from twenty-four years ago, Mr. Randall." Andrew could be just as blunt. "You have any thoughts on that?"

"No one's convinced me yet that my daughter ran away. Could have been she was forced."

"The evidence doesn't support that."

"But twenty-four years ago the evidence supported that she'd been murdered by that Beale kid." Franklin snorted derisively. "Enough evidence then to support a guilty verdict and a death penalty."

"Right now, I can't explain how that conclusion was reached, though I do have some theories. But if you look at the facts—"

"Well, which facts are the FBI looking at this time?"

"The facts Shannon gave her roommate, Mr. Randall."

"Shannon told this girl she ran away to become a whore?"

"She told her roommate she ran away, yes."

"And this girl, she's a whore, too?"

"She's been working as a prostitute, yes, but—"

Franklin waved his hand at Andrew as if dismissing him.

"Can't believe anything she says, then."

"Mr. Randall, stop playing this game with me," Andrew said calmly. "We both know Shannon ran away and I think we both know why she left and why she never came back."

"What are you talking about?" Franklin snapped.

"I'm talking about the fact that someone had been sexually abusing your daughter. She ran away to escape further abuse."

Franklin's jaw all but dropped onto his chest.

"*What*? That's the craziest thing I've ever heard." His face went from pale to scarlet in a heartbeat. "Who would have done such a disgusting thing?"

"I was hoping you'd tell me," Andrew replied levelly.

Franklin stared at Andrew for a very long moment before his eyes widened.

"You are not suggesting . . . you couldn't possibly think that I . . ."

"Most abusers are members of the family, or someone well known to the family." Andrew spoke firmly, calmly.

"No. No. The very thought of it"—Franklin shook his head—"No. No one would have . . . no." He covered his mouth with a badly shaking hand. "God, no . . . not my little girl . . . no."

"Mr. Randall, we're fairly certain someone was abusing Shannon," Andrew repeated. "If it wasn't you, odds are it was someone close. Was there a family friend who maybe spent a lot of time with your family back then, who would have had access to your daughter?"

"No, no." Franklin's arrogance was gone. In its place was a pain that Andrew could almost feel reaching out to him from across the desk. "There was no one. We did everything as a family back then; I don't think any of us were hardly ever alone. And being so busy at the church—I spent every day there. We were an active church, you understand. There was something going on there every day." Franklin's voice grew quiet as he seemed to look back in time. "There was hardly a day when I wasn't there from morning through evening, working side by side with my father. That was his church, he started it in a small place over on Sunset. Built the new church back in 1980, mostly with donations from his congregation."

"You served as assistant pastor?"

"I did. I assisted my father in every way I could. He was starting to slow down back then, you see. It was his dream—and mine—that I gradually take over for him. The plan was that someday, we'd reverse roles, and I'd be taking the lead and he'd be assisting me." He appeared totally defeated now. "That wasn't to be for long, as you can see."

"Surely you could have continued to preach . . . ?"

"I was in therapy for a very long time after my accident, Agent Shields. The church needed someone who could fully minister to the congregation. Thank God my Paula Rose was ready and able to step in and serve."

"Did your father spend a lot of time in the company of your daughter, Mr. Randall?" Andrew asked pointedly.

"Of course he did. Shannon helped out in the office."

"Alone?"

"Well, certainly, she sometimes—" He stopped in midsentence as Andrew's meaning became clear. His eyes narrowed and he gripped the arms of his chair with knuckles that had gone white. "My father was a man of God, Agent Shields. I won't have you maligning his name. He no more would have done such a thing than I would have."

"Are you willing to take a lie detector test, Mr. Randall?" Andrew asked coolly.

"Get out of my house," Franklin said darkly. "Get. Out. Of. My. *House.*"

"I'll be asking formally for the test." Andrew stood. "In the meantime, if you think of anyone else I should talk to, you have my card."

Andrew turned and left the room, and the magazine Franklin flung after him hit the doorjamb and flopped to the floor.

16

"Agent Shields." Judith stood near the front door, gazing out, watching as the last of the reporters packed up and left.

"Excuse me, ma'am." Andrew attempted to walk around her to get to the door, but she placed one hand on his arm to detain him. He held his breath. If she'd heard any of the conversation he'd just had with Franklin, she'd be unloading on him all over again.

"I was thinking about what you said when you were here last time. Wondering if maybe Shannon had tried to contact us and we didn't realize it." She swallowed hard and looked up at him. "I snapped at you, threw you out of my house."

"It's all right, Mrs. Randall. I understand that you've been through a lot—" He opened the door to leave.

"I'm thinking maybe I reacted a little too hastily. Should have thought that through some before I jumped all over you." She followed him out onto the porch, still holding on. "I'm thinking now maybe . . . at least, I've been wondering if maybe . . ."

"Maybe?" He paused at the steps. Apparently she

hadn't overheard his conversation with her husband after all.

"Maybe she did try, and we just didn't know." Another hard swallow. "There were hang-up calls, but you know, everyone gets those. Wrong numbers and such. But there were times when it seemed that whoever was on the other end stayed on for longer than you'd expect for a wrong number. Well, I always figured those for kids playing a prank, you know how they do? I'm wondering now if . . . do you think that maybe . . ."

"I think it's possible, in retrospect. I think if you were my mother and I was far from home, I'd reach out to you," he said as he patted the hand that gripped his arm.

"There was something else, I'm wondering now if maybe it should have made me think a little. Maybe I should have given more thought to it at the time."

"What was that?"

"For a while there, envelopes came to the house that had just a tiny something in it, if anything at all."

"What kind of things?"

"One time it was a little white clover flower." Her eyes welled with tears. "Most times it was nothing at all."

"Do you remember where they were postmarked?"

"The one with the little flower was from Nashville. I remember that one because I always wanted to go there, never did. Didn't know anyone there, either." She forced a half-smile. "I always used to say that in my next life, I was going to come back as a country-western singer. That I was going to sing at the Grand Ole Opry."

"Do you remember where the others were from?"

"Not really. Just places." She was crying now, tears spilling onto her face. "There was a postcard from Memphis once. It came on my birthday, about eight years ago. It had a picture of Graceland on the front. The girls used to tease me because I'd told them I was a big Elvis fan back when I was just a girl."

"Did you recognize the handwriting?"

"No. It wasn't Shannon's, if that's what you mean. I would have recognized that. I would have known."

"When did you receive the last envelope?"

"Oh, it's been some time now." She gazed upward as if searching for the answer. "Maybe four years or so."

"And the phone calls? Do you remember the last time someone called and hung up?"

"Oh, it seems we always get those, but maybe just a few months back there was one like the others. Like someone was there and didn't want to hang up but they wouldn't speak." She shook her head. "Wouldn't that have been something, if that had been Shannon?"

"Mrs. Randall . . . the empty envelopes. Who did you think they were from?" Andrew couldn't help but ask.

"I don't know. I didn't think much about them at all. I just figured someone had sent us something and it had fallen out because it wasn't sealed in the back.

The flaps were tucked inside the envelope, not sealed."

"How often did these envelopes arrive?"

"Oh, every few years or so. Not frequent enough that it would make me think about it so much." She took a tissue from her pocket and dabbed at her face. "Though that clover . . . that did make me wonder some. It never occurred to me that it could have been from her, that she could still be alive. But it should have made me think just a little."

It was the second time she'd used that phrase.

"Think about what?"

"Shannon always made those little clover chains, you know? She used to fashion them in a big circle and I'd have to wear it on my head." Judith was openly weeping. "She used to say I was the clover queen, and she was my princess. . . ."

Andrew took a step toward her, to comfort her, when Franklin appeared in the doorway.

"I told you to leave! Get the hell away from my wife. Get off my property!" He banged furiously at the closed screen door. "Judith, get in this house immediately! Do not speak to that man!"

"Franklin, what on earth . . ." Judith turned to her husband.

"Thank you, Mrs. Randall, for sharing your recollections with me," Andrew said quietly.

"You stay away from my wife, stay away from my family!" Franklin rolled his chair out onto the porch and wheeled past his stunned wife. "You hear me? Bastard!"

*   *   *

With Franklin Randall's curses following him all the way to the end of the block, Andrew was more than happy to reach his car and escape the harsh aftermath of his interview with the man. He turned the key in the ignition and pulled away from the curb. He could have sworn he could still hear Franklin yelling.

He turned on the radio to drown out the voice ringing in his ears, but it didn't help, so he snapped it off. Suddenly, he felt very tired, and wished he was home. Or if not home, then someplace, anyplace, where kids weren't abused by people who were supposed to love and protect them, where kids didn't cut themselves, didn't prostitute themselves, didn't give up bright futures in attempts to bury their horrible pasts.

He drove through quiet Hatton, his stomach rumbling. He called Dorsey to let her know he was on his way back and was grateful to learn she had in fact saved him some pizza. He parked his car in a space between her room and his and ignored the reporters who'd returned to the motel in hopes of getting some extra tidbit from him. He walked toward her room, prepared to knock, but when he raised his hand to the door, she opened it while keeping out of sight.

"Sorry," she said as she closed the door behind him. "Nothing personal, but I figured the last thing you needed right now was speculation on who the redhead in the motel might be."

He laughed ruefully and took off his jacket. "I have a feeling they might already know."

"What do you mean?" Dorsey stood with her hands on her hips.

"I mean you've been outed." He hung the jacket on the back of the room's lone chair. "Please tell me you have beer."

"In the bathtub." She nodded in the direction of the bathroom. "What do you mean, 'outed'?"

"One of the reporters asked how many agents had been assigned to the case and I told him one." Andrew disappeared into the bathroom. "Oh, wow. You know, you just might be the perfect woman."

He came back out with a dripping wet bottle of beer in his hands. "Ice in the bathtub. Brilliant."

"Thanks. It's going to make for a damn cold shower later, but hey, at least the beer isn't warm." She directed him to the desk. "The pizza might still be, though. I wrapped it in a blanket."

"You really are brilliant, did I already say that?" He sat wearily at the desk and opened the lid of the pizza box. "I'm so hungry right now I could eat the box."

"The pizza tastes better. Go on and eat." Dorsey sat crossed-legged on the end of the bed. "Finish the part about me being outed."

"I said, one agent had been assigned. Me. And Chief Bowden said, 'Oh, but what about Agent Collins?' "

"And you said?"

"I said," Andrew chewed and swallowed, "Agent Collins wasn't officially assigned. Which would have been fine, except that after the mics were turned off, I heard the reporter asking Bowden about you."

"What did you do?"

"What could I do? I went inside to interview Franklin and hoped that the reporter didn't think anything more of it."

"That will depend on how good the reporter is. How curious."

"Right. But anything else I said at that point would have had him wondering what the big deal was, so I acted like it was nothing. Sometimes the more you say, the more they want to know." Andrew licked tomato sauce off his thumb. "Did I ever tell you that my favorite pizza was sausage, sweet peppers, and mushrooms?"

"Just a good guess on my part. Now talk. What happened?"

Andrew filled her in on his remarks to the reporters and his conversation with Franklin.

"What was your gut feeling about him?" she asked. "Too much protest? Overly indignant?"

"Neither. To tell you the truth, I didn't get that vibe from him."

"The vibe that says, I'm lying through my teeth, or the vibe that says, you're way off base."

"The lying vibe. I think he was telling the truth. I don't think he was the one Shannon was running from."

"Who do you think it was, then?"

"I think it might have been his father."

"Reverend Paul? Founder of the church? The man who, according to Paula Rose, brought truth, justice, and salvation to the good people of Hatton?"

Andrew shrugged. "You asked me what my gut was saying, and that's it. Look, he was there at the church that day, we know that for a fact. Shannon was in his office."

"Martha said he had an appointment."

"Maybe Martha was lying." He polished off the first slice and took a long pull from the bottle. "A little more pizza and I might turn back into a human being again."

"Hmmm. Grampa Paul as abuser." She rubbed her chin as if considering the possibility. "I like it."

"I'm thinking the other sisters knew about that."

"Probably. If it was the old man, I'd be real surprised if he started with the third sister."

Andrew took another bite and chewed thoughtfully. "It would be unusual, with those two older sisters around, for him not to have started with one or both of them."

"It's certainly something worth exploring."

"You know, you're awfully calm for someone whose cover has just been blown."

"We knew it could happen." She shrugged. "But you never know, the whole thing could have gone right over this guy's head."

"Your name is out there. All it takes is one reporter with a contact in the Bureau to find out who you are."

"Well, let's hope this guy was slow on the draw. I'm not really ready to back out of this yet. Too many questions remain unanswered. I'd like to be around to answer a few of them."

"I'd like you to be, too." He caught her eye and held her gaze. She looked like she was trying to think of a snappy comeback and couldn't. He let her off the hook by adding, "It's a complicated case. Of course you'd want to finish what you started. See how all the pieces fit together in the end."

She nodded thoughtfully, eyes downcast. Then she looked up and grinned. "So how long exactly was it before Franklin kicked you out?"

"Maybe twenty minutes or so." He laughed. "About average for the Randalls."

He grew sober then, and related Judith's recollections of hang-up phone calls that lasted a little too long, of envelopes that often contained nothing at all.

"I'd bet anything that was all Shannon," Dorsey agreed. "But boy, the empty envelopes speak volumes, don't you think? Wanting to connect, wanting to reach out, but not wanting them to really know. . . ." She shivered. "That's one of the saddest things I've ever heard in my life."

"Everything about this case is sad." Andrew went into the bathroom. "Can I get you another?"

"Sure. Thanks."

He emerged with a bottle in each hand, and passed one over to her.

"Do you ever think about doing anything else?" Andrew asked as he sat back down at the desk.

"No. I don't know what I'd be doing if I didn't do this."

"Doesn't it ever get to you?"

She thought about her last case, about the two

young men now sitting in a federal prison awaiting trial. Over a period of three months, they'd kidnapped, raped, and murdered seven girls in the Florida panhandle. Seven Dorsey knew of, anyway. Who knew how many others there might have been?

"Yeah." She took a drink from the bottle. "Yeah, it gets to me."

"You see these families, they appear so solid. And then you find out there was something underneath it all that just was not right, and you wonder what went wrong."

His gaze went distant. To bring him back, she asked, "You're talking about the Randalls or the Beales?"

"Neither. Both." He focused on the pizza, as if debating whether or not to have another slice. "Maybe I was thinking about the Shields."

"Your brother."

"All of us. We came from this great, tight-knit family. We had two parents who loved us. Yeah, Dad was gone a lot, but Mom was no pushover, believe me. That woman ran a tight ship. She was strong, the real anchor of the family. I look back and remember how close we all were, how we were all such good friends. Me, Brendan, and Grady. And how protective we all were of Mia. She was the only girl in the entire family, you know? The baby sister. Even Connor and those guys doted on her." He looked up at Dorsey with haunted eyes. "I just don't understand what went wrong with Brendan. How he could have turned out so bad, when everything he came from was so good."

He cleared his throat and added, "I read somewhere that 45,000 women and children are trafficked into the US every year. My brother was responsible for some of those kids. He arranged for them to be sent here so they could be sold like puppies in a pet store. He didn't give a damn about them. About what was going to happen to them. I just want to understand how he ended up without a conscience. I just would have liked to have asked him why."

"We're used to finding answers, that's what we do. There's a case, we solve it. We try to find out who is responsible and we try to find justice for the victim, justice for their family." She sat up a little straighter so that her eyes could look directly into his. "It's hard for us to accept that sometimes things happen and there are no answers, no explanations. So we deal with it the best we can."

The label on the beer bottle had gone soft in the icy water, and she began to pick at it.

"You get called out on a case and you never know what you're going to find. Last year we arrested a guy who liked to collect thumbs. He had a whole shoe box full of them in his refrigerator. A few months back, we caught a case, two men, nineteen and twenty-one, stopped by a deputy sheriff for speeding. The cop thought they were acting strange, so he called for backup. Walked around the back of the car while he was waiting and noticed the blanket on the backseat seemed to be moving. The backup arrived, they looked under the blanket, and find a nine-year-old girl who'd been missing for five days. In the trunk was the body of another little girl. I probably don't have to tell you the rest."

"Jesus," Andrew swore and put down the pizza, his appetite gone that fast.

"The first thing the mother of the twenty-one-year-old said when she found out what sonny-boy'd been up to? 'He's a good boy, my Jon. It was that Rodriguez boy that put him up to it.' They're all good boys, though, right?" Dorsey made a ball out of the paper shreds from the label and tossed it at the wastebasket five feet away. It missed the rim and she got up, retrieved it, and tried again. This time she hit her mark. "Shit happens every day. We just deal with it."

"It's still easier to deal with someone else's shit than with your own."

She started back toward the bed when Andrew reached out and grabbed her by the arm.

His eyes on her face, he removed the wide silver bracelet that was always wrapped around her right wrist and exposed the lines that were etched into her skin.

"What was it you were dealing with?" he asked. "What did you tell me a few days ago, that you cut so that you can control the pain? What hurt you so much that you had to do this to yourself? What was it you had to take control of it?"

"Not what you're probably thinking." She made no effort to pull away.

"So you're telling me your father didn't have anything to do with this?" He tugged lightly on her hand.

"I didn't say he didn't have anything to do with it.

I meant he didn't molest me, because that's the obvious."

"Then what did he do?"

"He abandoned me," she said simply.

"He . . ." He let her hand drop.

"Abandoned me." She nodded without emotion. "After my mother died he just"—she shrugged— "pretty much forgot about me."

"How can you forget about your child?"

"He was in shock for a long time, I think."

"What happened?"

"Short version? My mom was hit by a car as she crossed the street." She spoke calmly, but melancholy settled into the lines around her eyes and her mouth. "One of the neighbors saw it happen, and he ran to our house to tell us. When we got to the scene of the accident, someone held onto me so that I couldn't see, but I saw." The control began to crack ever so slightly. "There was a mound in the street with a blanket over it, blood seeping out from under the blanket. I knew it was her. They put her on a gurney and carried it into the ambulance, and I couldn't understand why they didn't hurry more, why they weren't rushing. Years later I realized it was because she was already dead."

"How old were you?" He thought she might have told him once but he didn't remember.

"Nine," she said matter-of-factly. "I was nine."

"Where was your father?"

"He was with her. There on the street, then in the ambulance. He went with her. He stayed with her that night, or most of it, stayed with her body. At least I'm guessing that's what he did."

"He didn't make arrangements for a neighbor to stay with you?"

"I kept waiting for him to tell me to come with him, that I could stay with her, too. Or to tell me to go home. But he never even turned around to look at me. He forgot I was there."

"Did he know you were there? You said he left the house after the neighbor came to tell him about the accident."

"It wouldn't have mattered. He never gave me a second thought."

"So what did you do? Did you go home alone? To a friend's?"

"I went to the church, and I hid in the choir loft. I stayed there for the rest of the day, and through that night. It was so cold in there. . . ." She bit her bottom lip, which had begun to tremble. Andrew wondered how long it had been since she'd last talked about it, if she ever had. "Anyway, I went home when the sun came up. He was home, but he never noticed I wasn't there."

"Didn't any of your neighbors—?"

She waved him off. "Not their fault. No one knew where I was. I think everyone thought I was with someone else. But to me, it was as if I'd become invisible. No one could see me. It was like I wasn't there at all."

"Don't you think your dad probably thought you were at a friend's house?"

"No, Andrew. That's the point. He never even thought about me at all."

He started to say something and she stopped him. "He admitted it, years later. He admitted he never gave me a second thought that night. He was embarrassed by it, and humiliated and apologetic as hell. At least he didn't lie."

"Who took care of you?"

"My Aunt Betsy—my dad's sister—came to stay with me, because he left."

"Where did he go?"

"I had no idea at the time. He just said he had to leave, and he did."

"How long did he stay away?"

"I don't know. It seemd like six months, maybe. A long time. He took a leave from the Bureau, went . . . wherever it was he went—I still don't know—and when he came home, he went right back to work."

"And your aunt stayed with you? Took care of you?"

"She did, yes. She was very good to me, very kind, very loving. I was a huge pain in the ass, but she stuck with me anyway."

"I'm guessing you and your father worked things out."

"Over time, we did, yeah. A few years later, he was wounded—shot in the leg—and he was home for a while." She finished off the beer in one long swallow. "I understood how hard it was for him to be in that house, because I saw it on his face. He seemed to be in pain all the time, and not from the wound. I guess it was then I realized just how much he had loved my mother. I finally began to understand how much he'd lost."

"But you'd lost, too."

"That hadn't occurred to him until he was off on medical leave."

"You forgave him, though. You worked things out with him."

"He's my father. He's the only parent I have."

"And you began cutting after your mother died?"

"No. After my father came back." She looked at him with eyes that suddenly seemed old. "I was so afraid, I kept waiting for him to leave again. Every day I'd wake up holding my breath. Was he still there, in the room at the end of the hall? And every afternoon when I came home from school, I'd have pains in my stomach. Had he left while I was gone? Would I ever see him again?"

"How did you know how to do that?" He pointed to her wrist. "I mean, what made you think it would help?"

"I saw another girl doing it. I walked into the girls' room at school and she was in one of the stalls, but hadn't locked the door. She was standing over the toilet with a razor in her hand, and the blood was streaming into the toilet."

"I'm surprised you didn't run screaming from the room."

"I was mesmerized," she admitted. "I asked her what she was doing, and she told me. A few days later, I tried it. It helped."

"How long did you cut?"

"Five, six years." She smiled sheepishly. "Not so long, by some standards."

"Why did you stop?"

"I just didn't need to do it anymore."

"Did you ever talk to anyone? Your aunt, a school counselor, a therapist?"

"I was in therapy for three years, starting when I got to college." She hastened to add, "Of course, that's not on my official record. I didn't put that on my app when I went to the Bureau."

"You really think they couldn't have found out if they wanted to?"

"Maybe. But I went through the clinic at school, which was free, and completely confidential. My dad didn't even know. No one did."

"You never talked about it?"

"Not until now."

"Why now, Dorsey? Why tell me?"

"Truth?" she asked.

"Truth."

"I have no idea. It just seemed like it would be okay."

"It is okay." He got up, went to the bed, sat behind her, then began to massage her shoulders. "Thanks for trusting me."

"Ditto."

"Damn, but your muscles are tight, girl."

"It's been a tough week."

Dorsey let her head drop and he massaged the back of her neck with his thumbs for a few minutes before leaning back against him. It felt so good to have someone to lean on that she just rested there for a while.

"That feels so good. Don't ever stop."

"I wish, but we have a case to solve," he reminded her.

"Guess you're on your own from here on out."

"Not necessarily."

"If my name is out there, it's out there. Mancini can't be too happy about that."

"John doesn't know yet. I thought I'd wait until the morning to call in." He locked his hands in front of her and just let her lean. It felt solid and right, letting her rest against his chest, and he felt her relax. He realized he'd wanted his hands on her from the moment he'd first seen her on the dock that first day.

He wished he didn't need sleep as much as he did.

"I'm wondering if I shouldn't just leave tomorrow instead of waiting for the other shoe to drop," she said, thinking aloud.

"Let's just wait and see. There's a chance the reporter's already forgotten about you."

"If he's anything like the reporters I know in Florida, that's one slim chance."

She turned to say something else, lifting her face to his. Her mouth was so close, so pretty. He leaned toward her just as his cell phone rang.

He glanced at the clock and frowned. It was ten minutes after one in the morning. He eased her forward so that he could get up to retrieve the phone which he'd left on the desk.

"Shields."

He listened without saying a word.

"But—all right. Yes, I understand." He closed the phone. To Dorsey he said, "There's something John wants me to check for him. I'll see you in the morning."

He averted his eyes and grabbed his jacket from the back of the chair. "Thanks for the pizza and beer. And the conversation. And the company."

He went to the door and stopped. "Come lock up after I leave."

"I will." She got up off the bed and followed him, her eyes on his face. "Are you going to give me a hint?"

"It's nothing, no big deal," he told her. "Just something John wanted me to check into for him."

He smiled and paused, his hand on the door handle. He turned and leaned over just a bit and kissed her lightly on the mouth, a kiss meant to promise something more some other time. Her arms wound around his neck and pulled him close, demanding he kiss her for real, her mouth insistent and needy. He met her demand, his hands on either side of her face, and felt the heat rise between them. He broke away slowly, with the greatest reluctance, and kissed a trail from her lips to her chin.

He sensed she was waiting for him to say something more, to give some explanation, but he could not. Instead he held her at arms length and merely repeated, "Lock up."

He blew out a breath he didn't realize he'd been

holding and walked out the door, closing it behind him. He hadn't been able to look at her face, didn't want to see the questions he'd find there. There was nothing he could have said, no way he could have told her what he'd just heard.

He walked quickly in the general direction of his room. He stood in the shadows for a moment, scanning the parking lot for news vans or stubborn reporters who might have hung around hoping for some action. When he was satisfied there was no one there to follow him, he walked to his car, got in, and drove off into the night.

17

Something was going on, and she was being kept out of it. After they kissed—after that amazing kiss—Andrew had bolted out of her room as if he'd been shot. What the hell was up with that?

That had been the last thought in her mind when she'd finally fallen asleep the night before, and the first thought she'd had when she'd awakened the next morning. It rankled. One minute he was kissing her like she hadn't been kissed in a long time, the next, outta there.

She'd expected, sooner or later, to be cut out of the action. She'd accepted that if her identity became known, she'd back out gracefully. That had been understood from the start, and she had no problem with that.

The problem was that she knew her identity as Matt Ranieri's daughter was still under wraps. Sure, there was some danger of it coming out, what with Chief Bowden giving a reporter enough to figure things out with, if he were so inclined. But she hadn't heard anyone say it. It wasn't on the morning news. And if no one was saying it aloud, the story wasn't out there yet. Which meant she was being cut out of the investigation for another reason. And that had not been part of her agreement.

The question had nagged at her all night. What was going on, and why hadn't she been brought into it?

She'd called Andrew's cell phone twice already without a response. The first time she figured he might be in the shower, the second time had been within the last five minutes. Where was he?

She took a quick shower and towel-dried her hair. Since she wasn't working and could wear whatever she pleased, she dressed in a short jean skirt and a tank top. She brushed her hair out while she watched one of the network morning shows. There was a segment on kiddie-pool safety, followed by an interview with a popular romance novelist who was on tour with her latest book. When the show went to a commercial, Dorsey switched off the TV and tossed the hairbrush into her suitcase.

Dorsey tied back her hair, slid her feet into a pair of flip-flops, and grabbed her purse. She'd stop at Andrew's room and see if he wanted to join her for breakfast. Assuming, of course, that he was there.

Which he was not, she discovered when she knocked on his door. She glanced around the parking lot and realized his car was gone.

Damn, she thought. *He's not back yet. Where the hell did he go?*

She fished the keys from the bottom of her bag as she walked to the car. The least he could have done was given her a heads-up that he wasn't coming back.

It was obvious there'd been something on the tip of

his tongue before he'd left her room the night before, something that had nothing to do with the electricity that had passed between them when he'd kissed her. It had something to do with the call from John, any idiot could figure that out.

"It was nothing," he'd said.

Right. At one in the morning? Your boss calls at 1 A.M. and it's nothing? Who did Andrew think he was kidding?

Dorsey drove to the diner she'd seen a few blocks from the motel on the way into Hatton and took a seat at the counter. She wanted a real breakfast, one with toast and eggs and bacon and home fries—not grits, she specified to the waitress who took her order—and coffee.

While she waited for her food, Dorsey tried again to reach her father without success and was forced to leave another message. "This is your daughter. Please call me as soon as you get this message."

What the hell was it with the men in her life today?

Not that Andrew was a "man in her life," she reminded herself.

When she was alone, she could admit to herself she liked him a lot more than she'd expected to. More than she really wanted to. Her fingers traced the path his lips had taken the night before, from her mouth to her chin. Best not to dwell on that. She recalled in excruciating detail what happened the last time she got involved with someone she worked with. Of course, she apparently wasn't working with Andrew, not anymore.

She finished her breakfast and paid her bill, then walked outside from the cool air-conditioned diner into the muggy morning. What to do with herself now, was the question.

She drove back past the motel to see if Andrew had returned, but he had not. She drove past the Randalls' house on Sylvan to see if anything was going on there, but all appeared quiet. She swung around to Paula Rose's street and drove slowly past the church. Kids were gathering outside, with backpacks over their shoulders, and coolers at their feet. Judging by the number of adults who had gathered around the church van, there was some sort of picnic or outing planned. She slowed again as Paula Rose came out of the back of her house and walked across the parking lot to the church next door. She chatted with the maintenance man Dorsey and Andrew had spoken with.

When Paula Rose disappeared into the church, Dorsey turned off the engine and watched for a while. When ten minutes had passed, she started up the car again and drove off, with no particular destination in mind. She wasn't even sure why she'd driven to the church, except to have a place to go.

She drove hesitantly, not knowing which way to turn when she reached the stop sign at the end of the street. She was restless and feeling put out, and wondering if perhaps she shouldn't go on back to Florida, back to working on her own cases. "Fat chance," she muttered. She wasn't going to leave until she was sent home.

A right turn would take her back toward the Randalls'. A left would take her out of town. She took the left, the road less traveled, and all that.

She wondered if John Mancini had given any thought to her request to join his unit. She had the feeling that her time here in Hatton might have been a test, and she couldn't help wondering if she'd passed or failed.

Her cell phone rang and her hand reached out to grab it before it could ring a second time. She couldn't answer it fast enough.

"Collins."

"Miss Collins?"

Dorsey's heart fell just a little. It wasn't Andrew's voice, but a woman's.

"Who is this, please?" Dorsey asked.

"Miss Collins, this is Edith Chiong. Shannon's roommate."

"Yes, Edith, of course. I remember you." Dorsey paused. "How are you?"

"I am fine. I'm trying to reach Agent Shields, but he hasn't returned my call. Then I remembered I had your card."

"What can I do for you?"

"I, I have something I want to—you see, I'm leaving for Cincinnati and I want to make sure . . . but I don't know . . ." She spoke quickly, then stopped.

"What is it, Edith?"

"I need to see you or Agent Shields before I leave Deptford."

"When are you leaving?"

"Tonight. I have a ticket for the bus that leaves at six o'clock."

"Where are you now?"

"I'm at the apartment. It's on—"

"I remember."

"Do you think you could come here? There's something I have to give you."

"What's that?"

"Shannon's diary."

"I'm on my way."

"Teach you to ignore my calls, Agent Shields." Dorsey made a U-turn and headed back through the center of Hatton, then stepped on it once she got to the open highway. By noon she was knocking on the door of the apartment Edith Chiong had shared with Shannon Randall.

"I should have called before," Edith said when she opened the door. "I should have told you before."

"You're telling me now." Dorsey stepped inside and noticed the two small suitcases that stood in the middle of the living room. The furniture was gone except for a folding chair and the coffee table.

"I sold almost everything," Edith explained.

"You mentioned you were going to Cincinnati. Do you have relatives there? A friend?"

"No." She shook her dark head. "I heard about this place they have there. It's for girls like me. Working girls? They help you make changes in your life."

"Off the Streets?" Dorsey had heard of the program, newly begun in several cities across the country, that was formed to help prostitutes find another way of life.

"Yes, that's it." Edith smiled shyly. "A girl downtown told me about it. She left a few months ago and I heard from one of the other girls that she's doing real good. She's staying there at the shelter they have. She said the people there are real nice. I thought it might be worth a try."

"It's definitely worth it. Good for you, Edith."

"Shannon and I used to talk about it, getting out of the life, you know? She didn't get the chance." Edith's eyes welled.

"But you can. You're taking it."

Edith wiped her face with the side of her hand.

"You're going to do fine, Edith. It's a good first step."

"I hope so. I hope I can." She cleared her throat and stuck her hands in her pocket, and suddenly looked very young.

"You said on the phone . . ."

"Shannon's diary." Edith nodded. "Yes. I have it." Edith reached into a large white leather handbag sitting on the floor near the door leading to the kitchen.

"I knew I had to give it to you. I just wanted to read it a few more times. When I read it I can hear her voice in my head, you know?"

She handed it to Dorsey.

"I wanted to keep it."

The diary had a dirty white faux-leather cover and a lock that had long ago been broken.

"I don't know if there's anything in there that could

help you find the person who killed her, but I thought maybe you'd see something I didn't."

"Thank you, Edith." Dorsey slipped the diary into her own bag.

"What will happen to it?" Edith asked anxiously.

"It depends on what's in it. If she talked about the night she left Hatton . . ."

Edith shook her head. "She didn't write about that."

"Then maybe there's no reason for us to keep it. Look, I'll read it through, and if there's nothing in here that can help us solve the case, I'll see what I can do about having it returned to you."

"You will?"

Dorsey nodded. "Just make sure I know where you are, once you get there."

"I will. Definitely." Edith smiled. "It's just that, I don't have a lot of her, you know? She didn't leave much behind."

"By the way, where did you find the diary?"

"It was under her mattress. In an envelope." Edith laughed. "The envelope said *Carnival* on it, so I wasn't sure what was in it."

"Edith, do you still have that envelope?"

She nodded. "Did you want that, too?"

"If I could."

"Sure." Edith took the brown envelope from the bag and gave it to Dorsey. "If you think it could help you."

"I don't know if it will, but maybe it will come in handy." Dorsey smiled her thanks.

*   *   *

Dorsey had driven six miles out of Deptford before stopping at a convenience store. She went in and purchased a large soft drink with a lot of ice, then drove to the back of the lot and parked under a live oak with a huge sheltering canopy. She moved the seat back as far as it would go, got comfortable, and began to read. Shannon Randall had been twelve when she'd started to write in her diary. In it she'd recorded all the things that are important to girls of that age. What happened at school. What movies she saw. Who said what—did what—to whom. Who liked who that day, that week, that month. What grade she got on her history test. What silly thing happened in homeroom. What it was like to go from junior high to high school.

Dorsey sipped her cool drink and read it, cover to cover. When she finished, she closed the book gently and placed it on the seat next to her.

Before starting the car and heading back to Hatton, Dorsey placed another call to Andrew.

"I have Shannon's diary. I found one of the missing pieces of the puzzle. Not a big piece, maybe, but still, it's something. Guess you're going to have to start returning calls if you want to know what it is."

Dorsey headed back toward Hatton, but couldn't get there fast enough. Her first stop would be her motel room. She needed the list of names and addresses Judith had given them the first time she and Andrew had visited the Randall home. She hoped it was among the notes she'd kept in her folder, and not in Andrew's briefcase.

She all but flew into the motel parking lot, kicking up some pebbles as she rounded the corner. She turned the key in the door and went right to the desk where she'd left the notes she'd been making all week. Relieved to see that the information she needed was there, she was back into her car within minutes of having left it. She drove straight out of town, following the directions Judith had given them. She turned right two blocks past the center of town; at 1813 Meadowlark Lane, she parked the car and got out.

The two-story colonial was perhaps a decade old and well landscaped. Dorsey admired the flowering shrubs and lush flower beds that lined either side of the walk as she approached the front door. She rang the bell and waited. The woman who answered appeared to be in her mid-thirties. She was trim and pretty and held a toddler in her arms.

"Yes?" the woman asked.

"Kimmie White?"

"Kim White was my maiden name, yes." She tilted her head slightly, as if about to ask a question.

"I'm Special Agent Collins, FBI." Dorsey held up her badge for the women's inspection. "I'd like to talk to you about the Shannon Randall investigation."

18

"I saw that press conference over at the Randall's last night, and I don't mind telling you, I just could not believe my ears. 'Course, there have been rumors flyin' around town these past few days, but I didn't pay them any mind. I mean, who would ever have thought . . ."

Kim Holbrook, the former Kimmie White, held her sleepy two-year-old in her arms, her voice barely above a whisper as she swayed slightly from side to side to lull the baby, whose eyes were all but closed. "Poor Miz Randall, I bet she'd like to die just about now."

She continued to speak softly as she led her visitor into the living room of her beautifully appointed home.

"I was more or less expecting someone to come over, sooner or later."

"Why is that?" Dorsey asked.

"Well, I was one of Shannon's best friends. I testi-fied at the trial." She shook her head. "I just cannot believe all the things that FBI agent was saying on the news last night. I told Art—my husband—that finding out now, all these years later, it's like Shannon died all over again."

She realized what she said, then laughed nervously. "Well, of course, she did. Die, I mean. That just did not come out right." She rolled her eyes before heading toward the steps. "If you would excuse me for just one minute, I need to put her down in her crib. . . ."

Kim climbed the winding stairs to the second floor before Dorsey could respond, but she didn't mind. A few minutes alone would give her an opportunity to look around a bit.

The Holbrook home was lovely. There were photos of three towheaded children on the ornate mantel, including the youngest one in her mother's arms, but to look around the handsome room, one would never suspect a child lived in this house. There were no toys on the floor or behind the chairs that flanked the large fireplace. The sofa and chairs were expensively upholstered, the drapes on the room's three large windows raw silk. The carpet was oriental, and looked antique. All in all, Dorsey would have to say that Kimmie White had done quite well for herself. So much better than her childhood friend had. Dorsey felt a flush of anger for Shannon's sake as she looked around at all the dead woman had been denied. The children, the beautiful home, the good life in her home town.

"Sorry," Kim said as she came down the steps. "I was just about to put her down for her nap when the doorbell rang. Can I get you some coffee? A cold drink, maybe?"

"Nothing, thank you." Dorsey had returned to her seat when she'd heard her hostess's footfalls on the stairs. "Your home is lovely."

"Oh, thank you. We've only been here for about six months now, but it seems we've been working on it forever." She took a seat at the opposite end of the sofa from Dorsey. "This was my in-laws' house, and when my father-in-law passed two years ago, my husband inherited it. We've been renovating all that time—Lord, but it needed everything, nothing was up to date. . . ." She stopped and stared at Dorsey for a moment, then said, "But you didn't come to hear about that. You came to talk about Shannon."

"I understand you were with Shannon the day before she disappeared."

"We were at my house working on some project for school. I don't even remember now what it was we were doing," Kim told her. "Shannon left to go to the church for choir practice that night, just like any Wednesday. The next day she wasn't at the bus stop before school, and she wasn't in homeroom. Me and Heather—she was our other friend—called her house at lunchtime, thinking she was sick? But no one answered the phone. Then later that day, we heard she was missing."

Kim crossed her arms over her chest. "It was just the worst feeling; the worst thing that had ever happened to any of us, finding out that Eric Beale had killed her."

She visibly shuddered. "But of course, we know now that wasn't true. . . ."

"Was there any point over the years, when Shannon might have tried to get in touch with you?" Dorsey asked. "Phone calls, for example?"

"No." She shook her head adamantly. "No. If she had, I would have told someone. I can't help but wonder why she didn't, though, if she'd been alive all that time. We were really close, you know? I just can't get over how crazy this whole thing is. That FBI agent on the news last night, he was saying how Shannon had been a . . . a prostitute? Is that true?"

"Yes."

"Do you know why? When?" Kim floundered. "I'm sorry, I'm just having such a hard time imagining her doing something like that. Shannon was such a goody-goody. She didn't even have much interest in boys back then."

"But you did."

"Well, yes." Kim laughed self-consciously. "But we were in high school, after all."

"Did Shannon ever give you any indication that she was thinking about running away? Leaving home?"

"None. Honestly, no." Kim shook her head from side to side. "I swear I would have said something back then, if I'd thought she ran away. But no, it just wasn't something she would do. At least not that any of us had seen. It just all seems so out of character, you know? It makes me feel as if maybe I didn't know her at all—but I know in my heart I did. It's all very confusing."

"Was she having any problems at home that you know of?"

"No. Oh, her little sister used to get on her nerves a lot, but little sisters do that. God knows mine did, too. But no, she was happy as far as I remember. She had a pretty good relationship with her family, especially her mother. They were real close. Miz Randall used to bake cupcakes for school, cookies for the girls when they came home in the afternoon. Pretty birthday cakes. I always thought Shannon had it really good, frankly." Kim laughed. "I still find it hard to believe she ran away from all that."

"Did she ever mention that she was being abused by anyone?"

"Abused?" Kim's eyes went wide. "Oh, uh-uh. No. She never—I don't think she was ever—oh, no . . ."

Kim rubbed the back of her neck with her right hand.

"I'm sorry," she said. "I'm still having a hard time with all this. This is just all so crazy, you know?"

She got up and paced slowly. "If something bad was happening, she never let it show."

Kim wrapped her arms around herself and said, "Honest to God, if Shannon was being abused, she never let on. No one would ever have suspected something like that."

"Just like no one suspected that you were lying when you told Chief Taylor you'd seen Eric's car heading out to the lake with Shannon in it?" Dorsey asked.

Kim stared at Dorsey.

"I have no idea what you're talking about," she

said, a flush creeping from her chest to her face. "I would never have lied about such a thing."

"Of course you would. You did. I read Shannon's diary, Kim. I know that you had a 'powerful bad crush' on Eric Beale," Dorsey said calmly, her eyes never leaving Kim's face. "That's a quote from Shannon's diary. I believe she may have been quoting you."

Kim's face took on that deer-in-the-headlights look.

"You asked him to the winter formal and he turned you down," Dorsey went on. "You were plenty pissed off when you heard that someone else had asked him a few days later and he'd said yes."

Kim shrugged. "It was just a dance."

"You were one angry little girl, according to Shannon's diary. 'Kimmie says she's going to show him.' That's what Shannon wrote, just a day or two before she disappeared."

"That's just something you say when you're angry." Kim dismissed it with a careless wave of her hand.

Dorsey leaned forward.

"Well, I guess you sure showed Eric, huh? Putting the police onto him, making him out to look like a liar to the cops sure did show him, didn't it?"

"No, no, I . . ." Kim froze.

Dorsey stood, her hands in the pockets of her skirt. "Shannon disappears, and you have the perfect opportunity to get even."

"It wasn't supposed to . . . I mean, he'd been with her that afternoon, he never denied that. And there was that shirt they found in his car, with her blood on it."

"You put him in Chief Taylor's head, Kim. If you hadn't done that, they wouldn't have suspected him of lying. They would have looked for other explanations for her disappearance."

"That's not how it was. They would have blamed him anyway. Everyone knew that he had a thing for her. Sooner or later, his name was going to come up. I never thought they were going to arrest him. I thought they'd just question him, scare him a little. Listen, it never occurred to me that Shannon wasn't going to come back. I thought she'd show up and the whole thing would just go away. Until he said he knew she was dead and that Eric killed her."

"Who do you mean, *he*?"

"Chief Taylor." Kim's eyes were welling and threatening to overflow.

"Chief Taylor told you that?" Dorsey fought to keep her voice even.

Kim nodded. "He said he knew Eric was lying. He said he knew Eric killed her, that Eric had to pay for it. He said if I was any kind of real friend, I'd—" She bit her bottom lip.

"You'd do what?"

"I'd help him get Eric to confess."

"By lying about having seen Shannon in Eric's car where and when you did?"

"I told Chief Taylor that I'd seen Shannon in Eric's car that afternoon. And I did. I walked Carrie and Heather partway home, to Fifth Street, then I turned around and started walking home. That's when I saw them. Eric and Shannon. They passed me out near where Fifth Street runs into the park."

"And that's what you told Chief Taylor?"

Kim nodded. "Yes, but he kept saying, 'Well, they could have been going through the park to the lake, couldn't they?' " She shrugged. "Sure, you can get to the lake by going through the park. So, I said, 'Sure, I guess.' Then the next thing I knew, he was saying that I saw them on the road that leads out to the lake. Which isn't really what I said."

"I'm confused. Tell me what the difference is?"

"The road you generally would take if you were going to the lake is Lakeview. It only goes to the lake. You can get to the lake by driving through the park, and that's what I said. But that's not what the chief ended up telling people. He was saying I saw them on Lakeview." She began to cry. "Before I knew it, everyone was saying Eric took her out to the lake and killed her and hid her body somewhere out there. Everyone was making such a big deal out of it, that I was the one who saw them last. That I was going to be the one who helped the police get Shannon's killer."

"You helped set him up, Kim."

"For God's sake, I was fourteen years old. I didn't understand that it would make a difference. It was like, once Chief Taylor said that, it seemed like it could have been true."

"And eight years later, when they were about to execute Eric? You were twenty-two." Dorsey stared at her with contempt. "What was your excuse then?"

"It never occurred to me that it would make any difference. Everyone believed Eric had killed her. Everyone said it was true. . . ." Kim's voice dropped to a whisper. "Honest to God, I believed he killed her. Chief Taylor told me I had a chance to help catch her killer. Shannon was my friend, and I believed he'd killed her. I didn't think it mattered."

"The truth always matters," Dorsey replied.

"What"—Kim licked her lips nervously—"what's going to happen to me?"

"I'd like to see you prosecuted for perjury, but realistically—and unfortunately—something tells me that isn't likely to happen after all these years. Though you never know what the D.A. is likely to do in an election year. This case being as big as it is, he might come after you to prove he's really tough on crime, regardless of how old that crime might be. He might want to make an example out of you, Kimmie." Dorsey started toward the door, then turned and asked, "Did you know what was going on between Jeff Feeney and the Beale brothers?"

"I know they hated each other, but I never knew what it was all about." Kim's bottom lip was trembling, her eyes brimming with tears again. "All I know is that Jeff gave them a hard time whenever he saw them."

"Jeff gave *them* a hard time, not the other way around?"

Kim nodded her head. "I don't know about Tim, but I always had the feeling Eric went out of his way to avoid Jeff, but I never knew why."

"Thanks," Dorsey said curtly as she turned the doorknob to leave.

"Agent Collins?" Kim still stood in the center of the room, crying softly. "I'm really, really sorry. I can't tell you how sorry I am."

"Tell that to Eric Beale's family."

Dorsey let herself out without looking back.

19

Dorsey did her best to hold fast to the reins of her temper. That Kim had been blithely getting on with her perfect life while Shannon had been working the streets and Eric lay dead stung her in the way that injustice always did. She would have loved to have been able to tell Kim she could expect the chief of police to show up any day to arrest her for perjury, but she knew that was unlikely. She'd be lucky if she could get Chief Bowden to go to the D.A., especially when Chief Taylor was long gone and the new version of Kim's story could not be verified.

On her way back to the motel, she made one more swing past the Randalls', but Andrew's car still wasn't there. Where the hell was he? His silence seemed like just one more good reason to be pissed off.

She wasn't going to call him again. She'd left messages, he knew she needed to talk to him. She had Shannon's diary, and though it contained no smoking gun, it had put her on to Kimmie's lie. And it could serve another purpose. No one knew what was in it, and if they let it be known it was in their possession, would someone step up to try to find out what was in it?

Right, that'll happen, she snorted. Only on TV and in murder mysteries did the guilty party try to steal such potential evidence. In her experience, it just never happened the way it did on TV. Still, when it came to the Randall family, they might want to call her bluff. Who knew how they might react?

She pulled into the parking lot just as her phone began to ring.

Her father's home number appeared in the caller ID, and she answered with a demanding, "Where the hell have you been, Pop?"

"Ummmm . . . is this Dorsey?" a woman's voice inquired.

"Yes. Who is this?"

"My name is Diane Coleman, I'm a friend of your father's."

Diane of the "last weekend was fun" message on her father's answering machine?

"Yes, Diane. How are you? What can I do for you?" She immediately regretted how impatient she must have sounded, but at that moment, she was in no mood for small talk.

"Well, frankly, I'm a little concerned. About your father."

So much for idle chitchat.

"What about my father?" Dorsey asked cautiously.

"Well, he left here yesterday morning and I haven't heard from him since. Normally I wouldn't think twice about it, but he promised to call as soon as he got there because he knew I was worried—about where he was going and how he'd be received, you know?"

"Actually, I don't know. Where was he going?"

"To meet with a man named Timothy Beale. He said it had to do with a case he'd handled a long time ago, and—"

"Wait, stop." Dorsey couldn't believe what she'd just heard. "Pop went to see Tim Beale?"

"Yes. And he gave me a number to call, in case I didn't hear from him by midnight. Well, when I hadn't, I called the number—"

"Whose number did he give you? Who did he tell you to call?"

"Someone he said he knew when he was with the FBI. John Mancini. I'm sorry to bother you, but I'm getting worried and I thought maybe he'd called you."

"I haven't heard from him. But you're saying he's in South Carolina?"

"Yes."

"And he told you to call John Mancini if you hadn't spoken with him by midnight last night?"

"Right. And I even waited a little, I waited till almost one this morning before I called. I know I'm probably being silly, but I just feel really uneasy. I hope you don't mind that I called you. Your number was on Matt's phone, so I thought I'd take a chance."

"I'm glad you did. You did exactly the right thing." Dorsey's mind was racing. "Did you speak with John?"

"Yes. He thanked me for calling and told me not to worry. He said he'd take care of everything."

Dorsey had a feeling she knew how John had taken care of it.

"Diane, thanks for letting me know. I'll check into this, and as soon as I talk to Pop, I'll have him give you a call. Are you going to stay there at the house?"

"I hadn't planned on it. Let me give you my cell, just in case." Diane rattled off the number and Dorsey scribbled it on the back of a card she found in the bottom of her purse.

"Got it," Dorsey told her. "I'll have him get back to you."

"Thanks, Dorsey." She paused. "I hope we get a chance to meet sometime soon."

"I'd like that too. Soon, I hope," Dorsey said sincerely. Any woman who would look out for her Pop was okay in Dorsey's book. "Look, let me see if I can catch up with Pop."

"Right. Talk to you soon."

Dorsey hung up, her gratitude toward Diane instantly replaced with an anger so strong she could barely see straight.

Bastard.

Shields, you bastard.

"It's nothing," he'd told her calmly when his phone rang just after one that morning. "Just something John wants me to check into."

He lied to her face and never blinked. Son of a bitch.

He'd known her father had been at Tim Beale's all this time.

It was noon, almost twelve hours later. What the hell was going on? And why was Andrew called into it? And why did she have to hear about it from her father's . . .

What was Diane to Matt, anyway?

Dorsey dialed her father's cell phone but got no answer. In spite of her earlier resolve not to, she tried Andrew again, but wasn't at all surprised when he didn't pick up.

"What the hell is going on, Andrew?" She all but spit her words out. "Did you really think I wasn't going to find out my father is meeting with Tim Beale? You son of a bitch."

She hung up the phone and dropped it into her bag, wishing she hadn't disconnected quite so quickly. She had a few more curses left for Andrew.

She drummed impatient fingers on the steering wheel, then forced a few deep breaths to calm herself. She could scream and curse all she wanted later. Right now, she had to find her father and if she held on too tightly to her anger, she would be distracted from that task. Focus, she reminded herself. Find Tim Beale, and she'd find her pop.

Chief Bowden had said Tim Beale was living someplace not too far from Hatton. Had she been smart enough to make a note of it? She rummaged in her bag for her small notebook, and went back through the last entries. *Naylor's M.* was noted next to Tim's name. What the hell did the *M* stand for? She didn't want to call Bowden; he'd want to know why she was asking.

She'd have to stop and ask someone, maybe at that convenience store on the way out of town, the one with the gas station attached. Surely there'd be somebody there who knew of a place called Naylor's *Something-that-began-with-M*.

She hoped to God someone did, and could tell her how to get there. She wasn't really sure what she was going to do once she arrived, but she knew she wasn't about to sit home waiting for film at eleven.

"I'm not kidding, you assholes." The voice from the trailer sounded shrill and short-tempered. "I told you to keep your distance. Ain't no one coming in or going out until my momma gets here. Unfortunately for y'all, she's driving from Kentucky so it's going to be a while. I told you that when y'all got here. This ain't no party, and you ain't been invited anyway. This here's between me and old Matt and my momma. The rest of you can all go to hell or you can hang out, but keep back from the door or I swear, I'll put a bullet right between his eyes and be happy as shit to do it. Any questions?"

"None," Andrew called back.

"Good. Now y'all just be quiet for a while, and no one's going to be hurt. Just . . . be quiet."

"Gotcha'," Andrew replied in a voice too low to be heard from the trailer. He turned to John Mancini and asked, "You okay with us waiting for Jeanette Beale to arrive?"

"We don't have much choice." John checked his watch. "She should be here soon. We waited this long, we might as well wait it out. Not much we can do anyway, with Matt in there."

"You think he's armed?"

"Matt? If he was, Beale's got whatever Matt had with him by now."

Andrew's phone rang and he checked the number. It was Dorsey again. He shoved the phone back into his pocket. He felt like a heel, not telling her what was going on, but John had been very specific in his instructions not to let on to Dorsey what was happening. He'd repeated it twice, as if he wasn't sure that once had been sufficient. "You're not to tell her anything, understand? I want as few people as possible out here. And I specifically do not want her here."

Yeah, right. That worked. Andrew eyed the gathering crowd.

A deputy from the county sheriff's department had been driving past and stopped to find out what was going on with all the cars out here by the trailer that sat alone on a wide vacant lot. The deputy, a hunting buddy of Tim Beale's, was curious. Once he found out what the FBI was doing, he'd called back in to the sheriff—and anyone with a police-band radio, including the local press, heard about the FBI's presence out at Naylor's Marsh. From the looks of it, most of them had headed on out to take a look. John kept the locals busy by having them keep back everyone else who'd stopped by to see the show. Andrew had twice suggested to John that they let Dorsey know what was going on, and got rebuffed both times.

"I think she ought to know," Andrew had argued.

"Not until we see what's going down," John said. "I don't want Matt's daughter here if Beale is going to put a gun to his head and pull the trigger. I promised Matt I'd keep Dorsey out of it. I'll not go back on that."

Andrew has shoved his hands in his pockets and started to walk away.

"You disagree," John said. It wasn't a question.

"For the record, yeah, I disagree. I don't think she should be treated like a child, and that's what you and Matt are doing. She's a pro, John. She's as good as anyone we have on our team. She shouldn't be cut out of this."

"That sounds more like an emotional reaction on your part than a professional one," John had observed. "Not a good sign, in my opinion."

"I've been working with her for the past week. At your insistence, if you need a reminder. You're the one who sold me on her, you're the one who wanted her here in the first place. It's not fair to cut her out now."

"Fair isn't the issue," John had reminded him stonily.

"I'm just saying." An angry Andrew bit his tongue before he was tempted to say something to his boss he might regret later.

"Noted," John had said as he'd watched Andrew walk away.

They both turned to look when an old, pale blue

Oldsmobile pulled up and was stopped by the sheriff's deputy who'd stationed himself nearest the action. After a few words, he waved her through. As the
agents watched, a woman who appeared to be in her
mid-fifties got out from behind the wheel. She wore
white Capri pants, a purple tank top, and huge round
sunglasses. Strawberry blond hair was piled atop her
head and held there by a large black clip. She sur-
veyed the area around the trailer, her gaze stopping
when it reached the small cluster of FBI agents standing halfway between the cars and the trailer.

"That would be Mrs. Beale," John told the two
agents who'd accompanied him on the plane from
Virginia. He started toward her as she started toward
him.

"Mrs. Beale, I'm John Mancini, FBI." He approached
her with his hand out.

She met his eyes and ignored the hand.

"I figured the FBI would be here. You smell blood
again, Mr. Mancini?" Her face was hard-lined and
angry. "You here to take another son from me?"

"Mrs. Beale, there is nothing I or anyone else can
say that can make right what happened twenty-four
years ago," John said. "Sorry doesn't even come close
to what I wish I could say. What happened was a total
travesty, the most tragic—"

"Save it. Or better still, write it down for me. So
that I can take it into court when I sue your sorry
asses." She started to push past him just as another
car pulled over to the side of the road, twenty-five feet
from where they stood.

Dorsey got out of her car and started across what passed for lawn. She was stopped by the same sheriff's deputy who minutes before had flagged down Tim Beale's mother. The small group gathered around him parted to make way for the latest arrival.

"Miss, I'm sorry, but I can't permit you to—" the deputy began.

Dorsey waved her badge in his face. "FBI."

He stopped her long enough to look over her credentials, then said, "Go on over, Agent Collins. The others are straight ahead there."

"I see them, thank you." She tucked her badge back into her bag.

"Agent Collins?" someone called her from behind. "Are you Dorsey Collins?"

She turned to face a short, slender man wearing glasses and a Carolina Panthers cap turned brim backward. "Who are you?"

"Robert Kerlin. I'm with Channel Seventeen out of Charleston. I was at the press conference last night." He stepped closer. "I was wondering why Agent Shields said he was the only agent assigned to the Shannon Randall case, since Chief Bowden was pretty adamant that you were working the case as well."

Dorsey stared at him for a moment before muttering "I don't have time for this" as she pushed past him.

Robert Kerlin took a digital camera from his pocket and took a few shots of her back as she walked away.

"Dorsey." Andrew was standing a few feet away

from John Mancini and Jeanette Beale when he saw her.

She ignored him and continued on toward the trailer.

"Dorsey, don't," he called to her. When she refused to acknowledge him, he started after her. "Dorsey, you can't go there. Beale has a gun. He's threatened to shoot your father if anyone gets too close."

She spun around to face him. "You knew about this. You knew he was here. You looked me straight in the face and lied through your teeth."

"I understand how you must feel," he said, hoping to reason with her.

"Oh, do you? You think you do?" Her anger was palpable in the thick summer air. "Is that your father in there?"

"I know what you must think. . . ." Andrew pushed a hand through his hair. He'd been hoping to have this conversation later, away from everyone.

"Then you know I hope to God I never have to see you again after today." Her hands were shaking with anger and she crossed her arms over her chest in the hopes of steadying them. "This is the 'nothing' John called you about, right?"

"I wanted to tell you."

"Then why didn't you?"

"Because I would not permit it," John responded before Andrew could open his mouth. "If you're going to blame anyone, blame me. I ordered him not to tell you, as I promised your father I would. He was afraid you'd do exactly what you're doing now, which is putting yourself in harm's way. I agreed with him, by the way. And since I'm Andrew's boss, his job depends on following my orders."

"You're John Mancini?" Dorsey hesitated.

"Yes." John walked toward her, Jeanette Beale momentarily forgotten. "And you're Dorsey Collins. I'm glad to finally meet you. Andrew has had nothing but good things to say about you."

She refused to look at Andrew, and could think of nothing to say except, "Shit."

"Sorry?" John came closer.

"So am I. Glad to finally meet you." Swell time and place to meet the man she'd hoped to work for. She suppressed a grimace. Not much she could do about that now.

"I was hoping you'd come in for an interview next week. Maybe we could save you a trip, take some time to talk now."

"Please don't treat me like I'm an idiot. Don't try to distract me with a job interview, hang it out in front of me like a carrot. I need to talk to my father. I need to know he's all right."

"You're Matt Ranieri's kid?" A woman Dorsey had not noticed approached from somewhere behind John.

"Yes." Dorsey nodded.

"Your father is fine," the unsmiling woman told her. "At least he was about ten minutes ago."

Dorsey frowned. "How do you know?"

"I'm Tim Beale's mother. You want to go in, that's fine with me."

She took Dorsey by the arm. "More than fine. I'd say this just about balances things out, wouldn't you, Mr. Mancini?"

Jeanette Beale looked straight ahead and called out, "Timothy, you open that door now, hear? Me and my new friend are coming on in—"

"No. Uh-uh. No way." Andrew shook his head and raised his hand to pull his gun. "She's not going in there."

"I don't think that's a decision for you to make." Jeanette Beale stared at the gun, then started toward the trailer, still holding Dorsey by the arm. She called out to her son, "Timmy, you keep that gun pointed right at Matt's head. If there ain't two of us coming through that door in about thirty seconds, you blow his brains out, hear?"

"I hear you, Mamma," Tim Beale called back. "I got him right here."

The door swung open, held there by Tim's foot. Through the doorway, everyone could clearly see Matt Ranieri seated in a chair at a small square table, his hands tied behind his back. Tim Beale stood over him, pressing a gun against the former agent's forehead.

No one outside the trailer moved, except Dorsey and Jeanette Beale, who climbed the three steps into the trailer. The door was pulled closed and slammed from inside.

Andrew's hand was still on his holster. Dorsey and her father were captives of the family Matt had un-wittingly helped destroy, and there wasn't a damned thing anyone could do about it.

20

"Well, now, isn't this nice?" Jeanette Beale stood in front of the closed door facing the table that stood in the middle of the tiny living space her son called home. "Mother and son, father and daughter. I'd call this cozy. Timmy, I think it's time to put on the tea."

"Dorsey, what in the name of God are you doing here?" a weary Matt said loudly. "I specifically told John I didn't want you here. For this very reason."

"I should be here." She forced a calm, steady tone into her voice. No need for anyone—her father or the Beales—to know how hard her heart was pounding at that moment. This wasn't exactly what she'd had in mind when she arrived at the trailer. She had no idea her father was being held at gunpoint by Eric Beale's brother.

"And I'm here because Mrs. Beale thought it was a good idea."

"Very funny." Jeanette pointed to Dorsey's shoulder bag. "I want to see what's in that bag. Hand it to me."

The urge to swing the bag at the woman's head was almost overwhelming, but Tim still was holding a gun on her father, though he'd moved to the other side of the table. How quick would he be to fire off a round? How accurate was his aim? Dorsey didn't think she wanted to find out. She passed the bag to Jeanette and watched as the woman rifled through it.

"Now, this isn't a very ladylike thing to be carrying around." Jeanette held up Dorsey's Sig Sauer and tsk-tsked.

"Maybe we should search her." The woman's son stared at Dorsey. "She might have another gun hidden someplace."

"She's wearing a tank top and a short skirt. Where do you suppose she's hiding a gun?" Jeanette asked with a touch of sarcasm. "You watch too much TV, Timmy. I've been saying that from the time you were three years old."

Tim shifted his weight from one foot to the other. He was tall and slim with thinning, light brown hair and pale, vacant eyes. He seemed to have inherited the same air of poverty and desperation worn by his mother.

Jeanette leaned on the counter in the miniscule galley kitchen, the gun held loosely in her hand. She pointed it in Dorsey's general direction and looked Matt in the eyes and said calmly, "Give me one good reason why I shouldn't take your daughter's life, same as you took my son's."

"We could start with the fact that there are several of her fellow agents outside along with some local law enforcement officers. That might be something for you to consider. You've dealt with the legal system before, both of you." He looked from son to mother.

"You know there's no chance you'll walk away. You'll either die here or you'll be arrested and face murder charges." He addressed Jeanette directly. "You want your daughters to have to deal with that?"

"My daughters would understand," Jeanette told him. "That the best you got?"

She was in control and liking it, but Dorsey noticed she'd shifted the gun slightly so that it pointed downward.

"No pleading for the life of your child, Agent Ranieri?" Jeanette asked.

"I don't suppose that would be very effective, Mrs. Beale. And for the record, I'm no longer with the Bureau, so I'm not Agent Anyone anymore."

"Ahh, that's right. So I'll just call you Matt. And you can call me Jeanette, since we're all so cozied-up here." She narrowed her eyes. "I seen you on TV. You're the big expert they call in to talk about all them tough criminal cases, aren't you? The guy they always bring in when they want a professional, *expert* opinion on those big cases no one can solve? The man they go to when they want to figure it all out, right?" She snorted. "Well, I'm bettin' that's one job you wished you never signed on for."

"You have no idea," Matt told her solemnly.

Jeanette slammed her fist on the table hard enough to make Dorsey flinch.

"My son was innocent, *Matt*. You and that dumb shit of a police chief we had back then railroaded that boy." The woman's small body shook with fury. "You killed my boy. You, Matt Ranieri. You built up a case out of nothing. You made it all up." She wiped tears from her face with a shaking hand. "You told the jury Eric murdered that girl, and you made them believe you. My son was killed for a crime he did not commit, because of what you made up. The Bible says an eye for an eye."

She turned the gun onto Dorsey and repeated, "So tell me again why I should not take your daughter the same way you took my son."

"Momma, let me do it." Tim touched his mother's arm gently. "He's right. Someone gets killed here, it's murder one. I been in before, I can handle myself. You'd get eaten alive in that place." He took a deep breath. "You want her to pay the price, I'll do it. I'll do him, too"—he pointed at Matt—"if that's what it will take to end this for you."

Before Jeanette could reply, Dorsey spoke up boldly.

"Before you blow either of us away, I'd think you'd want to know the truth about what happened back then."

"We know the truth," Tim told her, his face twisted with anger. "Your father figured he'd come into this little town, take over this case, show Chief Taylor how it's done, solve the case just like that"—he snapped his fingers—"make a big name for hisself, ride right on back out of town and onto a big career on the TV. So he sets up Eric, he—"

"No," Dorsey said. "It was Chief Taylor who set up Eric, not my father."

"Why would he have wanted to do that?" Jeanette sneered. "What'd he have against Eric?"

"I'm not sure, but I'll bet he knows." Dorsey pointed at Tim. "Go ahead. Ask your son."

"I don't know what she's talking about, Momma, I swear," Tim protested. "She's just saying anything she can think of to save her ass."

"Both you and Eric had run-ins with Jeff Feeney," Dorsey reminded him.

"Yeah, so?"

"So what were the fights about?" Dorsey met his eyes levelly.

"I don't remember," Tim muttered.

"Isn't that funny?" Dorsey said. "Jeff doesn't remember, either."

"What's so funny about that? It happened a long time ago."

"I remember the bar fight that got you sent away, but I don't remember hearin' nothing about no fight with Jeff Feeney." Jeanette turned her attention to her son. "What was it you was fightin' about?"

"I said I don't remember."

"Timothy Beale, you have never been a good liar. You look me in the eyes and tell me what that fight was about," Jeanette demanded.

"It was something personal between me and Jeff, okay?"

"And the fight with Eric was personal between him and Jeff?" Dorsey asked.

"Yes. I mean, I suppose so. I don't know."

"You were already in prison then. When Eric and

Jeff got into it, you were already serving time," Dorsey reminded him.

"Was there something going on back then I didn't know about, son?"

"Momma, this ain't the time," Tim told her.

"I'm standin' here with a gun on this man, and I'm thinkin' about pulling the trigger. If there's something I need to know, if something else happened back then, damn it, I need to know it now."

"Jeff was always on me. Always gettin' in my face back then. First me, then Eric."

"About what?" Jeanette's voice had dropped to almost a whisper, as if she knew what his answer might be. When he started to shake his head, she snapped, "Say it."

"It was about you, Momma," Tim told her. "He was always goin' on about you. Tellin' the most awful lies about you. I can't even repeat them, they was so bad."

Jeanette stared at her son for a very long time, her color fading until her skin lost its early-summer tan and turned pasty white.

"You argued with Jeff Feeney about me. Eric argued with Jeff about me," she repeated.

"About the lies he was sayin'. Every time he saw me, he'd say it. And he was always teasing Eric."

"It was all about me?" Jeanette appeared dumbstruck.

"It was all about lies, Momma." Tim raised his voice to his mother for the first time. "If you knew

what he was saying about you—" He stopped himself.

"I want to know what he said."

"He said you were . . . said you were a whore,"
Tim whispered, as if saying it would make it so. "Said
he . . . said he even seen you one time with his own
grandfather. I knew it was an ugly lie."

Jeanette crossed to her son, sat down, and buried
her head in her hands. After a few minutes, she raised
a tear-stained face and whispered, "It wasn't a lie,
Timmy. It wasn't a lie."

The silence in the room grew as seconds ticked on.

"If he told you he saw me and Roy Feeney together,
he was most likely telling the truth. Me and Roy, we
were together for a long time, Tim." She wet her lips.
"If that makes me a whore, well—"

"That can't be true." Tim stared at his mother as if
she were a stranger. "You and that old man . . ." Tim
screwed up his face in a look of disbelief. "You . . .
you had an affair with him?"

"Might as well get it all out on the table, since it's
come up." Jeanette wiped the tears from her eyes and
took a deep breath. "Roy Feeney was Eric's father."

"That can't be true, Momma."

Jeanette nodded. "I'm sorry, son. I never meant for
anyone to find out."

"Wait . . . is this Mrs. Taylor's father we're talking
about?" Dorsey broke in. "Chief Taylor's father-in-
law?"

"Yes," Jeanette answered.

"But he died right about the time Eric was arrested,

right?" Dorsey frowned. "I remember someone saying that Mrs. Taylor inherited big time from her father."

"Roy was pretty well off, it's true," Jeanette said. "I imagine he left quite a bit to her and to his son."

"I bet if Mrs. Taylor found out her father'd had another child, she would have been one angry lady. She might have wondered if Eric—or you—might be thinking about making a claim on the estate," Dorsey said thoughtfully.

"I never would have done that. Besides, Eric didn't know," she said, speaking to Tim now.

"But Mrs. Taylor wouldn't have known that," Dorsey thought aloud.

"You think maybe she thought Eric knew?" Jeanette frowned. "Boy, she sure wouldn't have wanted that story goin' around town. She was pretty uppity, you know?"

"She still is."

"You met her?"

Dorsey nodded. "We went to ask her about the chief's file on the case. We wanted to read over the witness statements but the file was missing. Chief Bowden suggested we ask Mrs. Taylor if any of the old files were still in the house, but she wouldn't give us the time of day."

"Why were you wanting to read the file?" Jeanette asked.

"Because it looked like somehow the evidence had been slanted to make everyone believe that Eric had killed Shannon. And since we know that Shannon didn't die in 1983, I was trying to figure out what really happened back then, and why."

"I'm sorry, but I am totally lost," Matt said.

"When you arrived in Hatton, what were you told by Chief Taylor, Pop?"

"That Shannon had been murdered, her body hidden, and they were pretty sure Eric had killed her. Taylor had the bloody shirt, he had Eric's admission he'd picked up Shannon that afternoon, and Taylor told me Eric had all but confessed to him." Matt thought for a moment, then added, "And there was a witness who said she'd seen Shannon in Eric's car about an hour after Eric swore he'd dropped her off."

"We now know that was a lie," Dorsey turned to her father. "Kimmie White admitted to me she made that up. The chief told her that all he needed was an eyewitness. She was pissed off at Eric for turning her down for a school dance, and then going with someone else. She said she just wanted the police to scare Eric, bring him in for questioning, then they'd let him go."

Matt put the rest together. "And when they searched his car and found the bloody shirt, which Kim had no way of knowing about, they figured they had the killer."

"You mean that bitch—" Tim clutched at the gun.

Dorsey nodded. "Yeah. She lied."

"But why would Chief Taylor go after him like that? Why was he so convinced that Eric . . ." Matt started, then paused, nodded, and said, "Oh, Christ. The wife."

"Mrs. Beale, you said Roy Feeney died around the time Eric was arrested. Do you remember if it was before or after?" Dorsey asked.

"Roy died two weeks after Eric was arrested, but he'd been very sick for a while," Jeanette told her. "It had been months since I'd seen him, but I'd heard he was just going downhill every day. He was in and out of a coma for weeks, and no one knew if he was going to survive or not. I don't believe he was ever aware that Eric was arrested."

"Did Roy ever talk about adding Eric to his will?" Matt asked.

"Yeah, plenty of times," Jeanette said, nodding, "but I kept telling him I wasn't sure it would be worth all the trouble it would cause for Eric and for me, after he was gone. I figured Eric would make his way in life, just like everyone else had to. Roy's wife had been gone for about eight years before we ever got together, but he had those two grown kids. I wouldn't have wanted to tangle with either one of them. They're both nasty things." She grew thoughtful. "I always thought it was so strange that such a sweet man could have such awful kids. Anyway, I figured with Eric not being the wiser, we should just let it be. And of course, there was the fact that my husband would have killed me. We were still living together back then. He would have killed me and Eric without a second thought, if he'd known about me and Roy."

"But Roy's two adult children wouldn't have known

that. So if he mentioned to his daughter that he was going to add another heir to his will, she'd probably have been pretty upset, right?"

"She wouldn't have wanted to share Roy's money, that's for sure." Jeanette nodded. "Everybody in town knew she had her heart set on that big house, on fixin' it up and livin' like royalty once she came into money."

"So didn't it ever strike you as odd that Eric was arrested by Chief Taylor—Roy's son-in-law—just weeks before Roy died?"

"No." Jeanette shook her head. "If I'd known that Eleanor knew, yeah, maybe. But I had no idea that anyone knew except me and Roy. I figured that Taylor being married to Roy's daughter was just an unfortunate coincidence."

"And wasn't it convenient that Shannon just happened to go missing right around that time," Matt said. "Then when Kimmie set Taylor onto Eric and they found the bloody shirt—"

"Roy's daughter saw her chance to eliminate the competition," Dorsey said, finishing Matt's train of thought. "Roy probably hadn't added Eric to his will by then, he was in a coma, but there was no guarantee he'd stay that way. If he survived and wanted to change his will, his daughter would tell him, look, this kid is a murderer, why would you own up to him now? You don't want anyone to know he's your son."

"She must have been counting on Roy dying without coming out of the coma, so the secret would end with him." Matt nodded. "Even if Eric was acquitted and Jeanette made a claim on the estate, who'd have believed her?"

"But why would Taylor call in the FBI?" Dorsey wondered.

"Easier to wash his hands," Matt replied. "No matter what happened, he would be clean. He knew Eric was innocent, but if he was convicted, it wasn't Taylor's fault. And if Eric got off, he could tell his wife the FBI had screwed up. He eases his conscience, either way."

"But wouldn't he be afraid you'd learn the truth?" Jeanette asked. "Make him look stupid?"

"If I'd done my job the way I should have, yeah, he ran that chance," Matt admitted. "But as it was, there were no other suspects, no reason to think Shannon would have run away or that Kimmie had lied. The lake outside of town has a lot of caves underneath it. The word was that Shannon's body had been dumped in the lake and had gotten into one of them. We had divers go in, but there were too many caves and passages between them to search them all. The police searched the woods for days but came up with nothing. There was no trace of Shannon anywhere except in Eric's car. If it turned out otherwise, he could always say, he couldn't override the FBI."

"Lie upon lie, secret upon secret," Jeanette muttered. "Sin upon sin . . ."

Matt reached across the table for her hand. "I'm so sorry," he told her. "I'd give anything to go back in time and make this right, for Eric and for you, to do what I should have done."

She stared at him for a long thoughtful moment. "I believe you would."

"Momma?" Tim spoke up. "What are we going to do now?" He waved the gun as if to remind her he still had it. "You see any point in shooting him?"

Jeanette sighed. "Hell, I guess I don't want anyone to die. But I did want someone to answer for what happened to Eric. I guess you've done that, best as anyone can."

"I think the ones we need to be shootin' are Kimmie and Mrs. Taylor," Tim said.

"We're not shootin' anyone. Let it go, son." Jeanette stood. "It's time to just let it go. We got some answers, that's more than we had yesterday."

"What about them?" Tim waved the gun at Matt and Dorsey. "We just let them go?"

"Yes, and put that damned gun away."

"How do you figure we're gonna get out of here without *them*"—Tim pointed toward the yard—"blowin' our heads off?"

"I can take care of that, if you'll give me my bag," Dorsey said.

Jeanette handed over the bag and Dorsey searched inside for her cell. She dialed Andrew's number.

"Tell everyone to stand down. This has all been a big misunderstanding. We're all coming out now, and I want your promise that Mrs. Beale will be free to leave, and that no charges will be filed against her or Tim."

"Are you kidding?" a skeptical Andrew asked.

"No, I'm not kidding."

"Are you sure everything's all right? They're not making you say this at gunpoint?"

"No, it's fine. I swear it."

"All right. I'll take care of it, if you're sure."

"I'm sure. Thanks, Andrew." Dorsey hung up and turned to Mrs. Beale. "He just needs a minute to get everyone calmed down."

She looked at the gun Tim was still holding. "You plannin' on puttin' that away before we open the door? Someone might get the wrong idea, they see you walkin' out with that thing in your hand."

"How do I know you're not trickin' us?" Tim asked Dorsey.

"Agent Shields gave me his word. He'll keep it."

"Don't know that I'm ready to trust you. Either of you."

"Then you can sit in here on your butt by yourself," Jeanette told him. "I'm goin' out with them."

She stood and handed over Dorsey's gun. Dorsey slipped it into her bag.

"You satisfied?" Jeanette turned to Tim. "If she was going to do something, she'd have turned that gun on me right then and there." She softened slightly. "Put it away, son, untie the man, and let's go."

Tim reluctantly did as he was told, removed the cords from Matt's wrists, then put his gun in one of the kitchen drawers and opened the door. He turned back to Matt and asked, "You comin' with us?"

"I'm right beside you." Matt gratefully followed Tim out of the trailer, followed by Dorsey and Jeanette.

Dorsey looped her hand through Jeanette's arm as

they crossed the yard, the entire gathering of law enforcement watching for one misstep on the part of either of the Beales. When Dorsey reached Andrew, she said, "Have you met Mrs. Beale?"

"Not formally. Andrew Shields." He shook her hand. "We're all so sorry for what happened. Believe me when I tell you that any one of us would do anything to undo this."

"That's pretty much what Matt said, back in there." Jeanette nodded slowly. "I appreciate that."

"Dorsey, the county sheriff is down there and he wants to know what we're charging them with," John Mancini asked as he approached.

Jeanette Beale went white.

"They're not being charged," she said, and as she turned, the sheriff walked up with his hands on his hips.

Before he could say a word, Dorsey told him, "This has all gotten out of hand. No one had any intention of hurting anyone. Tim and his mother just wanted some time to speak with my father without being disturbed. All the press here spooked them, and they had questions they wanted to ask." She gave him her best smile, then turned to John and said, "And Mrs. Beale provided us with some important information. I'm pretty sure I know how it all went down back then, thanks to her."

John and Andrew pretended they didn't see Jeanette's eyebrows raised in question.

"So you're telling me that boy threatened to put a

bullet in your father's head just so he could have some time to talk?" The sheriff wasn't buying it.

"That was all blown out of proportion," Dorsey assured him calmly. "There was never any real danger."

"I think we're fine here, Sheriff." John extended his hand to the man and shook it soundly. "I appreciate your backup. Sorry to have called you out on a false alarm."

"Right." The sheriff shook his head as he walked back to the road.

"Mrs. Beale, please introduce me to your son." John took Jeanette's arm. "He's right over here with Matt and a few of our other agents."

Dorsey started to follow, but Andrew grabbed her arm.

"I want you to know I'm really sorry. I wouldn't have cut you out if I'd had a choice."

She waved off his apology. "It worked out okay. I understand the position you were in."

"So you think you have the whole case worked out?"

"I am ninety-nine percent certain."

"Want to tell me about it over dinner?"

She glanced at her watch. "It's four in the afternoon."

He shrugged. "We'll be just in time for the early-bird special at the diner in town."

Dorsey laughed. "My father—"

"Is more than welcome to join us."

"I'll ask him what his plans are." She started toward

her father, but the reporter who'd stopped her earlier was there when she turned around.

"Was the FBI trying to hide your presence in Hatton because your father was involved in the original Shannon Randall case? Wouldn't you call that a conflict of interest?"

She walked past him without responding, but he followed.

"You're not denying that you're Matthew Ranieri's daughter, right? What part did you play in the investigation? How can you justify not telling anyone here in Hatton that you're really Dorsey Ranieri?"

She continued to ignore him even as he persisted. John realized what was going on and calmly reached out to the reporter. Nodding to Dorsey to continue on her way, John told the reporter, "This is an ongoing federal investigation, so I'd appreciate you not trying to question my agents when they're not permitted to respond. Thanks for your time."

Dorsey mouthed a thank you to John as she reached her father. She tapped him on the shoulder.

"Pop, do you have your phone on you?"

"Yes." He patted his pocket. "Why?"

"Use it," she told him. "Call Diane and let her know you're okay. She's been worried. Oh, and Pop?"

He paused before he dialed and looked up at his daughter.

"Tell her I said thanks."

21

Dorsey folded the long knit shirt she'd slept in the night before and put it in her suitcase, wishing she wasn't going back to Florida just yet.

Over dinner the night before, she and her father had a chance to go over with Andrew everything that they'd figured out while they were in the trailer with the Beales. He'd agreed that all the pieces seemed to fit. He also agreed Dorsey and Matt had been very lucky. The situation could easily have turned out very badly for everyone involved.

"With Tim holding that gun, things could have been very different," he reminded her.

"In the end, the Beales really only wanted the same thing we wanted. The truth. And we feel we have that. Except we still don't know how and why Shannon left town that night, and who beat her up." She frowned. That still rankled, that they hadn't been able to nail that down. "And we'll probably never be able to prove that her grandfather was her abuser."

She hated leaving before she'd seen the entire case through to the end, when Shannon's murder was solved—but she wondered if it ever would be. That part of the case was ice cold at the moment, and unless there was a break, it was likely to remain so.

Still, she reminded herself, she'd accomplished what she'd set out to do in the very beginning: she'd found out why her father had traveled down the wrong path twenty-four years ago. That was something she and Matt both needed to know.

Funny how things had worked out. Matt had needed to speak with Jeanette Beale every bit as much as she needed to speak with him. There'd been questions—and guilt—on both sides. To deal with his own culpability, before Matt left Hatton he'd made a call to Owen Berger and arranged to be Owen's only guest on his Friday evening show.

"There are things that need to be said publicly," Matt told his daughter before he'd left. "Someone needs to step up and take responsibility for Eric Beale's death. That someone is going to have to be me. I'm just telling you ahead of time, there may be some fallout."

"I can handle it," she'd told him, "but are you sure you want to do this?"

"There's nothing else I can do, honey. I screwed up big time. I didn't do my job. I should have reinterviewed every witness, I should have personally checked out every fact—"

"You were part of a team," she reminded him.

"I was the leader of that team." He shook his head. "For years, I took the glory when it appeared Eric had been guilty. Now that we know he was innocent, I have to stand up and take the heat."

"Think that will cost you your career as a crime expert?" she wondered aloud.

"What's that worth, compared to what Eric Beale lost?" he countered.

Matt took the first flight out of Charleston back to Philly. Back to Philly and Diane, Dorsey reminded herself. Diane, who'd unwittingly saved the day—and probably Matt's life—when she'd called Dorsey the day before.

There were still issues Dorsey needed to discuss with her father, but those would wait for another day. The past twenty-four hours had left them both with plenty to think about. Right now, she was happy they'd both come out alive, happy that there'd been resolution and closure of a kind for him, happy she'd been there to share that with him. Soon, though, they'd have to speak of other things. She wondered if she'd ever be able to talk to him about her self-mutilating. They'd long since talked about her mother's death and the aftermath, but she still wasn't sure how to talk about her cutting without making Matt feel guilty, making him feel he'd failed her. Maybe when things settled down, she'd be able to talk to him about how she'd been driven to take a razor and slice her flesh, but not now.

Maybe not ever.

Did it matter? She didn't know.

Dorsey tossed her toothbrush into the suitcase, then took one more look around the room. Satisfied she hadn't missed anything, she zipped the case closed, then turned off all the lights. One hand dragging the suitcase, the other searching her bag for the car keys, Dorsey paused at the door. Shannon's diary and the envelope were still in her bag. She'd meant to hand them over to Andrew the night before, but it had slipped her mind at dinner. She'd do it now, before she forgot.

She walked outside and went directly to her car, where she opened the trunk and put her suitcase inside. She slammed the trunk and went to Andrew's room. As she raised her hand to knock, the door opened, and Andrew stepped out. She backed up to avoid a collision.

"Hey," he said. "I was just on my way to see you."

"I beat you to it." She opened her shoulder bag and took out the items Edith had entrusted her with. "Shannon's diary. Unfortunately, there's nothing in here about her being abused. Nothing, really, to help the case, except those remarks about how mad Kimmie was at Eric."

"Good move on your part, getting her to admit to her lie." He took the diary and turned it over in his hand. "I guess I should give it back to her mother." He tapped it in the palm of his hand. "Then again, maybe it really belongs to Edith."

"It's your call," Dorsey said. "Me, I think it means more to Edith. It's all she has of Shannon. Oh, and she's leaving the life. She's moving to Cincinnati and getting into a program there that's designed to help hookers become former hookers. Teach them their self-worth, get them off the streets, help them to find other means of employment."

"I'm really glad to hear it. She just didn't seem to belong there."

"I agree. Oh, and there's something else." She gave him the envelope. "What I wouldn't give to be a fly on the wall when you return this to Martha Randall."

He opened his mouth to say something but his phone rang. He excused himself to answer it, but hardly said a word while he listened. Finally, he said, "Where is she? I'm on my way."

He turned to Dorsey and said, "Aubrey Randall was admitted to the hospital about four hours ago."

"An accident?" Dorsey followed him to the parking lot where he was headed toward his car.

"If trying to kill yourself with pills is an accident. I'm smelling a guilty conscience here."

He got to his car and she walked toward hers. So much for my big good-bye scene, she thought wryly.

"Where are you going?" He stood next to the open driver's side door.

"Well, back to Florida. I thought—"

"Come on, get in. Until someone tells me you're out, we're going to assume you're in."

"John didn't say, get her the hell out of here?"

"Nope. Not his style, anyway." He waved her on. "We'll figure out how we want to play this between here and the hospital. I'm thinking we'll have the three sisters all to ourselves."

She got in the passenger side and he handed her the diary. "Here, hold on to this. It just might come in handy."

*   *   *

Aubrey Randall lay on the hospital bed, the head of which was slightly elevated. In spite of the day's heat, a blanket was pulled up to her chin. On her right sat her sister, Natalie, and at the foot of the bed stood Paula Rose, who appeared to be in the middle of saying something when she glanced up and saw Dorsey and Andrew in the doorway.

"I thought you'd be gone by now," she said to Dorsey. "Didn't that reporter on the news last night say something about it being a conflict of interest, you working on Shannon's case?"

"He was referring to the old case—which she wasn't assigned to. The case we're here to talk about, Shannon's murder, has nothing to do with Dorsey's father," Andrew responded.

"How's that going?" Paula Rose asked. "Any progress on finding her killer?"

Dorsey just smiled, then turned her attention to Aubrey. "How are you feeling?"

Aubrey wet her lips slowly. "I've felt better."

"Why the pills, Aubrey?" Dorsey stood next to the bed.

Before Aubrey could respond, Paula Rose said, "She just can't cope with everything that's happened. She's simply collapsing under the stress of having Shannon turn up dead, after all these years."

Dorsey pulled over a chair and sat across the bed from Natalie. "How are your parents taking this?"

"We haven't told them. Aubrey's been admitted

under a different name to keep it from the press," Natalie told her.

"Well, I suggest you get used to it. The press, that is. It's going to get worse before it gets better." Dorsey looked from the woman in the bed to her two sisters. "So. Which one of you answered the phone when Shannon called a month or so ago?"

The silence was thick enough to slice.

Andrew stepped farther into the room and said, "She called your parent's home, like she's been doing all along. She hadn't intended to speak, but this time, she was caught off guard. She was expecting your mother to answer. She didn't mean to speak your name, but she did. And you recognized her voice. What was it that gave her away? What had she said?"

"What makes you think she called the house?" Paula Rose asked, a challenge in her tone.

Andrew tapped Dorsey on the shoulder, and from her bag she pulled out the diary and waved it slightly.

"What is that?" Natalie asked.

"I think you know that it's Shannon's diary." Dorsey nodded.

"Where did you find it?" Aubrey asked.

"Her roommate had it. She thought it might be helpful in solving the case," Dorsey replied.

"May I see that?" Natalie reached for it, but Dorsey dropped it into the bag saying, "Sorry, but it's evidence."

"So I ask once again. Who answered the phone the day Shannon called?" Andrew studied the faces of the sisters.

"It was me." Aubrey's voice was weak and breathy. "I answered the phone."

"Shut up, Aubrey," Paula Rose snapped. She turned to Andrew. "Aubrey isn't herself, she's coming out of a near coma. I'm afraid she's very susceptible to suggestion right now. She's liable to say just about anything."

"Paula Rose, stop it." Aubrey attempted to sit up. "Just . . . stop."

"Careful, Aubrey," Natalie cautioned her. "My sister really is quite ill, Agent Shields. She could have died. I don't think this is the time or the place for this."

"It's okay, Nat," Aubrey told her. She turned to Paula Rose and said, "It's no use. I just can't carry this pain around inside me anymore."

"Aubrey, we're all in pain over Shannon." Paula Rose went to her sister's bedside and took her hand.

"Please." Aubrey squeezed her eyes shut. "Just stop pretending it didn't happen. I can't pretend, Paula Rose."

"Aubrey." Paula Rose took her sister's chin in her hand and forced her to look into her eyes. "Shut. Up."

"No," Aubrey whispered. "I'm really sorry, honey, but I can't. I thought I could, but I can't."

"Whose idea was it to meet with Shannon?" Dorsey cut in, smelling a confession.

"Mine," Aubrey told her. "I couldn't believe it was really her. I drove down to Deptford one day by myself, to meet her for lunch in this little restaurant. I had to see if it was really her. I just couldn't believe it.

She looked so old, and so sad. I mean, we're all twenty-four years older, but you always have this image of someone looking just like they did the last time you saw them. I knew she'd look older, but I wasn't expecting her to look so hard. So tired and worn out." Aubrey shook her head. "Then when she told me what she'd been doing all those years, the kind of life she'd led, it just broke my heart. My sister, my little Shannon, selling herself on the streets like a common whore."

"She was a common whore," Paula Rose told her. "I believe that's already been established."

"She could have put it behind her," Aubrey protested. "She could have come home and started over."

"And when the story got out about her coming back from the dead, everyone would want to know where she'd been all those years, what she'd been doing."

"Not necessarily," Natalie spoke up. "No one needed to know the truth."

"She was going to tell, Natalie." Paula Rose snorted. "She said she was going to tell *everything.*"

She stared into her oldest sister's eyes and repeated, "*Everything,* Nat. She was going to tell it all."

Paula Rose held her sister's gaze for a long time, for as long as it took for that flash of understanding.

"Now, don't you think that would have brought on an awful lot of uncomfortable moments come election time, *Senator?*"

"I could have handled it," Natalie told her calmly.

"Right. Just the way *she*"—Paula Rose jerked her

thumb in Aubrey's direction—"thought she could have handled it when the news teams from the network that carries her show started interviewing some of Shannon's street pals. Some of her johns."

The silence returned. Finally, Andrew asked, "Whose gun was it?"

"Daddy's," Aubrey told him. "Paula Rose took it from his desk."

"Aubrey, for the love of God—" Paula Rose growled.

"Strange time to be bringing up God, Paula Rose," Natalie said very softly.

Aubrey's eyes brimmed with tears. "I swear to you, I didn't know she had it. I didn't know what she was planning to do."

"Tell us what happened, Aubrey," Dorsey said.

"Paula Rose said the next time Shannon called, we should make plans to go see her, so I told her we'd drive down, pick her up, and go for a picnic out in the woods, like we used to do when we were kids. We were going to talk about the best way to tell Momma and Daddy she was still alive—we all agreed that if she just showed up at their door, it would be the death of them both. Paula Rose said she had an idea about that, that we could plan it together."

"So you picked her up and drove someplace where no one could see what you were going to do to her." Andrew closed the door behind him as Paula Rose appeared to be inching in that direction. He leaned back against the frame, his hands in the pockets of his jacket. "When did she realize what you were going to do, Paula Rose? Did she cry? Did Shannon plead for her life? Beg you not to kill her?"

Natalie hid her face in her hands and wept.

"She was going to tell everything. She thought she'd be on some TV show. *Larry King* or *Oprah*, maybe. The woman who returned from the dead." Paula Rose grabbed Natalie's arm to force her hand from her face. "Do you understand what I'm saying? She was going to tell everything."

"You mean about your grandfather raping her?" Dorsey asked. "And I suspect you, too, Natalie? And Aubrey . . . and Paula Rose?"

"This is all my fault." Natalie's voice was heavy with pain. "My fault. If I'd told . . . if I'd spoken up, that first time, I could have stopped him. It could have stopped with me." She held her hands over her stomach as if holding in a horrible pain. "I was such a coward. If I hadn't been such a coward—"

"I could have stopped it, too, Nat. I'm just as guilty," Aubrey told her.

Natalie looked up at Paula Rose. "How could you have thought of protecting him, even now, after he's been gone for so many years, after everything he did to us?"

"You want to be known around the capital as the senator who was screwed by her grandfather? The senator whose sister liked it enough to make it her life's work?" Paula Rose taunted her.

"Surely you don't believe that." Natalie looked up at her. "Any fool can see that Shannon was running from him. And if she turned to a life of sin, it was because he set her on that path."

"She was a whore at heart," Paula Rose said calmly. "She tempted him."

"Oh, for the love of God," Natalie whispered. "You just don't get it, do you?"

She stood and faced her youngest sister. "He *raped* us. Do you understand what that means? To have someone you love and trust force you to do things that hurt you, things you don't understand, terrifying things you know are wrong and shameful?" She stared at Paula Rose. "No, you don't. You were the lucky one. He stopped after Shannon. She did you a big favor, you know that? Running away when she did? Maybe that scared him into stopping. Maybe he left you alone because of what he thought had happened to her."

"Y'all are going to burn in hell," Paula Rose said, staring at Aubrey and Natalie. "Sullying the name of that righteous man. Sticking up for that whore who was setting out to ruin all of us. I saved us all, can't you see that? I did what I did for all of us."

"Her blood is on your hands, not mine." Natalie took Aubrey's hand. "Not Aubrey's. Only yours."

"One thing I don't understand," Dorsey asked Aubrey. "Why try to hide the gunshot wound?"

"She wasn't trying to hide it. She wanted me to do it. She said we were both there, we were both responsible, we both killed her." She began to sob. "She walked right up to her. Shannon thought she was going to hug her. She put her arms out to hug Paula

Rose back," Aubrey said, spreading her arms open as if embracing someone the others couldn't see. "But instead, she put the gun right to Shannon's chest and pulled the trigger. Just like that . . ."

Natalie dropped her sister's hand and crumpled into her chair.

Aubrey gasped and her body shook, but she continued. "She gave me the knife and told me to stab her. Shannon was there on the ground and she wasn't breathing. I said, *'For God's sake, Paula Rose, you killed her.'* She said I had to do it, but I couldn't. She took the knife and stuck it in Shannon's chest to show me what she wanted me to do, but I started to throw up, and she got mad and started stabbing Shannon, over and over. . . ."

The imaginary knife in Aubrey's hand pumped up and down, stabbing at the air.

"Then you put the body in what, plastic, Paula Rose? Wrapped it up, drove it to Shelter Island so you could dump it?" Andrew asked. "You drive that church van yourself, or did you get the church gofer to do that for you?"

"I don't need anyone to do for me. I can do what has to be done." Paula Rose turned to Aubrey. "I never suspected you'd be so weak. I never should have trusted you. I should have just taken care of everything myself. No one would have known. She would have been just another dead whore."

Andrew took his phone from his pocket and held it to the side of his face. "You heard enough?" he asked.

"You're forgetting Edith," Dorsey said to Paula

Rose as the police chief and two officers came through the door. "Shannon's roommate—she knew who Shannon really was, and there was no way she'd let her be a Jane Doe."

"Who'd have thought she'd have kept on the cops like that," a suddenly docile Paula Rose murmured. She stared at Chief Bowden as if he were a stranger.

She said nothing more as she was led from the room.

Aubrey sat still as a stone on her bed, Natalie motionless beside her. Both appeared shell-shocked.

"I'm sorry, Nat, I couldn't live with myself anymore," Aubrey told her sister, but Dorsey couldn't tell if she was apologizing for admitting Shannon had been murdered, or for her attempted suicide.

"I know, honey. You did the right thing." Natalie got out of her chair and patted her sister on the head.

"Where are you going?" Aubrey asked.

"Someone's going to have to tell Momma." Natalie stopped in front of Dorsey, who now stood. "Am I free to leave?"

"What was your role in this?" Dorsey asked.

"Aubrey came to me the day after Shannon . . . the day after. She told me everything," Natalie admitted.

"You'll be held for withholding information, obstructing justice. We'll need to send an officer with you now."

Natalie nodded. "I understand."

"You went to Deptford to identify her because you were the only one who wasn't there when she died." Dorsey touched Natalie's arm as she passed by.

"Paula Rose . . . I didn't want her to go. And Aubrey, she could never have handled it. It was the least I could do for Shannon. Someone who cared for her had to be there for her," Natalie told her. "Someone had to say good-bye."

She turned to Andrew. "What's going to happen to Aubrey?"

"She's cooperating. If it weren't for her, we'd still be wondering what the hell happened. I doubt Paula Rose would have confessed on her own. I think it's pretty clear Aubrey didn't have any part in the murder," Andrew told her. "I'll speak with the prosecutor on her behalf. I promise to do the best I can for you and Aubrey."

"Thank you. I appreciate that. But Paula Rose? Y'all can let her fry." Natalie shook her head as if it were beyond understanding. "How do you do such a thing to your own flesh and blood?"

"You're asking the wrong person," Andrew replied. "That's a question I ask myself every day."

22

"So where to now?" Andrew eased the car into the parking spot in front of his motel room.

"I guess back to Florida, as I'd planned before you hijacked me this morning," Dorsey replied.

"Hey, it was worth missing the plane—admit it." Andrew grinned. "Seeing the look on Paula Rose's face when she realized there was no way out, that was worth a missed flight any day, right?"

"Absolutely." Dorsey nodded.

"By the way, I asked Chief Bowden to talk to the handyman at Paula Rose's church about that van. It bothered me that the van was blue, when the witness swore it was a light color."

"And?"

"And the man was telling the truth. The van we were looking at had always been blue. What he hadn't said was that the church had only had it for about two weeks. They'd traded in the old one." He shook his head. "I could kick myself for not grilling him better."

"It didn't occur to me to ask him how long they'd had it, either."

She stared out the window.

"I really feel for this family, you know? Aubrey having to live with that scene in her head; that moment when she realized what Paula Rose was going to do must haunt her. Watching one sister murder the other. And Natalie, caught in the middle like that. I guess blood really is thicker than I'd realized."

"What do you mean?" Andrew asked.

"At some level, I just don't understand why Aubrey or Natalie didn't blow the whistle on Paula Rose. Then on another, I understand the whole self-preservation thing."

"Everyone suffers when one member of the family turns on another. You never stop asking why," Andrew said, "even when you know you'll never find the answer."

"Sometimes, there isn't a credible answer, Andrew. Paula Rose's excuse was that she didn't want to deal with all the ugly truths Shannon's return would have made public. Superficial, yeah, but that was the bottom line with her," Dorsey told him. "Maybe in your brother's case, it was something deeper than that. Then again, maybe even Brendan didn't know why he did what he did."

"But Paula Rose was here to face her crime. Here to be prosecuted, here to answer for what she did." Andrew sat behind the wheel, his hand on the key, still in the ignition. "Brendan wasn't around to deal with the aftermath. Wasn't here to see how much pain he caused. Didn't see our family crumble, didn't see Grady just fade away."

He turned to Dorsey. "I told you, right, that it was

Brendan who set up Grady's wife to be killed? The woman his brother loved, the woman he wanted to raise a family with, spend his life with. She was nothing more than a nuisance to Brendan, so he had her removed. And then the bastard died without having to look Grady in the eye and admit what he'd done. Or explain to the rest of us how he could sleep at night, knowing how many children's lives he'd destroyed. The bastard died without having to answer to anyone for anything."

"Anyone in this life, anyway."

"True. If there's a hell, I know he's got a little corner all to himself." He pulled the key from the ignition, tossed it in the air, and caught it in the palm of his hand. "That's some consolation, however small."

He opened his door and got out, then waited for her to meet him in front of the car.

"What time was your plane, anyway?" he asked.

"It left about an hour ago."

"Any chance I could talk you into staying one more night? We could go out for a nice dinner, maybe get some champagne to celebrate having wrapped this up."

"I could be persuaded. A little celebration does seem to be in order." She smiled. "I'd just feel better if there weren't any loose ends."

"What loose ends?" he asked.

"Who beat up Shannon that night? And how did Shannon get out of Hatton?"

"I doubt we'll ever know now. I was hoping her diary would tell us, but it appears Shannon never wrote in it again after she left home. Maybe the truth was too ugly for her to put in words. Maybe she just brought it with her to remind her of the good things she was leaving behind—her childhood. Her innocence." Andrew shrugged, then added, "You know, you can't help but think that someone in this mix had to have been the one who'd driven her to wherever she went that night."

"Everyone connected to the case has an alibi," she reminded him, then paused, thinking. She slapped herself on the forehead. "Not quite everyone."

She tugged at his arm.

"Come on, back in the car. I know how Shannon got out of town that night. I think I might know what happened. . . ."

Dorsey stood in the doorway and knocked lightly on the wall.

"Mrs. Randall? Do you have a minute?" she asked.

"Well, Agent Collins is it? Or is it Ranieri?" The old woman stared at Dorsey from the opposite end of the sunporch where she sat enjoying the afternoon. She waved Dorsey closer. "You can come in, but I don't have much to say to you."

"There's really only one more thing I have to talk about, Mrs. Randall," Dorsey said as she walked closer.

"What's that?"

"You must have known what he'd been doing to your granddaughters. How could you have kept silent all those years? How could you have permitted such a thing to go on?"

The old woman stared at Dorsey but did not respond.

"Shannon told him to leave her alone that day, didn't she? Said she'd tell her father what he'd done to her if he didn't, right? So he slapped her around, gave her a black eye, made her lips bleed. And all the while, you knew. When she disappeared, did you think he killed her? Did you ask? If he denied it, did you believe him?" Dorsey leaned down to force the woman to look her in the eye. "How could you ever believe him again, knowing what he'd done to her? Or did you pretend not to know?"

Martha Randall's eyes narrowed to slits.

"Of course, he couldn't afford to have the truth come out, you'd have known that. So even though you thought he killed your own granddaughter, you still kept your mouth shut. How long had you known the truth about what he'd done? Did he ever tell you the truth, that he drove her out of town?"

The woman would neither confirm not deny anything. Dorsey suspected she was wasting her time. She started toward the door.

"It was me," the voice from behind her said.

"What?" Dorsey turned back.

"I did it." Martha's chin jutted out defiantly. "I slapped her. I don't know how many times. I lost count. She was going to tell. I couldn't let her do that. He was a good man. We had a good life. She was going to ruin it with her filthy lies."

"So you beat her until she bled?"

"She fell against the side of the table in the kitchen. She was running through the basement of the church when I came in. She ran to me, she was crying, shaking, saying terrible, terrible things." Martha sat calmly, her hands folded in her lap. "Those horrible things, ugly, ugly lies—she was going to tell, she was going to tell my son."

"And when she disappeared and everyone thought Eric had killed her, what did you think happened?"

"Oh, I knew what happened," she replied smugly.

It was Dorsey's turn to stare.

"When she ran from here, well, I had to find her. I could not let her go home to Franklin. Not ever again, unless she promised never to repeat those ugly things again. But she wouldn't." Martha's face went red, a trace of the anger she must have felt that night resurfacing. "She said she was telling her father and she didn't care what I said. Well, I just couldn't let that happen, now, could I?"

"So you drove her someplace?"

"To Calhoun. I gave her some money—"

"The cash from the carnival." Remembering the envelope, Dorsey pulled it from her bag and held it up. "She'd saved the envelope you gave her, all those years. Her roommate found it."

"I gave it to Shannon, all of it, plus some money I had of my own. I told her to wait for me in the kitchen while I went to the office, but when I came back, she was gone. I rode around town until I saw her getting out of that boy's car, then I followed her as far as the woods at the corner. I made her get into the car. I gave her one last chance to repent, but she refused. So I told her to take the money, that she was going to have to leave Hatton and never come back. She was a godless little liar and she didn't deserve the wonderful family she had. She had no right to be part of our family any longer, and I told her so. I drove her to the bus station and told her she'd never be welcome here again."

"She was fourteen years old." Dorsey was almost speechless. "You turned a fourteen-year-old child, your own flesh and blood, out onto the street to protect a pedophile?"

"Don't you *dare* use that word! My husband was a man of God!"

"You let a young man die for a murder he didn't commit."

"Sacrifices must sometimes be made for the greater good. Compared to the many souls my husband brought to the lord, what was one life?" Martha sniffed self-righteously.

"How could you have done such terrible things—"

"How could I let my family be destroyed?" the old woman snapped. "My husband would have gone to prison, we'd have lost everything. Our church, our standing in the community, the respect of our son. . . ." She shook her head. "There was no way I could have permitted Franklin to hear such ugly lies about his father."

"But you knew they weren't lies and you protected him. Your son lost his daughter because of you. How do you think he's going to feel when he hears all this now?"

"I suppose *you're* going to tell him?" She laughed. "The daughter of the man in charge of the investigation back then? The man who got a big TV career out of it? Looking back, your father was the only one who profited from that mess, wouldn't you say?" She waved a dismissive hand in Dorsey's direction. "You don't really think Franklin would take your word over mine, do you?"

"Maybe not, but there is this." Dorsey reached into her pocket and pulled out the small tape recorder. She rewound for a second, then hit play.

"There was no way I could have permitted Franklin to hear such lies about his father . . ."

The woman froze in her seat for a moment, then laughed.

"I know you can't just record a conversation without me giving permission," the smug old woman told Dorsey. "I watch all the shows, you know. You can't use that as any kind of evidence."

"Sorry, but that's not quite true," Andrew said as he stepped into the room. "The law varies, state to state. Here in South Carolina, the law says that only one of the parties has to be aware of the recording."

He turned to Dorsey. "You were aware that your recorder was on, weren't you?"

"I sure was."

"See?" He held up his hand and Dorsey tossed the recorder to him. He caught it midair. "No law broken here."

"I haven't broken any law," the woman reminded him.

"Well, assault on your granddaughter, we'll probably have to let that one go. The theft of the money from the church, I'm thinking we'll have to let that one go, too. Statute of limitations has run out. Withholding information? Don't know where the D.A. would stand on that, all these years later." He nodded. "So there may be nothing you can be arrested for, that's true. But facing your son, your daughter-in-law, the rest of your family"—he held up the tape—"well, now, that's going to be a problem, don't you think?"

Andrew turned to Dorsey. "Anything else?"

"No, I'd say my work here is done." Dorsey turned to leave. "Enjoy your old age, Mrs. Randall."

23

"Well, I'd say a toast would be appropriate right about now."

Having decided champagne would be an appropriate way to end the meal he and Dorsey had shared in the only really nice restaurant in Hatton, Andrew poured from the chilled bottle the waiter had just brought to the table. He handed a glass to Dorsey, then poured one for himself.

"To Shannon," he said solemnly. "May she rest in peace."

"To Shannon."

"And to us. For batting a thousand here in Hatton." Andrew tilted his glass in her direction.

"Another good one." She took another sip.

"To Jeanette Beale. For not pulling the trigger."

"Here, here."

"To Edith Chiong and her new life."

"Definitely." Dorsey raised the glass to her lips once again.

"And to many more."

"Many more what?" she asked.

"Many more cases solved in a week or less."

She put her glass down. "You know."

"Know what?" He pretended to examine the stem of his glass.

"You know John called me."

"He might have mentioned it." Andrew shrugged nonchalantly.

"Then I suppose he mentioned he has an opening he'd like me to fill?"

"I seem to remember having heard that."

"And that he wanted me in Virginia by the first of the month?"

"Sounds familiar."

"Thank you."

"For . . . ?"

"I know you put a word in for me. After I showed up at Tim Beale's trailer and went off on John the way I did, I figured I had less than a snowball's chance to ever work for him."

"Actually, I think that was when he decided to bring you on. He said you showed initiative, courage, determination, understanding of what the situation called for—"

"Stop! Stop!" She laughed. "You're going to give me a swelled head."

"Well deserved, though."

"Thanks. I can't deny I'm excited at the prospect. I've been hearing about his unit for years. The best of the best, and all that. How you get all the best cases. . . ."

"Oh, that we do," he said wryly. "The best of the serial killers. The craziest of the crazies."

"Doesn't sound too different from some of my cases in Florida."

"I'm sure your experience was a factor in John's decision. And for the record, he's had a lot of applications ever since the position became available."

"So it's true? He only has so many spots in his unit?"

"Yes. Only way to get in is if someone leaves."

"Who left?" The minute the words were out of her mouth, she knew.

Andrew's brother, Grady.

"Oh. I'm so sorry. Andrew, are you all right with me taking the job?"

He nodded. "That's the only reason John called me. He doesn't make it a habit of discussing new hires with anyone else, but he wanted to make sure both Mia and I knew he'll have a place for Grady when he decides to come back. If he comes back."

"Do you think he will?"

"I have no idea. He's not very communicative these days. Mia wanted to take some time off and spend it with him, but he told her not to come. Said it was a bad time."

"What would he do if you just showed up?"

"I don't know. I've thought about doing just that, but I hate to put either of us in that situation. You know, him not wanting me there, me being uncomfortable forcing myself on him. I think we're just going to have to wait for him to come around, and pray that he does."

Andrew tore a small piece of the napkin that sat under his glass.

"Nothing can screw you up like your family, you know that?" He wasn't really expecting an answer. "I couldn't help but draw parallels between Paula Rose and Brendan. Both betrayed the people who loved them the most, and all but destroyed their families. Poor Shannon got a triple dose. Her grandfather, her grandmother, her sister." He looked up at Dorsey with tired eyes. "Some family, eh?"

"And the scariest thing is that compared to some other families I've seen, the Randalls look like the Waltons."

"You know it's going to be worse," he told her. "Some of the cases we get are so gruesome they never even make the news."

"John said." She nodded. "I'm going to meet with him in two weeks—to make sure I know what I'm getting into, he said. I couldn't tell if he was kidding or not. I can't imagine there's anything he could say that would make me change my mind. Then I'll only have a few weeks to settle up my old cases as best I can, pack up my stuff, and move."

"Let me know if there's anything I can do to help," he said.

"Maybe you could suggest a good place to live. I'll be looking for an apartment while I'm up there."

"My complex always has a few openings. It's well located, the rents aren't astronomical, and the maintenance people are available 24/7. Just let me know which days you'll be around, and I can take you on a tour."

"That would be great, thanks. But do they allow dogs?"

"In some apartments, they do." He drained his glass. "You have a dog?"

"I'm thinking I might get one, once I get settled."

"Big dog, small dog?"

"Don't have a preference. I figure I'll go to a shelter and I'll know the right dog when I see it."

"That's exactly how I picked out my last dog."

"You didn't mention you had one. What kind?"

"He's a retriever mix, but I don't have him anymore."

"What happened to him?"

"He went with my ex-girlfriend."

"What?"

"He sort of belonged to both of us. When we broke up, well, only one of us could have him."

"So you let her take him?" Dorsey's eyebrows raised in surprise. "Didn't you like him?"

"I loved him." Andrew didn't look the least bit sheepish at the admission. "But she did too, and it would have been harder for her to give him up. She was transferred shortly after we broke up, so it was good for her to have the dog. You know, something familiar she cared about in a new city, with a new job."

He tried to make light of it. "Apparently she found me easier to give up than the dog."

"Amazing. You let her have the dog. . . ." She shook her head. "When my ex and I broke up, he took our dog. I just came home from work one day and bam—no dog."

"Bastard."

That he really seemed to mean it made Dorsey smile. "Thank you."

"You're welcome." He smiled back. "Maybe when you're ready, I can go to the shelter with you. Just to look."

"Sure. Just to look."

The ringing of his cell phone interrupted them.

He looked at the number of the incoming call, then frowned.

"Shields. Yes . . ." He fell silent for a moment, listening to the caller. "All right. When—"

He made a face.

"Sure. I'll give him a call when I'm ready." He hung up, looking decidedly unhappy. "Slight change in plans."

"That was John," she guessed.

Andrew nodded. "He's sending a plane to Charleston. It should be arriving in about an hour."

"Destination?"

"Alaska."

"Alaska." She sighed. "I always wanted to go there. What's the case?"

"You ever hear of Robert Hansen?"

"Sure. The 'big-game hunter' who took women into the wilderness, released them, and told them to run. Then he'd hunt them down like animals. I heard he killed at least seventeen women that way, though the number is probably higher."

"Looks like there's a copycat."

"Damn." She frowned. "I wish I could go."

"And I wish I could stay." He reached across the table for her hand. "I wasn't really ready to leave."

The waiter returned with the check, and Andrew handed over his card.

"I was hoping we'd have a little time to ourselves, get to know each other a little better." His thumb slid under her bracelet to touch her old scars. "I was thinking we'd go over to that park on the way into town and watch the swans for a while. Maybe take another bottle of champagne with us. Just to celebrate . . . things. Maybe talk about something other than work and dysfunctional families."

"I would have loved that. It sounds very romantic."

"I was thinking it might be." He was clearly disappointed.

"What time does your plane leave?"

"It leaves when I get there."

"Well, who knows how long it will take you to drive from here to Charleston? If there was an accident on the highway, you'd be delayed, right? A flat tire? They're not expecting you to be there within the hour, are they?"

"No. And I won't be driving. John left one of the agents he brought with him to Beales here to help tie up loose ends. I'm supposed to call when I'm ready to leave and he'll pick me up." He drummed the fingers of his free hand on the table, a slight smile on his lips. "You know, on second thought, I probably have a little time."

"Good." She smiled, then turned to look for their waiter. Catching his eye, she motioned him back to their table.

"We'll have another bottle of champagne. And we'd like that to go, please. . . ."

Read on for a sneak peak at

Last Words

Prologue

He leaned a little closer to the mirror, checking for signs of five o'clock shadow, tilting his head this way and that to satisfy himself there was no stubble to sully his image. He washed his hands and dried them on the beige hand towel his wife had hung on the bar that morning, then adjusted the collar of his polo shirt and straightened his shoulders.

He did look fine.

"Honey?" his wife called from the hall. "Are you watching the time?"

"Not closely enough, apparently," he called back, taking one more glance in the mirror before turning off the bathroom light.

"Don't forget to say good night to the kids," she called over her shoulder.

"I won't." He fought to keep the touch of annoyance from his voice. As if he'd forget.

God, but she was annoying sometimes.

He poked into the kids' rooms. If he'd been an honest man, he'd have admitted that the delay was more to let the excitement within him continue to build than to have an extra ten minutes with his children. But he was far from honest, and so divided the time equally between them before reminding both to finish their homework and say their prayers before they turned off their lights at bedtime.

"See you at breakfast," he promised as he headed downstairs.

"I wish your out-of-town clients could show up during normal business hours." His wife complained when he came into the kitchen. She was rinsing the dinner dishes before stacking them methodically into the dishwasher and didn't bother to turn around when he came into the room. He fought an almost overwhelming urge to bash in the back of her skull with a heavy object. Which fortunately—or unfortunately, depending—was not within reach.

"What's the big deal?" He patted her on the butt with what he hoped would pass as affection, "It's barely seven. And you know very well it's not unusual to see clients in the early evening hours. You have to, if you expect to compete."

"Well, it just seems you're out more and more in the evenings." She turned to him. "But I guess I should be grateful you get home every night to have dinner."

"You know how strongly I feel about families sitting down at the table together at the end of the day." He opened his briefcase and pretended to be looking for something. "And I probably needn't remind you that you work through dinner more often than I do."

"Not my idea," she protested.

"Not the point." He closed his briefcase with a snap.

"I don't get to set my own hours," she reminded him.

"I'm aware of that. I'm not finding fault. I'm just saying that sometimes if I leave work early in the afternoon to spend time with the kids, I'll have to make up that time later, which is what I'm doing tonight. It's a trade-off, that's all. I know you don't have that luxury." He checked his watch. "I've got to get going. I'll try not to be too late."

He kissed the side of her face and walked out the door that led to the garage. On the way, he took a deep healthy breath of fresh air. It smelled of lavender and early summer roses, and underneath it all, it smelled of freedom. Of promise. Of something wicked and yet oh so fulfilling.

He drove carefully, stopping at the stop sign at the end of his street, waving casually to a neighbor, then drove purposefully through town. He made a left at the first light and went on to his place of business, where he parked his car and went inside. Leaving the lights on inside—anyone passing by would think he was working late, as he often did—he slipped out the back door and walked to his destination. It took him a while, and he was mildly winded by the time he arrived.

Unlocking the padlock he'd installed after his last visitor had almost departed on her own, he stepped into the dark.

"Honey, I'm home," he sing-songed as his hands

reached up for the flashlight he'd left on a hook on the right side of the wall. "Did you miss me?"

His footsteps echoed on the wooden floor and he walked slowly, following the stream of light deeper into the building, letting the anticipation build in him—and the fear in her. He stopped when he came to a doorway, and stood still, sniffing the air, as a dog might do, seeking the scent that a woman gave off when she was terrified.

There, there it was.

Lovely.

He stepped into the room and paused to light the candles on the makeshift dresser that stood along one wall. Inside, her clothes were folded and stacked. She would no longer have a need for them but he didn't have the heart to toss them out, so he'd washed them and put them away neatly.

"I missed you all day, sweetheart. I couldn't think about anything or anyone except you." He knelt down next to the bed. "About being here with you, just like this."

She struggled against the restraints, her eyes wide with fear, her cries muffled by the gag that protruded from her mouth.

"Oh, look at you," he tsk-tsked softly. "You've soiled yourself again. What am I going to do with you?"

He left the room for several moments, then returned with the garden hose.

"We're just going to have to give you a little

shower, aren't we." He smiled. "Can't have you getting all snuggly with your man, looking like that."

He unlocked the shackles on her ankles, then one of the restraints that tied her wrists to the bedpost. Forcing her to stand on unsteady legs, he moved her as far away from the bed as he could, stretching the arm that was still attached to the bed as far as it would stretch. When he realized that he couldn't hose her down without getting the mattress wet, he debated momentarily before releasing her other arm. He knew her legs wouldn't support her even if she had the strength to try to get away—which she obviously wasn't about to do—and led her several feet to the right before turning on the nozzle.

The first blast of cold water hit her right in the middle, and she cried out, raising her arms to shield her eyes as best she could.

"Now, now, sweetheart, this will just take a minute." He turned her around to hose off her back and the backs of her thighs. "And you know, if you hadn't been such a naughty girl, this wouldn't be necessary."

He walked around her with the hose, enjoying her efforts to avoid the harsh spray from getting in her face. When he was done, he dried her off with one of several towels he kept there for this purpose.

"The mosquitoes have really been feasting on you this week, haven't they?" He noted the red welts all over her body. "Maybe if you're nice to me, I'll bring something to put on those bites. They really are unattractive, you know."

He forced her stiff legs to carry her back to the bed. Tiny tears rolled down her face as she submitted to the humiliation of having her arms locked above her head once again. The shackles were not, however, re-fastened to her legs.

He stood and took off his polo shirt in one motion and placed it on the back of the chair he'd brought when he first decided to feather his love nest. His shoes were next, then his pants which were also care-fully folded and laid on top of the shirt.

"Like what you see, sugar?" He leaned down and touched the face of the woman on the bed. "I know you do, baby. And it's all yours. All for you . . ."

He eased himself down on top of her, his breathing coming faster now.

"And if you're a good girl, after I'm finished with you, maybe I'll give you some water. Would you like that?"

The woman struggled inside her bonds. The sounds she made were choked, incoherent.

"Yes, I know you would. Now, are you going to be a good girl?"

She nodded her head with as much vigor as she could muster.

He chuckled and pulled the gag from her mouth.

"Now, sweetheart, you know that . . ."

She spat in his face.

At first he froze, then he laughed. "Well, well, we still have a little fight in us, do we? Baby, you ought to know there's nothing that turns me on more than a little bit of fight."

He shoved the gag back into her protesting mouth. Before he forced himself inside her, he reached under the bed, seeking the recorder he kept there. Once located, it was activated with the touch of a finger.

"Later, baby," he whispered over her muted cries, "we'll have plenty of time to talk later . . ."

Turn the page for a bonus excerpt from

Last Breath

Prologue

April 2007
Somewhere in the mountains of Afghanistan

He lay on the ground and shifted his weight from his left hip, where a small pile of stones seemed to have imbedded themselves while he was sleeping. *Lie down with rocks, wake up with stones,* his tired mind paraphrased an old saw.

He inched quietly onto his back, one hand wrapped around the handgun he was rarely without, all his senses having gone on alert when he woke suddenly. He listened intently for any sound that might mean he was no longer alone on this mountaintop, but after ten minutes of barely moving, he had to assume it had been the dream that had pulled him from sleep.

For the fourth time in less than three weeks, Connor Shields had had the same dream.

He was in his favorite hotel, in his favorite city, leaning on the iron railing that enclosed the balcony overlooking the Moroccan coast of the Atlantic and watching the gulls circle overhead. The sky was as blue as he'd ever seen it, and the breeze as gentle as a caress. Coming on the heels of the past few weeks spent in a Middle Eastern desert, the peaceful morning was balm to his soul.

There was a rap on the door, and he answered it without hesitation.

"Your breakfast." The dark-eyed woman carried a rectangular tray in both hands and headed straight for the balcony. "You should eat here, in the sun. It will relax you."

"Magda, you're more like my mother than my mother was."

"Someone has to watch out for you," she said without smiling. "It might as well be me."

She placed the tray on the small glass table and removed the napkin to reveal a plate of warm croissants, figs, a thinly sliced pear, and a small mound of white cheese.

"Sit and eat. I'll be right back with your coffee."

"You're way too good to me," he said as he sat at the table.

"I certainly am." Magda went through the double doors into the room and disappeared into the hall. When she returned, she brought a second tray upon which stood a tall carafe and two cups. She poured coffee into both cups, placed one before him, then sat in the chair opposite his.

"Nice of you to join me." He offered her the croissants, but she waved him off.

"I eat early, at dawn. You know that. I need an early start if I'm to take care of you and the rest of my guests in the manner in which I've made you accustomed."

"There is no finer hotel in Essaouira. It's the reason I've come to love this city. The reason I spend any available free time right here." He tilted his cup in her direction before taking a sip. "And besides, there's no better coffee anywhere in Morocco."

Satisfied, Magda leaned back in the chair and raised her face to the sun, her eyes closed.

"There's a new guest who checked in two days ago. An American woman. She's an archaeologist, she says, on holiday."

"So?"

"So you should make her acquaintance. She's very pretty. Blond. Soft-looking. She doesn't go out much."

"So maybe she's tired. Maybe she sleeps a lot."

"Maybe she's lonely. Maybe she'd appreciate a little companionship from a fellow countryman."

"Why are you always trying to set me up?"

"Because you live like a mercenary."

"I'm not a mercenary."

"I know what you are. But you still need a nice girl in your life."

"I have a nice girl in my life. I have you."

"I'm old enough to be your mother, and if you ever looked at me that way, Cyril would slit your throat." She smiled, but her eyes remained closed.

"Your husband should be jealous of you. You're one in a million, Magda."

"I know."

She opened her eyes and stood, then patted him fondly on the arm as she walked past him.

"The American woman takes tea in the courtyard

every afternoon at four," she said without breaking stride. "Today she'll be seated at one of the tables for two, in the corner near the palms."

Magda closed the door behind her.

He'd made a phone call and spent several minutes discussing a case before disconnecting the call. From the balcony he could see into the courtyard, where right at that moment, a woman in a gauzy white dress had stopped to put a large hat atop her head. Before her hair had disappeared under the hat, he'd noticed it was blond, cut short in a choppy style, as if done without artistry or skill. She was tanned, almost as tanned as he was, and even from a distance, he could see she was very well put together.

The American Magda had told him about?

Tea in the courtyard at four might be interesting after all. He watched her disappear through the courtyard gates and hesitate, as if unsure of her direction. For a moment, he was tempted to join her, to offer her a tour of the marketplace, but he had a meeting in twenty minutes with a man who had information his superiors were quite eager to obtain.

He turned off the laptop, located his sunglasses, and locked the door behind him. The pretty blond would have to wait.

But it had been he who had waited, the next day and the one after that, watching from his balcony for a glimpse of her.

"You missed your chance." Magda shrugged when curiosity finally got the better of him and he asked if tea with the American archaeologist was still a possibility. "She checked out this morning."

He started to say something flippant, but she stopped him with a glance from those dark eyes.

"You should have met her when I told you to," Magda said smugly. "Now you'll have to wait till next time."

"Next time?"

"Of course. She'll be back." Magda smiled with satisfaction. "And so will you."

But the blond hadn't been there the next time he'd stopped for an overnight on his way back to the States, nor was she there the following trip.

"You missed her by three days," Magda told him the last time he stayed at the Villa.

"Missed who?" He tried to be nonchalant.

"Missed who." She glared at him. "Dr. McGowan, who do you think."

"Who's Dr. McGowan?" He frowned. It was not a name he recognized.

"The pretty archaeologist. The blond, the American. You know damned well who I mean."

"I didn't know her name."

"It's Daria. Daria McGowan. Dr. McGowan to you who couldn't bother to make time to meet her."

"She's been back?"

"Several times." Magda's eyes narrowed. "I thought you weren't interested."

"Who said I was interested?"

Magda had merely laughed at him, and her laughter rang in his ears, rousing him from sleep.

Connor's free hand rubbed the back of his neck, his other hand still holding the handgun, because in this part of the world, you literally did not know what you'd find hiding behind the next rock. He stared up at the sky, watched the stars flickering overhead, so vivid, so close he could almost reach up and touch them. There were no city lights to compete, no sounds of the civilized world here, just the occasional call of an owl, and the agonized scream of its prey.

He thought of the dream and of the woman, the elusive archaeologist, and wondered why she was still in his head. She certainly wasn't the only woman to have crossed his path, though admittedly, life was such these days that he'd rarely had the time to say more than *hello, nice to meet you,* to any woman who might have caught his eye. Which was just fine with him. Connor had an agenda, and he hadn't penciled in *find a woman.* Maybe someday, but not now. Then again, maybe never. Life was too complicated. Or, he mused, too simple.

There were reasons he volunteered for every dicey assignment the FBI had up its sleeve. For one thing, he knew the hills of Afghanistan as well as anyone in the Bureau. With so much of the Bureau's resources going toward fighting terrorism, more and more agents were finding themselves on foreign soil. Connor had been one of the first agents to volunteer for such work, and as such, had established his own network of contacts throughout the region. One in particular had proven to be a tremendous asset, and it had been this man Connor had traveled, mostly on foot, to see. His assignment completed, the information he'd sought secure, he was on his way back home. Hopefully, he thought, not for long. Home was just too painful a place to be, and had been ever since he'd learned that it had been his cousin Brendan who'd murdered Connor's own brother, Dylan, two years ago. The fact that Connor had been the target made him feel intense guilt rather than any sense of relief he might have felt at having been spared.

Dylan had been the best of the lot, had been engaged to marry the woman of his dreams, had a wonderful life ahead of him. If Connor had been given the chance to live that night over again, he'd have gone in his brother's place willingly. Connor had faced death so many times over the past fifteen years, he no longer feared it nor whatever would follow. He'd be forty on his next birthday, and had been a loner for most of those years. Dylan, on the other hand, had made a friend of everyone he'd ever met. Not a day passed when Connor did not wonder why the wrong brother had been taken. He couldn't help but think that Dylan had been the victim of a vast cosmic error. He, Connor, had never really been in love—not the way Dylan and his Annie had been, anyway. He'd never considered himself a permanent fixture in this world, whereas Dylan had had everything to live for. Connor hadn't had a real relationship with a woman in . . . he tried to recall how long and couldn't.

Which was why the recurring dreams about the blond Daria McGowan—Dr. McGowan—puzzled him so. He'd lost count of the number of times in the past year he'd had that same dream. And while he'd feigned disinterest to Magda, the truth was that the dreams had prompted him to look up a little info on the doctor's background. Strictly out of curiousity, of course.

He learned she was thirty-six years old and was an internationally recognized authority on ancient Middle Eastern civilizations, specifically, the art and artifacts from the region. He learned her findings had been published by a prestigious university press, that she had lectured widely in the U.S. and Europe, and was highly regarded by her colleagues. Respect for her was so high that she'd been invited to view findings in areas where her nationality and her gender were not usually welcomed. She was the daughter of a well-known anthropologist and an equally regarded archaeologist, so it would appear she'd been nurtured from the cradle to become what she was. In some circles, it would appear from several articles he'd located through the Internet, what she was, was larger than life.

He wondered if he'd ever see her again in real life.

Whatever. Experience had taught him that what would happen, happened. There were some things you just couldn't plan for. He was still three days from Kabul on foot, and then he'd be on his way to Morocco.

A stiff breeze picked up and he pulled the blanket around him against the cold. Three more days, then a warm, comfortable, familiar room at his favorite inn. Magda would coddle him and bring him wonderful food and endless cups of the best coffee he'd ever tasted. In the bar, her husband would drink with him into the wee hours of the morning and they'd trade stories over tumblers of scotch.

And maybe the pretty blond would wander in. If not this time, maybe the next.